PRAISE FOR

BEHELD

“Cevasco lays bare the extra[illegible] of
Lady Godiva and her age, melti[illegible]ring vision of
the birth to a[illegible]

Michael Livingston
award-winning medieval scholar
and historical fantasy novelist

“Christopher Cevasco channels a darker Bernard Cornwell in his audacious debut. At the same time a convincing and historical evocative thriller, a study of lust and obsession, and a bizarrely off-kilter love story. *Beheld* blew me away.”

Alan Smale
Sidewise Award-winning author of the
Clash of Eagles *trilogy*

“In this swiftly moving story with spectacular attention to period detail, Christopher M. Cevasco removes Lady Godiva from the chocolate box and deftly returns her to historical context—a distant, brutal age when viking was a verb and secret pagan cults littered England’s forests.”

Karen Essex
national and international best-selling author of
Leonardo’s Swans *and* Kleopatra

BEHELD

GODIVA'S STORY

CHRISTOPHER M. CEVASCO

Greenfield, MA

ISBN: 978-1-59021-714-6

Cover and Interior Design by Inkspiral Design

Published by Lethe Press.

Publisher's Cataloging-in-Publication data
Names: Cevasco, Christopher M., author.
Title: Beheld : Godiva's story / Christopher M. Cevasco.

Description: Greenfield, MA: Lethe Press, 2022.Identifiers: LCCN: 2022905267 |
ISBN: 9781590217146 (paperback) | 9781005727376 (ebook)
Subjects: LCSH Godiva, Lady, active 1040-1080—Fiction | Anglo-Saxons—England—Fiction |
Leofric, Earl of Mercia, c. 1057—Fiction | Coventry (England)—Fiction |
Great Britain—History—Anglo-Saxon period, 449-1066—Fiction | Voyeurism—Fiction |
Women—History—Middle Ages, 500-1500—Fiction |
BISAC FICTION / Biographical | FICTION / Fairy Tales, Folk Tales, Legends & Mythology |
FICTION / Historical / Medieval | FICTION / Literary | FICTION / Thrillers /
Historical |FICTION / Thrillers / Psychological
Classification: LCC PS3603 .E83 B44 2022 | DDC 813.6—dc23

for

MEGAN

N
Northumbria
York
Chester
Newark
Derby
Shrewsbury
Leicester
Wenlock
Severn
Mercia
Coventry
East Anglia
Ely
Wales
Leominster
Worcester
Avon
Warwick
Northampton
Hereford
Rollandriht
Deheubarth
Dyfed
Gloucester
Lea
Thames
London
Barking
Malmesbury
Bristol
Southwark
Sandwich
Canterbury
Wessex
Winchester
Dover
Bosham
Godgyfu's England
Normandy
Seine
Rouen
Jumièges

PROLOGUE

COVENTRY
11 OCTOBER 1028

GODGYFU SLUMPED TO HER KNEES. But for the nun's strong arms beneath her own, she would have fallen on her belly among the floor's dusty rushes.

"I can't die like this, weak and broken," she breathed … or thought she did; the nun made no response, so maybe Godgyfu had only thought it without giving it voice. *Am I dead already? My soul gone from my wracked flesh?* But that couldn't be true either; why then would she still know such pain?

"Don't …," she tried again, "don't think of me this way … after …" It sounded little more than a whisper, weak and forlorn. Godgyfu closed her eyes and wept. Though she had never been one of those great folk whose faring through the earthly kingdom left ripples in her wake, she had nonetheless always taken pride in holding steady on the oar, never flinching, no matter what storms or narrowness had beset her eighteen years. Now her *wyrd*—the lot God willed for her—had brought her body low, and she wanted to go into the hereafter with head high. Instead she wavered, she shied, and somehow, that was the hardest of it all.

"Just a little farther," Sister Eanfled grunted behind her, the nun's rosary dangling over one of Godgyfu's ears to trail across her mouth. Godgyfu kissed the beads with cracked lips and stepped toward the pillows and tangled, sweat-soaked bedclothes.

And there was Ruh, the old hound that had been her father's best-loved hunter! Godgyfu reached for him, and the hound lifted his long muzzle from among the crumpled bedding, tongue lolling happily.

"How could I have forgotten him?" she asked.

"Forgotten who?" the nun asked, helping to lift her.

But of course Ruh had come. When it had been his time to die all those years ago, they'd found the hound curled up in Godgyfu's own bed. Now he was back, waiting ....

Dull pain bloomed in her knee as she bashed it against the carved board beneath the bed-cove. She whimpered as she threw herself at last into the wall's hollow, wilting. Her knee would be bruised, but that ache was a drop in the flood filling her side and back, spreading into her groin like hellfire. Where had Ruh gone? She needed to borrow his old strength, but the bed was empty. Only her and the pain.

It was the worst pain Godgyfu had ever known. Worse even than what she recalled of her wedding night not so very long ago .... *Five years?* It seemed a longer, untold span. That night had likewise been soon after the harvest, mild and warm even as this night was cold and foggy. She'd been a little girl then, her blood having come but her body not yet ready for the wedding bed .... Now she was a woman grown, but she felt again like that callow, wide-eyed bride.

Shadows moved about in the house's eaves. Stalking. Closing in.

This is it? she thought, something almost like laughter making her tremble. *All I've lived for? To watch mother and father die, see my marriage crumble, bear no children, know no love but the love of Christ and Marie Ever Maiden?* She wondered why God had bothered to give her breath.

A chill crept in under Godgyfu's drenched linen shift, and she clambered to draw the bedclothes fast. The sheets smelled of the gall she'd been heaving up, of the water that had leaked out while her gut clenched. But she was beyond caring about such things. Eanfled hurried to help and, once she was settled back, pushed something into Godgyfu's hand.

For now, Godgyfu lacked the strength even to look and see what she held. A cow lowed outside, a gloomy sound. Cows seemed ever mournful to her, and she tried to call to mind if she'd ever seen a happy one? Wan light leaked past the room's dark beams through a spot of roof thatch wanting mending; daytime then—not night at all. It all felt the same.

Poor cows.

She suddenly wanted to weep over that frayed bit of thatch. This house was one of eight she owned across the Midlands, but like most of them she'd hardly spent any time here; when she was gone, who would be left to see to the roof's mending or milk the cows? Who would live here? *Some hairy thegn I've never met. Danish or English. Did it matter which?*

Blinking away unshed tears, she looked at last and saw a little silver-topped glass flask in her hand; something dark was pressed within.

"I brought it for you, dearie," the nun whispered. "A lock of Saint Osburh's hair. Ask her to speed your prayers to Christ the Healer, and she'll do what she may."

Godgyfu closed her fingers about the relic. She wished she had the strength to smile thanks. It was a sundry thing indeed for the old sister to have brought this from where Godgyfu knew they kept it in one of Coventry's little minster churches alongside a bigger chest holding the saint's head. Abbess Osburh died a martyr when Cnut's Danish raiders sacked her abbey. Godgyfu had been a wee child then, still full of hope. Now Cnut himself was king of Denmark and England both, and Godgyfu the widow of one of the raiders he'd set up as earl of the Gloucestershire Mercians.

Who'd have guessed I'd end up dying here in Coventry, of all steads?

"How long have I been here?" she asked.

Sister Eanfled sighed. "More'n a week, dear."

"I was to be at the earl's feast now," Godgyfu whispered, and again Eanfled seemed not to understand. She drew a deeper breath. The ache had abated somewhat at last; she knew she should find much-needed sleep, but she wanted talk … of anything and nothing. There would soon be time enough for stillness everlasting. "This Leofric, the Mercians' new earl …. He's been given sway over Gloucestershire too—my dead husband's spot. I wonder … will he be any good?"

"I'm sure the king would not have named him elsewise," Eanfled answered, wiping Godgyfu's brow with a soft cloth.

Godgyfu let her eyes close for a spell. "King Cnut must have thought my husband would make a good earl too, but that all went to hell." The sister's rubbings had begun to irk her, and Godgyfu wanted to bat her hand away but could only cling to the cloth with shaking fingers. "No matter. I shan't live to find out."

Eanfled made a shushing sound. "Pray to Osburh as I bid you. Christ will hear."

"God's truth." She looked back at the relic in her other hand and was ashamed. "I will pray." She wrapped both hands about it and sought the right words.

I don't want to die. Straightforward enough, she supposed.

When Eanfled rose to leave, Godgyfu called out. "Stay. Please! I don't want to be alone if ... if ...."

Eanfled leaned back against the cove, her smile coming easy as always, but Godgyfu knew the woman must be exhausted. She'd hardly left her side since the illness first gripped her, and Godgyfu knew she should let her rest but couldn't bear the thought of death bundling her off while she lay alone in the still room. "If you'd like to go to Newark to be with your own people, I'm sure a wagon could be—"

"No!" Godgyfu answered more loudly than she'd wanted to, making Eanfled flinch. "Thank you, but no. Newark holds only bad memories."

Don't think about it! But as ever, she couldn't stop herself .... She was twelve again. Word had come of her father's death. She was walking into the barn, calling for mother. First she found the piebald mare and hadn't understood the dark, sticky stains over its withers. Then she looked up. The rope. Her mother's eyes bulging above a torn neck. A single red drop fell upon Godgyfu's cheek ....

The pain came back all at once in a rippling wave pushing out and down from her back.

"Christ in heaven!" She folded over, retching on herself, bringing up what little broth she'd managed to keep down earlier. Her body tightened, then slackened in the lull between waves. She wiped at the yellow-green stains on her shift, careful not to get any on the relic.

"Here, love, let me." Eanfled tugged the shift, bringing it up and over her head with one deft pull. "Your handmaid has a fresh one drying in the yard for you. Just wrap these about you until I'm back."

Godgyfu gripped the sheets, shivering at the chill. But no sooner did she cover herself then the bedclothes grew stifling. A fire burned and pounded at her eyes and forehead. She threw off the sheets and sat naked, crouched over her shrunken belly. Eanfled was back with the clean shift, but Godgyfu waved it away.

"Rub my back again ... just here." She reached down to mark a spot between ribs and hip. But when the good sister touched her, it ended up being too painful, and she shied away. "Just talk to me. About anything." Somehow the talking got her through the worst of the ache, which already lessened somewhat again, coming as it did like the tide's ebb and flow.

Eanfled sighed. "So, not Newark. Maybe Cirencester, then? Your own bed?"

But Cirencester had never truly felt like home to her, no more than it had ever been her husband's. She shook her head, then met Eanfled's gaze. The woman had a kindly cast—ruddy cheeks, smiling eyes, big horse-teeth that came out over her lower lip when her mouth was at rest. For a moment it looked as though her cheeks glowed, but Godgyfu reckoned that was only a fever trick.

"Do you know … I only lay with my husband once." Maybe the fever also made her speak of things that had never before passed her lips. Maybe she merely thought to find some shrift for her misfarings.

Eanfled looked down. "My lady, it's not for me to know."

"Only the once," she went on. "On the night of our wedding, so none could ever say the betrothal hadn't been fulfilled. Eilífr would not even have done it then. He was in truth a kind man—a kind Danishman, if such a thing could be among their murderous lot. Mild of heart. He feared he might do me some harm, young as I was. Still twelve at the time."

Eanfled clucked her tongue.

"Do you know what he had me do ever after?"

"I'm sure it's not something …" Eanfled marked a cross upon herself. "Doings between wer and wife are none of my—"

"I …" she started, then trailed off. Eanfled was right. How could she speak of such a thing? "Sister, will I meet my husband again in the hereafter? Must I be with him again?" There were few worse things she could think of.

But Eanfled misunderstood. Nodding and smiling, the nun spoke words that filled Godgyfu with dread. "If he was a good man as you say, then he awaits you in heaven."

A sort of growl came unbidden to Godgyfu's lips. "Better I seek hell."

Eanfled crossed herself again and sputtered in bewilderment.

Should I tell her? Tell her of it all? The room grew wholly still but for Godgyfu's own rasping breath. Outside, the cow had stopped lowing. She felt her last strength draining away. Time ran short; she knew it, and she wanted nothing so much as to tell this woman, half a stranger, as much as she could so she'd leave some shade to linger after her passing. It was a wild, needful drive to speak before the gathered shadows—angels or devils?—stilled her tongue with their black, peering eyes. She saw them—eyes from the past—staring now from her sickroom's shadows. They were here in Coventry, meting her worth, damning her. The words almost fell from Godgyfu's lips, but she choked them back. *There are some things not fit to speak of even on my deathbed.*

Tears spilled from her burning eyes. When a sob came, it hurt her belly, and she retched again, this time bringing nothing up.

Eanfled put arms about her, shushing. Godgyfu felt awful for having shamed the good woman by even hinting at her sorry tale. *I should have taken it all with me …*

She must have slept then for a time, for when a knock sounded upon the little house's front wall, she started awake in the nun's arms, still clutching Saint Osburh's relic. Eanfled slumbered too, and Godgyfu had to nudge her.

The good sister had barely flung a sheet over Godgyfu's nakedness when the old priest from rickety Saint Michael's tottered in. "Blessings upon you," the grayhair said, then, "Christ! What a stink!"

"Godgyfu, you know Father Offa," Eanfled said. "You bid me send for him."

Had she?

"Yes," Godgyfu said. "Thank you." Behind the man's robes, a young boy lurked, the one Eanfled had sent to find the priest. The boy stared at Godgyfu with wide blue eyes, unblinking. His gaze briefly made her forget why she'd asked for the priest. The seed of pain grew again in her belly, and she knew she had little time before it bloomed into something that stole her wits.

"The chrism and the rites, Father Offa. But first, I'd ask you to bear witness to a gift. My lands …" She stopped, gritted her teeth, pushed away the fire with all her will. "My lands at Barking—it was my thought to make a bequest of them to the monks at Ely. I beg you to see it's done." *Maybe this is why God calls me now to His side, so I might give away all I have to His Church.* Had the ache not begun to overwhelm her, she might have said more, given away everything. But there was no time. She cried out, gripped the sheets so her nails tore through them.

The priest nodded, swearing to see it done. He smeared her forehead with holy chrism. Then he lifted one edge of the sheet to do the same on the balls of her feet, mouthing blessings as he did so. His cast came from the shadows above her, lit by a lone, bedside candle, every crease in his skin a deep crack in which the darkness pooled.

He put a hand all made from bony knuckles atop her head. "May the Lord God forgive you your sins, child." From his robes he brought forth the bread of Christ's body. He put it before her shaking lips, and she opened them just enough to take a small bite. It took all her strength to make herself swallow, but once she'd done so, she felt God's holy gift overtaking her. "May the Lord Christ lead you on your way to life everlasting." The words rattled in her ears.

Through a red fog, she heard the priest ask the nun to let him see her piss. Godgyfu pulled the bedclothes more tightly against her nakedness, bewildered. Eanfled lifted a bowl Godgyfu had filled earlier with brownish-pink water, the surface streaked with yellow rot. The monk smelled it.

"Brew some yarrow, and make her drink it all down," he told her caretaker. He made the mark of the cross over her one last time, thanked her for her gift to Ely, and turned to go.

Godgyfu grasped at the darkness, seeking Eanfled. She felt the woman's hand in her own and pulled herself upright. "I'm going to be sick."

When she was done heaving, she was on her hands and knees in the bed, shivering, staring down at the bits of holy bread spattered with gore. She tried moving from bed to floor. She found herself looking into the eyes of the little boy who stood alongside the bed-cove.

"Sweet God, Eanfled, get him out of here! He should not see such ugliness."

Eanfled drew him away, but the lad reached out to lay fingertips on the back of Godgyfu's neck. He leaned in to whisper, lips brushing her ear. "Brother Beocc says all who have faith are fair in the eyes of God. Only sin is ugly." Then he melted into the darkness so swiftly Godgyfu wondered if he had ever been there.

She wept, great wracking sobs, tears when she'd thought she had none left. The glass holding the saint's hair was smooth in her hand, and she gripped it all the tighter.

I want to live. Let me live, and I will be a better Christian. Help me, Saint Osburh, and I give my oath to build the Benedictines an abbey church to house your relics. An abbey more beautiful than any other ... with my own hands, my own pennies. All I have will be yours. All that—

A new pain blinded her, stealing thought. She lost hold of the relic. It fell, shattering against the floor.

My life is yours, Saint Osburh, now and for the rest of my days ....

Sleep's blissful nothingness washed over her, a freedom at last from the fire.

ONE

WORCESTER
12 NOVEMBER 1041

All around Earl Leofric, the town burned. Smoke drifted westward, long, snaking tendrils of gray. His eyes teared and his nostrils stung.

Leofric stood northwest of Worcester, in the market just outside the bank and ditch that made the town into a burh … just beyond the broken, smoldering remains of the gates he'd ordered torn down when he and his men came with the dawn. Behind him the western road descended to the bridge over the Severn; he'd considered burning that too, but until they worked out where most of the townsfolk had gotten themselves to, he wanted to keep all paths open. Even a rickety bridge was preferable to the mud of the ford.

"Hungry?" Osmund held out a filthy neep he'd fished from the wreckage of one toppled stall. The man was the leader of Leofric's housecarls—his household warriors.

Leofric grimaced at his friend as Osmund tossed the fat root back to the ground. His heavy ring shirt was rubbing his shoulders raw, and he was in no mood for laughter.

"Jarl, maybe this better," one of the king's own housecarls said in broken English, rolling a wooden vat before him. Every man the king had sent was a Dane, and Leofric found most of them loud and nettlesome.

"Leave it to a Danishman to sniff out drink," Osmund said, and even Leofric had to smile. A drop of mead was in truth the very thing he needed .... No, not a drop; more like a small lake's worth.

When Osmund handed him a horn, Leofric drained it in one long pull. He wiped the froth from his whiskers with the back of a hand and raised an eyebrow at his man.

"Nothing," Osmund answered, his own dark beard dripping. "If the folk are hiding within the walls, they're not in the hedge stead or anywhere north of the bull street. Our men have taken everything from the chapman haven to the market street and the king's housecarls are burning everything between there and the high street. Had the townsfolk merely hidden as well as this from the king's geld-collectors instead of killing them, all this bother might have been staved off ...."

"If wishes were feathers, graybeards would fly ..." Leofric grumbled, staring southward across the burh. Within the bank's ring, the land sloped up and away from him, sharply here by where the river curved into the town's western side, more gradually toward the middle of Worcester, until it reached the highest point where the minster grounds lay. They were to leave Saint Marie's church and its Benedictine house alone unless they met an answering strike there, but the rest of Worcester was to be shown no mildness. Already smoke from the nearby fires and those the other earls set in the burh's eastern and southern reaches had begun to fill Worcester so the minster looked like a low island in a misty sea. Soon it would be hidden altogether behind the wafting billows. Even the newly risen sun only managed to stab through in scattered, smoky-gold thrusts.

Barely past dawn, Leofric thought, *and already I'd hardly know the stead any more. What am I doing here?*

He chewed his lower lip and walked toward his eldest brother, Godwine, who everyone called Mouse, standing at the market's edge looking up at the grassy bank. Five townsmen—the only ones they'd found so far, all ceorls and thralls—had been spitted on wooden stakes overhanging the ditch. It was another warning about what happened to those who crossed the king. Somewhere in all the smoke behind the dead, the hundred men he'd brought with him awaited his word to get back to overrunning the place.

"I'm earl of the Mercians, am I not?" Leofric asked, coming up behind his brother, but didn't wait for an answer. "And this is a Mercian town. I should be warding it from such harrying, not adding my strength to the harriers ...."

The Mouse opened his mouth but then shut it with a heavy sigh and scratched at his shaggy mop of gray hair. They'd talked about it over and again on the ride to Worcester from Salwarpe, where the Mouse held five hides of land from the church. Mostly they talked about how it would be better for the Mouse and his son to leave Worcestershire for a time until ill will over the raid had waned; Leofric's brother was frightened near to death of what the fieldly folk might do if they got their hands on him, squeaking and crying enough about it to well live up to his unhappy nickname. But there'd also been talk of an earl's burden to his king, of oaths and the worth of men. What more was there to say? No talking could change Leofric's wyrd any more than it could grow back Æthelwine's hands or his ears and nose ....

"Where's Æthelwine gotten himself to?" Leofric asked.

The Mouse nodded his head toward the market's far side, where his broken shard of a son stood watching as a knot of king's housecarls had their way with two women found hiding in the town. Æthelwine was one of those unhappy reminders of the early days when the Danes first took the kingseat, an English troth-ward handed over as a boy to the newly crowned Sveinn Forkbeard. When Sveinn died and King Æthelred wrested his crown back for a spell, Sveinn's son Cnut sent the wards home; some without hands, some missing ears or noses, and some like little Æthelwine missing all three. It was a wonder the lad had lived, and looking thirty years later at his wretched shape and the unsightly hole in the middle of his face, Leofric thought it might have been better if the boy had died from his wounds.

One of the held girls screamed anew as another man stepped up to take his turn with her. Someone smacked her head with a bit of wood, and Æthelwine laughed with all the other men as the screams became muffled sobs. His nephew's laughter whistled through the puckered nose-hole. Leofric almost stepped forward to put an end to the whole business, but then he stopped himself. This sort of thing was to be foreseen, and besides the women were both thralls from Wales.

"Maybe we should send the poxy lasses back to their king when we're done with them," Mouse said with a grim little laugh. The Welsh king Gruffydd ap Llywelyn had killed their younger brother Eadwine in battle two years ago, and his death was still a fresh wound.

"Oh, you're so bold," Leofric mocked, "with Gruffydd back in Wales. But to the son of the man who hacked up your Æthelwine you happily bend your knee while cheering on his housecarls when they help themselves to some Welsh quim!" It came out harder than he'd intended, and Leofric knew he chided himself every bit as much as he chided his brother. Were Godgyfu here rather than back in Coventry, it wouldn't matter to her that the women were Welsh; his wife would see only the wrong being done. Leofric could almost hear her invoking her beloved Osburh, the saint who'd saved Godgyfu from death in her bygone youth, the saint martyred by reavers little worse than the men before him.

Leofric tossed his empty meadhorn to the ground, stalked toward the Danes, and began yanking them off the women. "Enough!" He kicked one of the housecarls who scrambled away on all fours. "We still have to find the God-cursed townsfolk!"

The men grumbled, and one stepped right up against Leofric's chest to glare at him—he could smell the man's foul breath. Leofric laid him flat with a sound elbow to the jaw. "You're here on the king's business, so find whichever Dane leads your sorry lot and be about it!"

The men slunk off, and Leofric spun on a heel, cursing whoever had let them fall into a such wild shambles with work still to be done.

One of the thralls was suddenly clinging to his leg as she crawled alongside him through the mud. "Thank you, lord. Thank you."

He looked down at her bloody, swollen face, then spared a glance for the other one who had not stirred from where she lay naked and witless atop a heap of cloth sacks. Leofric tugged his foot from the woman's grasp and spat as he strode away. *Damned, filthy Welsh.*

When he neared his brother, the man cringed as though waiting for Leofric to strike him too. Then the Mouse barked at Æthelwine to get away from where he still stood gaping at the women, and the wretch heeded his father's call, loping toward them in all his ghastliness.

Leofric turned aside—from his brother, from his nephew, and from the thralls. *Forgive me, Godgyfu.*

He wished the mead had been stronger; his head still felt cursedly clear.

All at once another cloud, darker than the smoke and fast moving, burst into the sky on the Severn's far bank. It changed shape, grew and shrank, into and away from the wind. A great moot of starlings, disturbed from their roosts by the smoke and commotion. The birds danced and wheeled in their sundry way that ever minded Leofric of molten silver. A lone shape shot up from below and tore a starling from the flock in midair, dragging it down and out of Leofric's sight. A dwarf-falcon. Its mate was likely nearby, maybe had even tried to flush the flock toward the other. He wished he had one of his own falcons to wrist. Better to hunt birds than men; leastwise his own men.

Those dwarf-falcons played the same game he and the other earls had worked out. Leofric and the Mercians were to have waited here at the northwest gate, the king's housecarls at the north, while Earls Godwine and Siward and the others came at the town from the south. The townsfolk driven ahead of the spears would have been caught by Leofric or run into the river. As yet, only the starlings had been flushed. Plainly most folk had fled the town before the king's men arrived. *So much for taking them unawares ....*

"Christ," Leofric snapped. He walked through the broken gates into the burh, the Mouse and his son hard on his heels and Osmund falling in behind. He paused for half a step alongside the little gate church where wayfarers could pray to the saints, but then thought better of it; how could he seek Christ's blessing for what they'd come to do? His men were all around him now, thegns and fyrdmen of Derby and Tamworth, Stafford and Shrewsbury, Warwick, and of course his own housecarls from Coventry. Mercians all. He stared at them as they stood awkwardly among the houses and lanes. They had been loath but had come to fight. Finding no foe now, there was almost a merriness about them, merriness grown into wild looting. Notwithstanding his earlier anger at the wildness of the king's housecarls, he knew he had little hope of holding his own men in steady lines any longer. They wandered where they would, taking anything that could be carried away and burning what couldn't. Leofric shook his head at one young Derbyshire man who seemed to have lost sight of this distinction dragging a heavy oaken table through the mud.

"Earl Leofric!" The lad he'd sent along the wall to bring word to the other earls ran up, naked steel in hand. "Osgod Clapa's men are back. They've found the townsfolk. Fled to an island in the Severn, and they have weapons."

So that's where they went—hiding with the beavers. Leofric snorted. "Weapons? What, mattocks? Sticks?" In truth there would have been a good many townsfolk with spears, maybe even a few swords—townsmen who betimes answered the fighting fyrd's gathering. But whatever they had wouldn't be enough to stop the king's own housecarls and the earls' combined strength. The only hope left to the Worcester folk was that the river would be shield enough.

My only hope too, truth be told, if I wish to stave off killing any more of my own commended men and followers. He wondered if he did wish that. *Or would I kill them all to kiss the new king's arse?*

"Do we take the island?" His man did not sound at all keen.

Leofric shook his head. "Not yet. Maybe all of them didn't make it there. For now we do as King Harthacnut bid. Take the burh, slay anyone we find, and reave at will. Move south and meet the other earls at the minster grounds." Saying the words left him cold. But they were the king's words. And he knew Harthacnut was not wrong given what had had happened when the king's housecarls came in May to gather the higher gelds he'd set. Rather than hand over the pennies, the Worcester folk set upon and killed the geldmen, nailing one to the abbey-church door, if the tales could be believed!

What else could the king do but send a gang of his housecarls and summon his earls from all over England to right the wrong? This was no local matter to be settled in the Fishborough hundred moot; Worcester threatened to break up the onefold ship so carefully crafted by King Alfred's sons and grandsons and held together for a hundred years by all the ealdormen and earls who had been the iron seam-nails in the kingdom's hull.

I know it, and yet I say the words over and again in my mind to bring myself under their sway. Leofric spat into the mud and led the way toward the middle of town. At least the wafting smoke hid most of what they had wrought here. The town was a wreck: wagons overturned, fires everywhere, cows slaughtered in their stalls, the streets choked with trash. In and out of it all, the men scuttled about like rats in a midden heap. Once, as a boy of no more than eight, he'd been with his father in the south of England when a great Danish host came a-viking in their dragon-headed ships. They'd barely gotten away and only because they'd had a fast horse at hand—Hræfn, he thought the horse's name had been. He remembered that long-gone southern raid looking something like this, only now he was with the Danes doing the viking.

Viking! Godgyfu had called it that before he left Coventry; the scorn in his wife's eyes had burned into him like a brand, and he'd been scratching at the wound ever since.

A swift wind from the south pushed aside some of the nearby smoke. Riders approached.

"Ballocks," Leofric grumbled as he saw Earl Godwine among them, Thuri and Hrani in tow.

"Who do you think looks more like a pig?" Osmund asked. "Thuri or Hrani?"

Leofric sniffed. "They've both gotten fat enough on the bits of my earldom Harefoot and Harthacnut gave them like so much slops. I'd be happy enough to see them both carved into backmeat."

"Backmeat!" Æthelwine snorted, snot flying from his nose slit.

"That's the Danes," Osmund whispered, for the men were nearly in earshot now. "Harthacnut may wear two crowns, but he's always going to help his Danish underfolk first, even when it means more ugliness for good Englishmen."

"Speaking of ugliness," Leofric shouted as Earl Godwine pulled back on his horse's bridle before them. Godwine was no Dane but had wedded one and still seemed ever to reap good hap under them.

The earl took no mind of Leofric's opening thrust. "You heard about the island?" he barked. "They were warned. They knew we were coming!" He stared at Leofric, eyes blazing above his straw-colored beard and blotchy weasel's face.

Leofric saw the unspoken accusation in his eyes, could almost hear it upon his lips. He met the man's stare, unblinking, daring him to say the words aloud. "Do you think so?" Leofric answered at last. "I thought maybe half the God-cursed town had been lucky enough to think this a good day for an outing on the water!"

Hrani and Thuri laughed, but Godwine only sniffed. Then he caught sight of Æthelwine, and his eyebrows climbed his forehead. "Christ's bleeding wounds, what is *that*!"

"My brother's son."

Godwine alit. "Ah yes, I've heard of this one. Been hiding him away, have you?" He stepped up to get a closer look at Æthelwine and gave an overblown shudder. "Had a little run in with King Cnut back in the day, did you? The whole business puts me in mind of that fellow from the old Welsh saga … the one who cut the lips and ears and eyelids off the Irish king's horses." Godwine stopped to laugh. "I've an outstanding gleeman back at my hall in Bosham who tells the tale wonderfully. You truly should come be my guest some time, Leofric, and hear it. Oh, but then I suppose you've no great love of things Welsh lately."

Leofric bit his tongue and stared back at Godwine with what he hoped was a stony cast.

His brother's own loud laughter broke in upon the awkward quiet. "I once saw a horse with no lips. Kept licking its teeth."

Godwine turned. "You must be Earl Leofric's brother with whom I share a name? I'm glad folk call you Mouse, as I'd hate to think anyone might ever mistake us one for the other."

"No, Earl," Mouse answered, casting a sidelong look at Leofric as though afraid he might have spoken out of turn.

Godwine laughed again and came over to slap Leofric on the shoulder. "Nothing like kin, eh?"

Leofric would have liked nothing better than to smack the haughty sneer right off the man's face.

Instead, he turned to Osmund, who stood gawking. "I thought I told you to go loot something."

"Yes, Earl." The man had the sense to run off without further words. The smoke thickened around them now as the wind shifted; Leofric breathed in too much, and a coughing fit overtook him.

"I must say you sound overwrought, Leofric," Godwine said. "Is this hard for you?"

Leofric turned at the sound of a roof crumbling behind him, watched it send up a swarm of burning embers. He cleared his lungs with a last hack. "I obey the king, as do you. Forgive me if I cannot summon the glee with which you blinded Alfred Aetheling."

Godwine ignored the barb. "Yes, like a worthy hound you are, licking at whatever hand feeds you, which now happens to be Harthacnut. But to see your own lands laid waste ...."

Leofric nearly choked again; *this* from Godwine, who changed lords like a lord's woman changed clothes.

The man's gloating smile was like two fat, pink worms in the nest of his beard. Leofric was a breath away from mashing a fist into that smile, when Osmund ran back, two others with him looking winded.

"There's a large gang who did not make it to the island!" Osmund yelled. "Earl Siward's just flushed them from their hiding-hole. But it's a true mess now; seems the fighting's spilling out over half the town."

As though summoned by his words, there came a clang of steel. Leofric looked and made out two men struggling alongside a burning wagon not far off. Swords flashed, one man fell, and the other melted back into the smoke.

"Right! Gather the men!" Leofric shouted to Osmund even as Godwine and the other earls shouted their own bidding. "I want half moving down this road with me, the rest following you down the high road. We'll meet up at the minster—"

More shouts and louder clanging cut him off. A heartbeat later, a tide of men came up the smoky road and washed over them, kingsmen and townsfolk both, locked in a running fight. Leofric spun, reaching down to tear his sword Bloodwreak from its sheath. He heard Godwine calling the king's name as a sort of war-cry. "Harthacnut! Harthacnut!" Then his sword met a Worcester man's spear butt, and he was ducking splinters. The man stared at him a moment, his mouth an open hole between hairless cheeks; a boy then. The lad leapt forward, making to drive his broken shaft into Leofric's throat, but by then it was too late. Bloodwreak took off the boy's lower jaw in a red spray.

A riderless horse nearly ran over Leofric, but he fell away from it and landed hard upon his right knee. An old wound from Assandun ever ached him there, and he winced at the fire now blossoming in his leg. *It's nothing!* he told himself and leapt back onto his feet. Earl Godwine stood straight before him in a tight knot of his own housecarls, each laying about him with blade and axe. One scar-faced man was shouting something, the words lost in the wider tumult of bellows and thick, wet smacks. Only when a louder sound, not of the whole, came to him did he think to turn. A new wave of townsfolk rushed from another byway between two burning granaries.

Leofric lifted his sword, and all became a blur of jarring blows given and taken, wide mouths screaming at him, wild eyes and thirsty blades. Afterward he remembered little; there had been an old man with rotten teeth whose nose he'd mashed with his hilt, another man who'd almost lost his head to Bloodwreak before Leofric recognized him as one of the king's own. At last he stood with no living foemen about and drove his sword hard into the earth so as to rest for a breath with his weight upon it. He found himself blinking and reached up to touch his eye. His hand came away red with blood, and he searched a little higher, wincing when he prodded a swollen wound above his brow he didn't even remember getting.

"What a thrice cursed heap of pig's bread," he grunted at no one. The smoke had swallowed him; he could see but a few steps ahead. There was still a din of fighting about him, but it seemed far now, ghost ripples. The whole thing had become a mess, and he wished for the more orderly lines of the shieldwall the men would have wontedly drawn up into for a true fight.

But this is no fight, he reminded himself. *Godgyfu's right. It's a bloody raid, a bit of Danish viking.*

Only … no viking was ever so quiet as the burh had now become. *Where have my men gotten to?* He dimly called to mind sending them off like a pack of hounds—pointing with his dripping sword toward where Earls Thuri and Hrani looked to be having a hard time keeping the townsfolk at bay.

"Osmund!" he called. "Mouse? Where are you, brother?" *Leave it to Mouse to have gotten himself killed!* He took a few steps, then found he couldn't tell which way he walked. The sun was straight overhead, a brighter glow in the gray-white all around him. *If I keep on, I'll find someone—friend or foe.* He swiped with his sword at the smoke, cutting his way through it. He called his wife to mind—her ruddy hair and smiling eyes—something to grab hold of, to ground him. *Help me, Godgyfu. Give me your strength.*

In a short while he felt turf beneath his feet and so worked out he must have been walking westward toward the river. He'd wandered into the hedge stead where once kingly halls and wooded yards had stood. Now it was mostly given over to warehouses. Taken by a wild urge to be away and back where his men were fighting, Leofric spun on a heel.

A shadow brought him up short, and he wondered whether he dreamt.

A massive white stag stepped out … antlers tall and rendered golden in the swirling smoke. It snorted once and tossed its head, eyes wide and wild. Again, the eerie quiet struck Leofric. He and the stag were the only living beings in all the wide world, or else he had stepped through the mist into another world altogether. Had the stag wandered in from the wilds, dizzy from the smoke? If so, it had to have forded the river.

Leofric touched his wound, which had swollen now to a great mass on the side of his forehead. He sucked a breath at the sharp ache, then rubbed his eyes with the knuckles of thumb and forefinger.

When he opened his eyes again, the stag was gone.

He took a step forward. Then another. The smoke thinned somewhat, blowing eastward with a new wind. Leofric quickened his step, eager to find the others. The ache in his head worsened, and a queasiness overtook him as his vision intermittently doubled. The world spun. He fell shaking to his knees and in one mighty heave brought up all the mead he'd drunk earlier. He gagged again but had nothing left in him.

How long he crouched on hands and knees, waiting for the spinning to stop, he could not say. In time a sound came. Shouts.

"Osmund!" Leofric called, lurching to his feet, steadier now. "Beorhtwine!"

But it was not his men. Hounds had found some of the dead and were gnawing at them, yipping and barking over their grisly feast.

Twice Leofric tripped over bodies. "These are no warriors," he whispered, peering at the slaughter he'd wrought. Some ten men lay within a few yards, most likely his own handiwork. There wasn't a scrap of chain byrnie or even a bit of boiled leather between them. And the weapons they still held in dead hands ... two axes of the sort woodsmen used to fell trees, one rusted sword looking old enough to have been some Roman centurion's, and the rest a sorry lot of cudgels and sticks.

"Talking to the dead?" words came from behind him.

Leofric turned toward a rider nearing on a big dapple-gray. He wore a hunting horn around his neck and a brownish-gray smock over his byrnie. "Earl Siward," Leofric shouted. He couldn't bring to mind the last time he'd been so happy to see a friendly face. Walking alongside and behind the Earl of Northumbria were a score or so of his men, hung in leather and ring, bristling with sword and spear. The earl alit from his horse and stepped up alongside Leofric to stare at the bodies.

"These are farmers," Leofric said. "If I turn them over, I reckon I knew half by name. This was no warrior's work. It's shameful. We are shamed before God."

Siward made a noise that might have been a laugh and fingered the old scar running from above one big ear down to his chin. "They thwarted their rightful king. The shame is theirs, and we are God's wrathful spearhead."

Leofric peered at his friend and tried to work out if he was being mocked. He knew Siward was half a Northern heathen himself, though the man put on a good outward show of faith in Christ. But he decided he'd had enough of fighting with men who should have been his friends, and he let the words pass. "Have you seen my brother or his son? Are they well?"

Siward nodded, then shrugged. "Leastwise as well as Æthelwine can ever be."

Leofric grunted. "And Earl Godwine?" He tried not to let the eagerness for a different answer show through his words.

"Earl Godwine's got the rest of the townsmen penned up to the east, and he's making the high street into a butcher's yard."

Leofric grabbed a scrap of torn cloak from a body at his feet. He used it to wipe blood from his sticky blade. His belly heaved, and he feared he would retch again. He did his best to shove his queasiness aside and turned the start of a gagging cough into a curse. "Christ. Bloody Christ."

Siward sighed and planted his own sword-tip in the earth. "You know what they did, friend. They brought this on themselves. Feader and Thurstan were good men, murdered on the king's business. Did you know *them?*"

Leofric made to spit, but his mouth was dry. "Aye. Thurstan I knew, his wife and son too. The other not but to look upon him. Their slaying was unworthily done ...." Whatever words he was about to say were stolen from him when his own men goaded a woman forward before a thicket of spears. She'd been stripped naked, her hair unbound to blow about her in the rising wind.

Leofric knew her. She was the daughter of a Worcester chapman he'd done business with often. No older than seventeen, not yet wed as far as he could bring to mind. And she was a comely maiden, with good skin and golden hair. Between her legs her hair was darker, he saw, and a warm flush rose in his cheeks. His breath quickened again, as it had when he fought.

A trembling overtook his arms and legs. *What's wrong with me?* This was no different than what was done to the Welsh thralls in the market. He'd seen scores of women taken by the winners after a fight—it was the way of war. But ... somehow this *was* different. This was no thrall or ceorl's daughter. This was a worthy young woman made to walk naked through the streets of her home. She had no doubt walked the very path she now took untold times, trading words with her neighbors, maybe sweet-talking some young man or another. But now, here she was, every bit of her bared, the men around her roughly jeering. One man had even opened his breeches to flap his manhood at her, thrusting his hips shamefully.

Leofric should have been wroth with his men over such a thing, should have knocked a few heads in and given his own mantle to the girl to put over her shoulders. Instead, he found himself burning with lust, quaking, overcome by a heat so strong it almost made him drop to his knees. *What's the matter with me?* He'd never had such ... awful, unseemly thoughts before. The girl tried to look away from the thrusting oaf, and the hopelessness of her bid for modesty only stoked the unwelcome fire growing in Leofric.

She was past him now. Soon she'd be out of sight beyond a ruined hall. He watched her buttocks working as she strode and tried to regain his wits by making himself think of the dread the unhappy girl's father would be feeling were he here—*his own daughter* walked about for all and sundry to drink in with their eyes. Likely the father was dead or dying somewhere beneath Earl Godwine's blade or would be soon if he was among those hiding on the island ....

Just before the girl melted away, someone threw a handful of dung at her so that her pale skin became smeared with it. *A dirty … filthy whore!* All at once Leofric's knees did buckle. He felt himself spilling his seed inside his breeches and stared down at himself, aghast. *What in heaven's name?* A great, screaming pain filled his head in answer.

"You should have your man see to that bruise," Siward said, squinting at Leofric's brow. "It looks dreadful and may need draining."

Leofric hardly heard him but brought to mind the earl's earlier words. *Siward is right. This is a godless burh.* It was a wanton stead in which the devil had come to play with men's minds and lead them down sinful paths. *Whores and forsworn wretches! Murderers!* He looked out over the burning town, fiery tongues licking at gray skies, and it was as though he looked upon the devil's reich in truth. All hell spread out before him!

"Devils!" he screamed aloud, though his own words sounded far off to him, buried beneath the blood-rush in his ears, the pounding ache in his forehead. The king had bid them scour the town—clean it of its blight. "Devils!"

He scrambled to his feet and ran, headlong like a bolting stag, into the swirling smoke, taking up a burning timber in one hand, his sword gripped tight in his other. When he came across a row of houses somehow unburned, he shoved his brand up under the overhanging thatch and watched the fire spread, a spill of crackling red, climbing, feeding. A man and a woman ran from a house, the light of God's fire driving them forth from … from where they must have thought to hide their sins.

The man saw Leofric and stepped between him and his woman, one arm raised to ward them from his wrath. The whore was crying out, screaming, the sound scraping against Leofric's ears. The man went down in a spray of red. Leofric sent the woman down atop him, Bloodwreak hacking over and again to stop her before she could tempt him further, drive him away from Christ. "Devils!"

He ran headlong through the town. All became red—fire, sin, blood.

COVENTRY
17 NOVEMBER 1041

THOMAS RAN FROM THE ABBEY building site with an urgency bordering on fear. It was the feast day of Saint Hilda of Whitby, but the weather was unwontedly mild for this late in the year, and Thomas knew his goddess would be basking in the warmth and sunshine as always. She'd walk along the Sherbourne's banks almost to where it flowed into the Sowe until she came to the old oak beneath which she ever loved to while her mornings south of town.

Thomas took a less winding path, following the London road until it bent eastward then cutting south through open fields. His passing bothered some sheep who lifted their heads to roll their eyes and bleat, but otherwise he went unmarked, which was well.

When he spotted the great tree with its spreading limbs and thickly leafed crown, he sighed with relief; she had not yet come, which meant he could hide himself well and near to her and not have to suffer watching from afar. He threw the sack he bore under a hedge and shoved the branches together to better hide it from passing eyes. Running, he came at last under the oak and put a foot to the bole, pulling himself up into branches he'd come to know so well. *Up and up and up again*, he sang to himself; high enough that he'd be well hidden in his rough-spun, brown woolens, but low enough that the leaves wouldn't fully block his view.

Finding his spot, he settled back against the forked limb and closed his eyes, hoping to reclaim the sleep he'd been robbed of with Earl Leofric off in Worcester. The soughing wind and a wren's whir lulled him, and behind his eyelids he saw her again as she'd revealed herself to him when first he'd come to Coventry late that Eastertide: a lady on a white horse, the morning sun rising behind her as she rode up the High Street. The horse's step had been slow and even, and bathed in that light, she'd seemed clothed in shining, golden silk. Thomas knew at once he'd found his long-sought beacon.

A twin half of himself.

A worthy haven for his soul ....

Some small sound made him start, and Thomas came fully awake, dizzy for a time with the dappled sunlight shifting through the branches. *How long have I slept?*

He looked down. Godgyfu had arrived.

She stood near the stream bank, face upturned and eyes closed to let the sunlight fall upon her marble skin. What a wondrous, comely thing she was: long neck, strong chin, full lips. Her wide mouth only seldom curled in mirth, but even in its downturned sternness, she seemed to smile, filled with an inner bliss. Her nose, too, was wide and proud between strong cheekbones, eyes set far apart so as to make her lordly and wise. From what he could gather, she was in her thirty-first year, had been born a little more than ten years before Thomas himself, but at an age when most women were well on their way to becoming crones, Godgyfu kept a youthful glow. Even the lines at her eyes gave her a happy, rather than aged cast. In truth, every maiden Thomas had ever seen was unlovely next to her.

She opened her eyes at last and dropped her gaze to the book she'd been holding—a boon-book with wooden boards bedecked with pretty stones. He'd seen her with it once before in past weeks but only from afar, and he welcomed the chance to look it over more carefully. She came within the tree's shade and settled herself on the ground. Her back against the bole, she hiked her long skirts up above her knees to fold her legs before her and set the book upon her lap. Her knees were even paler than her marble cast, the hair on her shins a fine down. Squinting as Godgyfu opened the book, Thomas saw the staff was blackened on the leaf in a fine, steady hand—a bit too far for him to make out all the words, but near enough to see it was English, not the Church tongue. He thought Godgyfu might indeed know a smattering of Latin, but only to speak it, not to read.

She turned the page with long fingers, and Thomas sucked a breath. More words filled the back of the first leaf, but the facing one bore a likeness of the Blessed Maiden in lively hues. Marie's crown and halo shone in the day's brightness, her eyes looking heavenward and her hands raised, set asunder, opened outward. This was Marie as Queen ... like the Lady of the Mercians, Æthelflaed; would that he had lived a hundred years earlier to have known such a woman. But the Marie likeness was even more: a queen, yes, but also a goddess, like Rhiannon of the Welsh. He should have known Godgyfu would have a book like this; she eagerly followed the Queen of Heaven, and she herself was Thomas's own Rhiannon come back to full-blooded life.

He saw her inner might and worth most at times like these, when she was alone and his being there was unmarked; that was when all women were at their strongest, when they were the wild wights he alone could see them as. Aware of him, they became something other, the way they were around other men. Smaller. Shadowed.

When Godgyfu uncovered her head, Thomas envisioned a golden crown atop it. *She should be clothed all in gold and cloth of gold and the soft cloth they make across the sea in Cambrai.*

"Hail Marie," her voice all at once rose toward him like a bell, "full of God's gift, the Lord is with thee ...."

The prayer's words washed over Thomas, a cleansing rain that rose from the earth and flew to the clouds. He felt his heartbeat quicken and had to close his eyes, make his breath come slower lest it give him away to Godgyfu's little ears. Then she grew quiet. For a long while she stayed so still, Thomas wondered if she might have drifted into sleep.

He watched her shoulders' steady rise and fall. His hand reached beneath his leather vest to stroke the linen folded and tucked away there. The day before, he had snatched an undertunic from Godgyfu's own washbasket ere her handmaid had a chance to bring it to the water. He brought it up to his nose as he kept his gaze settled upon her, breathing in the lavender she was wont to wear along with the sour-sweet smell of her sweat. He closed his eyes and saw himself lying alongside her; their bodies did not touch, but her long, rusty locks, dusted by the barest hint of gray, were unbound to cover and enfold him like an angel's wings ....

A loud crack nearly caused him to drop the linen. *She's seen me!*

No. He wanted to laugh when he saw she'd taken three red apples from a sack. Her teeth cracked a second time through the crisp flesh. She sucked at the juice, then popped the last bit into her mouth, chewing the seeds with great smacks. She even let out a happy sigh that minded him of the sounds she sometimes made when her husband took her as a man takes a woman—a wild-kin grunting as she exulted in the way her body made the great earl her thrall. *In a rightwise world, the earl would be her thrall even without such sullying of the flesh.*

Thomas smiled and watched her eat the second apple, then most of the third before she stopped and left a bit of the kernel-shell on the grass beside her. Doubtless she'd eaten her wonted hornfish and leeks with brown bread for morning-meal and now grew full.

Godgyfu was rising then, putting her hair back up and covering it in a pale green headcloth, richly broided with a band of blossoms along its edge. Thomas loved that his Lady always decked herself in such finery. In that she minded him of yet another woman—Saint Edith of Wilton, who had once been offered the crown of England. A man would have grasped at the offer; only a woman like Edith would have had the wit to forbear such a cursed hat. He'd met an old woman once in Malmesbury who had truly been there to witness Edith stand up to the Bishop of Winchester when that arse in jeweled head-linen thought to chide her for her bright, fair clothes. How he wished he'd been there too to see the look the bloated bishop must have worn when Edith told him a mind could be as clean and true under golden cloth as under his own tattered hides. Thomas nearly laughed aloud and had to put a hand over his mouth.

He glanced down; Godgyfu had left. He waited a while for her to make her way farther back along the Severn and out of sight, guessing she'd go to the abbey now to make her daily oversight of the building work. After, she'd make her rounds of Coventry, doing what she could to put down the waxing grumbles over what her husband had done in the Danish devil-king's name. In which case, Thomas thought he should do what he could to stoke the anger ....

He put a foot on a lower branch.

Earl Leofric was not back yet. But word of what had been happening in Worcester leaked in. It was shameful. All those men and women put to the sword! Maybe it was the very thing needed to turn anger into open rising. *Men who rise against their king are that much closer to rising against their God.*

From the lowest branch, Thomas leapt down and landed in a crouch, hands gripping the flattened grass where Godgyfu had left her mark. Perhaps he'd head a bit farther along the river to Allesley and see if he could spread some bile there among some of Coventry's nearest neighbors. He thought he might well sway a few of those folk to kneel to Rhiannon as a more wholesome lord than anything Denmark had to offer. Better than anything of the Church too, truth be told. The lad Coenwulf and his sister would be a good place to start; Sveinn Forkbeard's men had killed both their father and mother.

Thomas took up the apple core Godgyfu had left behind in the grass. He ran the tip of the little finger on his right hand along the teeth marks, slick with his Lady's own spittle. He brought the apple up to his mouth and traced the toothmarks with his tongue, tasting her. Lightning ran through him as he felt her strength enter him. Then he lowered the apple, held it out before him and let a line of his own spittle drip down to pool in the tooth mark. He thought about eating it, then deemed it more fit to bury it beneath the tree. He went to a knee, wriggled his fingers into the loam beneath the grass, and tore up a clump. Once he'd dropped in his offering, he covered it over again and made silent boon ....

Blessed Rhiannon, wife and mother, bestower of kingship, speak for us and do not scorn to give your help. For we trust always in your love.

Allesley could wait; Coenwulf wasn't going anywhere. Thomas rose. He wished to be near Godgyfu again—his queen and one day soon the goddess into which he would make her. The goddess already dwelling beneath her skin, though she herself did not yet know it.

He ran first to his hidden sack. Within was the coarse black cowl that would have hindered running and climbing, but now he shrouded himself once again as a novice of the Benedictines.

"*De gente fera Normannica nos libera, Domine*," he mouthed the old monk's boon against the Northmen's bloody wrath and crossed himself as his new brothers were forever doing.

COVENTRY
24 NOVEMBER 1041

For the first time, Godgyfu felt a hint of coming winter in what had otherwise been a blessedly warm November. She pulled her wrap tight and made her way among the market stalls, glad to see how busy the morning already was. She spotted folk she knew from Binley and Foleshill and Coundon, even two from as far off as her holdings in Appleby in the south of Derbyshire, likely come to pray before Saint Osburh's shrine. Of course, there were all the craftsmen and workers and their families, here to help build the abbey. It gladdened Godgyfu's heart to see it; before long Coventry would be one of the great towns!

"How are we with cole?" she asked Beornflæd, eyeing the stacked, leafy heads as they passed a stall groaning beneath its late-harvest weight.

Her old handmaid scratched her hip. "Ye mean yer husband's nephew? I think I saw him lurking about the lichyard with yer boy …."

Smiling, Godgyfu hit her playfully on the arm. "He can't help how he looks." *Which is an unhappy thing*, she thought. *Now's hardly the time for another reminder of the Danes' bitter bloodlust.* But she understood why her husband had brought the Mouse and his broken son home with him for the nonce. They were blood, and that was that. "And you know well what I mean."

Beornflæd shrugged, eyes merry behind deep wrinkles. "Could do with another few." She took some pale green heads for her sack.

"Those coles are from the abbey's own gardens," Abbess Tova said, stepping up alongside them and pushing back an edge of her wimple, which a sudden wind had threatened to blow over her eyes. She and Godgyfu were of a like age, and Tova the closest thing Godgyfu had ever known to a blood sister.

"Then keep another penny," she said, handing over more than was needed to the old fellow manning the abbey's stall.

"Bless ye," he said.

"God has already blessed me," she answered, "and I've our good Saint Osburh to thank for that."

All three women made the mark of the cross upon themselves.

"Shall I walk with you for a bit?" the abbess asked.

Godgyfu nodded. "We're done here anyway, heading over to see the work."

Through the gap in a hedge to the east, the market opened up into the wide minster grounds atop Coventry's middle rise. The yard swarmed now with stonewrights and craftsmen, gravers and treewrights. Everywhere men hauled stone, took careful metings with lengths of string or notched sticks, carved or hammered wood, dug holes and ditches, and worked at a hundred other deeds that made for a dizzying whirl. To an outsider first come upon it, the grounds might have looked like a trodden anthill—wild and thoughtless; but Godgyfu had come to see the pattern in the weave. She could look now at any man among the many and know what stitch he added to the greater whole. Among the workers, the black-robed Benedictines brought drink to the thirsty, gave blessings, and even betimes put their own backs to a shovel or to hauling baskets and barrows. Coming here always made Godgyfu glad. She smiled and crossed herself again. *Thanks be to God.*

Overshadowing it all was the new abbey Godgyfu and her husband were building for the Benedictines. Its climbing stone walls stood atop the spot where Tova's own little abbey had stood; the few sisters the abbess oversaw had been moved for the time being into an even smaller house on the rise's northeastern bend. Godgyfu hoped to work out a more lasting spot for them soon.

Beornflæd shaded her eyes with a bony hand and looked up at the abbey church decked in a skeleton of wooden boards for the workers to climb upon. "Nearer to done by the day. And a right pretty threesome it'll make with the other two."

Godgyfu looked across the nearby graveyard to the minster's smaller churches. To the south stood Holy Trinity, which she and Leofric had re-hallowed in Blessed Marie's name; it held Osburh's shrine and was where Godgyfu herself heard mass. Once the abbey church was done, this smaller church would be given over to do for the flock of folk living on abbey lands in and about Coventry. Still smaller was Saint Michael's a bit to the east. Lacking the cross-shape of the other two churches, Saint Michael's nave and chancel were a onefold box, but Godgyfu and her husband had rebuilt its wooden walls with stone some years back, and it would do well for the folk living on her and Leofric's own nearby lands. The monks, of course, would have the new abbey church to themselves.

"Another year," Godgyfu said, half to herself, "maybe two, and it will all be done."

"Come see how the cloister is coming." Abbess Tova led the women on a weaving path among the workers and around to the abbey church's far side. The groundwalls of the linked house in which the Benedictines would live had now been laid, and already it was easy to see what a wonderful thing it would be when done. Godgyfu almost felt tears come as she stared out over the low stones and down the sharp slope leading to Osburh's pool—the very spot where Cnut's raiders struck down the sainted abbess while she fled to bring the church's relics to safety. The Sherbourne snaked idly through Coventry, between scattered houses and farmsteads, flooding the pool before keeping on past Coventry's mill, then south and east. Past the pool and its wider marshes, the still waters of Swan's Well sparkled like a great penny in the morning sun, and beyond that the yellows, browns, and greens of late harvest-tide woodlands faded northward into gray mist.

As ever, the sight stirred her deeply. She felt her soul bound up in this stead—the town, its people, its saint—all these things together had saved her life and made her who she was today. It was something she could never fully give back in kind, though she had made it her life's work to do so.

A deep voice broke in upon Godgyfu's happy thoughts. "A gleaming fair sight, no?"

She turned and found the monk with bulging eyes standing alongside her. "Tova, have you met Mannig yet? He's only come yesterday from Evesham, but he'll be in Coventry through the winter."

The abbess nodded and smiled at the newcomer. "I've not yet had the good hap, but your fame comes before you, Brother Mannig. Men name you one of the greatest craftsmen of our time."

"Merely *one* of them?" the man asked, his eyes opened even wider in mock hurt. He gave a sly grin behind the gray scruff of short whiskers. "I must look into this slight."

Abbess Tova hid her own smile behind a hand, but Godgyfu and her maid laughed loud and merrily.

"Mannig's brought a gang of goldsmiths with him," Godgyfu went on. "They'll be crafting a new shrine for Saint Osburh under his oversight. I hope I might also sway him to hue the walls of the abbey church with some worthy likenesses once the roof's been laid. Do you know my boon-book, Tova? Mannig inked it himself—the words and the likenesses both."

Tova nodded. "It is a comely book, giving great worth to Christ and His saints. And we are blessed to have you crafting the shrine."

Mannig bowed his tonsured head in acknowledgement. "The least I could do for Godgyfu and the Earl, who gave so much to allow the renewal work at my own abbey. Speaking of which, I should find my men and be about my craft."

"As should I," Godgyfu said. "The house I've given over to you is to your liking?"

Mannig nodded. "Slept like a babe last night. And there's plenty of good, bright sunlight for my work."

"I'm glad." She bid the man a good day as he strolled off humming a lively song. *To think ... Mannig himself. Here in Coventry! It's all coming together now ...*

"I should go see to my sisters," Tova said. "Yesterday I caught young Eawynn making moon eyes through the window at one of the Welsh ditch-diggers."

Godgyfu gave Tova a parting embrace, then kept on with Beornflæd in tow. Before leaving the minster grounds, they bided a short while more among the southernmost of the graves, one of the few quiet spots atop the rise. There, Godgyfu knelt and withdrew the bundle she'd kept tucked through her belt. Drawing forth a fresh holly bough—bright green with plump red berries—she laid it atop the spot where dear old Sister Eanfled was buried; holly had ever been Eanfled's favorite.

"She helped forestall my doom every bit as much as the saint," she whispered to Beornflæd. "I don't know what I'd have done without her during that dark time."

"So ye've told me more times than I can reckon. Her and the priest both."

"Father Offa. Had God not sent him to me with his knowledge of foul brews to bring me back from the brink ..." She shuddered and broke off a single sprig of the holly and put it on the grave of the priest who lay alongside Eanfled. Then she wiped away the threat of tears, pushed aside her mother's shade who ever lurked at the edge of thought in times like these, and stared southward. She could just see her house peeking out from among the farthest trees beyond the High Street. The same house where she'd been laid up all those years ago, sick unto death, her life a sorry wreck. Back before ever she'd met Leofric. But a lone house then, now it was grown into a lordly landseat with a wide hall and a good handful of outbuildings—a worthy home for the earl of the Mercians. It was the only home she felt she'd ever truly known. When she lay dying there with Sister Eanfled at her bedside, the thought of breathing her last in that little house, in a backwater bit of nowhere like Coventry, had filled Godgyfu with dread. Now there was nowhere else she'd rather spend her last days on God's earth. "Let's go home."

They wended their way down from the graves to cross over the High Street. They'd hardly gone more than a few steps onto the road, however, when a voice called out: "The blessings of Saint Crysogonus upon you both."

Godgyfu half expected another of her husband's housecarls with a sack of pennies in hand. Since Leofric had come home, already three of the men he'd taken with him had come to her, all stinking of mead, to bestow the reavings they'd taken from Worcester; they told her to use the silver to help pay for the abbey. She knew guilt drove them all. Guilt over four days of wild viking while Leofric and the other earls made their bid to take the island. Thankfully the folk hiding there had held out until a peace was worked out to let them go home. *But home to what? Scorched earth and tumbled down timbers? Who but a Northman* berserkr *wouldn't feel guilty for what had been done?*

Whatever spurred them, at least those three housecarls had done the right thing in giving their ill-gotten pennies to the Church. It was more than could be said for most of the others. More than could be said for Leofric himself, who deemed the vast hoard he'd brought back fair payment for what he'd done for the king! Godgyfu was not of the same mind, which was why she'd forbidden Leofric from bringing even one penny of that hoard into their home. She wore the keys to their storeroom and their penny chests; as the woman of the house, their wealth was in her hands to oversee, and she was not about to dirty it with Worcester's blood. Leofric grumbled, but she held her ground, and the reavings had not come into their household. Wherever else he'd put it—some hiding-hole of his—she didn't know and didn't care.

But the man who gave his blessing that day on the street was not a housecarl; that much became plain as soon as Godgyfu turned. He was a Benedictine—a novice from the look of him. His face was familiar, and she realized she had reckoned him one of the builders—had she not seen him climbing the scaffolds?—but now here he was in a monk's robes.

"I'm sorry?"

"Saint Crysogonus," the novice said again. "Today is his feast day."

"So it is. And I thank you for—"

"Yes," the young man cut her off, and Godgyfu raised her eyebrows at his rudeness. "Yes, but do you know of the saint's martyrdom? Beheaded by the Roman caesar, his body thrown into the sea so it could only be buried once it washed up on the strand. Does that put you in mind of anyone we know?"

Godgyfu's limbs turned to ice. She knew very well what the fellow spoke of. King Harthacnut had done something very like that to his forerunner on the kingseat—his own hated half-brother Harefoot, whose body he dug up and dumped into a shite-filled ditch and later into the Thames. *Danes! Give them a crown, and they're still little better than Northmen a-viking.* But such words were not for the High Street. Not now.

"Putting aside anyone we know," Godgyfu said, "I don't believe I know *you.*" She did her best not to sound as bothered as she felt by the lopsided grin roosting between the monk's big ears. Even the floppy tuft of gold-brown hair hanging over his forehead and into his eyes seemed to mock her as a stray wind blew it about.

The novice made an overblown bow, then rose with a flash of teeth that made him look even younger than she'd first guessed. *More handsome too, if truth be told.* That she noticed this last thing bothered her all the more. "I am Thomas, Lady Godgyfu."

Beornflæd hid a laugh behind her palm.

"La—? Godgyfu will do. I am an earl's wife, not a queen."

"In that you're wrong. Rhiannon of the Welsh was known far and wide for her open-handed giving, and the greatness of a king is meted not only by his craftiness or the might of his sword but by the freedom with which he gives of his wealth."

Godgyfu cocked her head but did not ask further after his meaning; she began to think him rather odd. "Thomas, you say. An unwonted kind of name."

He shrugged. "My father was from Normandy."

"And your mother?"

"Welsh." His blue-eyed gaze dropped to the dirt for the first time. She thought she might have seen something of shame there. Likely he knew what the Welsh king had done to Leofric's brother Eadwine.

She gave the lad a heartening smile. "Your speech has little of the outlander about it, for all that."

"Indeed. Both my parents … died when I was but a child. I have lived in England most of my life, though I am only lately come back from long years in Wales. The Benedictines were ever kind to me, and I've thought to troth myself to them. I heard of your good work here to remake a house of God on the site of the gutted nunnery. Under the Danes, I find much of England dead and soulless even as Dyfed was under the Gray One's curse. Only here in Coventry have I found a haven from the wretchedness. It is a worthy thing you do, Lady. I can't help but wonder though if men such as Harthacnut truly give it the worth it's owed. Whether even the Church itself understands what a dear jewel it has in you."

She snorted before she could stop herself and did her best to hold back yet another smile threatening to stretch her lips. *Pride is a sin.* "Do you mock me now, Brother Thomas?"

"I am a monk's thrall, not a brother." He twinned the cadence of her own earlier words. "Not until I've taken my oath. I mean only to let you know this newcomer to the way of Benedict gives you his thanks. And to show I give you more than hollow words, I hope you'll think on letting me make you something. I see you well like brightly woven cloth, and I happened to work for a short while under a dressmaker in Winchester."

Godgyfu fingered her rail's broided hem. "You seem to have done a bit of everything, young Thomas."

"I'd be most happy to work out your lengths and make something if you bring me the cloth you like best."

Beornflæd asked him, "Yer burdens with the Benedictines let ye do this sort of work?"

He laughed, a bright, young sound. "Ah, but that's one of the great things about an abbey not yet fully made. The bridle is still somewhat loose." He winked at her then, bold as can be, and Godgyfu thought she'd had enough.

"Maybe that is something I should tell the brothers." She turned away and took Beornflæd's elbow. "We've lingered long enough."

"Indeed," Beornflæd agreed. "Leofric will be looking for us."

They fled the street. She did her best to cast the whole thing from her mind, but the froward monk's words against the Danes, her own earlier thoughts, and other whispered words she'd been hearing in town for weeks kept rattling about inside her head. More and more, she felt Coventry slipping down into the pit that had swallowed Worcester. Such grumbling would only lead to woe; before long one of her folk here would think to send the geld-men away empty-handed. Then Coventry would be overrun, drowned beneath a red flood of spears and swords. There had to be some way to stop such a thing.

"Thanks be to God the geldmen came to take the autumn pennies in October," she said aloud. "Had they come now, well might November have lived up to its name as the blood month, and not only for the slaughter of fatted sheep."

Beornflæd snorted. "Pennies to pay the Danes so the Danes can pay their spearmen to keep their Danish arses on our kingseat. Who needs 'em, I say."

"Beornflæd!" Godgyfu, shocked, stopped in her tracks and spun to face her. Things were worse than she'd thought; if her own handmaid was willing to give voice to such beliefs, then there was no one who wouldn't do the same.

There must be some way to ease the upset. If only the geldmen never had to come back, in this or any other month .... She slowed again in her tracks, almost missing a step. *God above, that might be the answer!* By the time she reached her house, she knew what she had to do.

Beornflæd went with her sack toward the kitchen, and Godgyfu made for the hall. She nearly ran into Leofric's man Osmund coming out. He muttered something about the Warwick road and hastened toward the horse stalls, likely bearing some word from Leofric to King Harthacnut in Winchester. Her husband had already left the hall as well, and she found him instead in their own rooms in the house's oldest wing. He sat at a table, a mead cup before him and his head in his hands, thick-knuckled fingers twined in the tangled mass of his gray hair.

"What word?" Leofric asked when he heard Godgyfu walk in. He lifted his head, the stitched wound above his right eyebrow still looking red and raw. A yellowing bruise from the blow spread across nearly the whole of his forehead, wrapping back toward his right ear. Still worse somehow, the bleary look he wore took Godgyfu aback—dark rings beneath his eyes, a hollowness to his cheeks behind his whiskers.

Godgyfu sighed and crossed to the larger of the room's two narrow windows. She leaned out on the sill and wondered how best to broach the subject of the heregeld. "The abbey grows more lovely by the day. And Mannig's eager to begin his work on Osburh's shrine. It will be a wondrous thing."

"If she stole you away from death," he said, coming up behind her, "then it's no less than her worth." His hands fumbled with her dress, lifting it so it rose up above her hips. Then his rough fingers kneaded her bare flanks, and she gasped.

"Someone will see," she warned.

"Let them," came his throaty answer. He nuzzled at her neck, mead and onions heavy on his breath. His hair still held the smoke reek from Worcester.

Wriggling like a trout in a net, she turned to look at him, wincing as a splinter from the sill clawed at her thigh's soft skin. "What's gotten into you? Ever since you've come back from Winchester, you've been starving for it." It was not altogether an unhappy shift, but it was unlike Leofric to say the least. Since his homecoming, he was in many ways a new man altogether—half a stranger. As though he'd gone over into the Otherworld, the faerie reich, and lost something of himself there or been trapped so that a fetch—some lustful changeling oaf—was sent back in his stead ....

"Can't a man miss his wife?" He tugged at her breasts through her clothes, and she batted his fingers aside.

"Betimes you've been gone longer and never had such a ..." she paused to touch the bulge in his breeches. "Such a hunger."

He no longer listened to her, solely bent on stripping away her clothing. When he tore off her headcloth and worked to unwind her hair, she shoved him away at last. It would not do for someone to see her with her hair unbound below her shoulders like some unwed girl. "Listen to me! I'll give you what you want, but first I've a boon to ask."

"Name it." He started fumbling at her skirts again, lifting them up with one hand even as he tore down her hose with another.

She closed her eyes, some of his fire beginning to work its way into her, and behind her eyelids the face of the young novice came unbidden. *Thomas.* Then the touch of air, a stray breeze from the window, brushed her hidden flesh, and her eyes went wide. *What am I doing?*

"Relieve Coventry of the heregeld," she said.

Leofric stiffened. "Do what?"

"You heard me." Godgyfu kept her eyes on his, not letting herself drop her gaze. Any weakness, and he would put this aside as womanly foolishness.

"And how in hell am I supposed to do that?" He reached up to rub his bruised head, which from the way he squinted looked to be aching him again. "Mind you, I'd love to become king if only to see Earl Godwine swallow his tongue in a fit. But I don't think Harthacnut will think to name me heir .... In fact, my guess is he already knows who'll sit the kingseat after him. I just got word he's asked Eadward to come back from Normandy."

"Eadward?" That did take Godgyfu aback. If Harthacnut named his half-brother and the rightful English aetheling to follow him, it would go a long way toward quieting the growing anger. "Why now after all these years?"

"No sons of his own, no wife to get with child, and the old sickness seems to have taken him anew. From what I hear he's coughing up blood with every other breath, and to look at him you'd think he was no more than bones clothed in skin."

Godgyfu shuddered, then shook her head. "It's of no matter to what I ask of you. Likely Harthacnut will outlive us both—that's often the way with men who seem sickly. It's men in the bloom of health who die young, I've marked, like as not in battle. But much as I'd well like being your queen, I don't ask you to steal the kingseat from the current thief."

"Watch what you say." He squeezed her shoulders and looked uneasily beyond her, more afraid some passing houseman might overhear a word against the king than that someone might have a look at his wife's bare flesh.

She rolled her eyes and laughed. "You can hear more and worse any day around the well, which you'd know if you spent more time among your folk and less with Harthacnut's Danish hired-men. Ask the king for a writ freeing Coventry from the geld. It's been done before by other kings—for burhs and abbeys both."

"Yes," Leofric granted, his cast showing his forbearance wore thin. "But always for some close kin to the king or for something whose root—"

"Are you not as good as kin? Did we not work out the betrothal between our little boy and the younger Ælfgifu for the very mark of linking ours blood to Cnut's? In a few years they'll be old enough to wed!"

"Little good that does us now with Harthacnut on the kingseat. Better if we'd betrothed our Ælfgar to one of Harthacnut's mother's kin than to Harefoot's mother's. You were the one who balked at throwing our lot in with the Lady Emma. Shameful you called it that Emma broke troth with her first husband's name by wedding the Dane who'd raided his kingdom and driven him to an early grave. Better we link ourselves to a good Mercian woman than to a Norman whore, never mind that the whore was King Aethelred's widow. By Christ, we made the wrong choice between Cnut's two bloody wives!" Leofric cast had grown ruddier as he spoke, his jowls quivering with every word by the end.

"There are other sorts of kinship beside those of blood or wedlock. You have done all Harthacnut's asked of you—shown your troth even when asked to strike down your own. Does that mean nothing?"

Leofric sighed, weary of being minded of what he'd done. "To most men it would mean something. But Harthacnut's not like most men. Have you heard what he did to Eadwulf of Bebbanburh for showing some backbone and balking at his orders? The king bid him come under oath of safe faring and then had his men murder the ealdorman. Murder, Godgyfu! As though his word had meant nothing."

Godgyfu shook her head. What could she say to that?

"Even if there were any hope of such a writ," Leofric went on, "now is not the time to ask—not in the wake of what happened to Harthacnut's two geld-men. And how could I ever again face the Worcester folk whose only crime was to balk at paying the geld if I then get freedom from that same geld for the stead in which I bide most of my time!"

"Face them?" Godgyfu felt a red heat rising to her cheeks. "From what I've heard you left few alive to face!"

He pulled away from her then, and she feared she'd gone too far. "That was ill said."

He was right. She knew how hard it had been for him to do what the king had asked. In truth what choice had he had? Refuse, and the king would have cast them both out from England along with their boy and Leofric's living kin—stripped them of all they'd built over the years. Or else Harthacnut might have killed them outright. He dealt death as most men drew breath. Never mind Ealdorman Eadwulf; she called to mind again the ugliness he'd shown his own dead half-brother. "Blessed Marie, at least think on it, Leofric."

He made a grunt that might have been a sound of assent and stalked off. At the edge of sight, a shadow moved against the small window on the far side of the room where no shadow should have been. She grew sharply aware then of her state—hair half unwound, skirts still up around her waist and hose askew. All at once she was a girl again, standing before her first husband Eilífr while he .... *No! Don't think of it!* She straightened her hose, tugged down the skirts, and strode over to the other window to peer out. No one was there. About to close the shutters, she caught sight of one of her linen undertunics lying in the muck outside.

"Damn that girl." *If Beornflæd's daughter can't even do the wash without losing it, what good is she?* She walked outside, glanced at the sky and saw rain was coming, and took up the cloth. She'd wash it herself.

FOUR

WINCHESTER
12 JUNE 1042

"DOES IT FEEL TO ANYONE else that kings have been dropping like apples at harvest-tide?" Earl Godwine asked.

Leofric grunted and wiped the rain from his eyebrows. It had been a sundry day—a weird week all told. Half the time he didn't know whether to feel gleeful or sick with fear.

King Harthacnut was dead. The wretch fell down in a frothing fit while drinking with his men at Lambeth and breathed his last not long after. They'd buried him earlier that morning in Winchester's great minster church where his father Cnut lay. Afterward, the new king, Eadward, bid them all a short ride northwest of the town walls and gather at the great home that was now his. Leofric and the other earls had gotten as far as the Durngate—where horses were to have been waiting to take them over the bridge spanning the swollen Itchen's banks—when a king's man came running to tell them Eadward was of another mind. With the rain pissing down heavy as it was, the king now thought it better merely to have them come to him at the king's hall nearby the minster. *Right back where we bloody well started.* Leofric half felt Eadward crafted the whole thing only to make them jump to his bidding, back and forth through the mud.

"Kings die like the rest of us," Earl Siward answered Godwine, pulling his cloak tighter about his dripping beard.

Godwine laughed; even the rain seemed unable to sour his good spirits. "You don't have to tell *me*. Eadward's the seventh king I've seen in my lifetime—same as you and Leofric. But that makes … what now? Three dead kings in little more than six years? And these last two so young? I thought the Danes were made of heartier stock."

Siward's growl seemed meant as a laugh. "My Danish stock's hearty enough, and I've a strong son back in York. So you can bide yet a while before thinking to win my earldom for one of your own brood."

Leofric smiled. Siward never failed to lay bare Godwine's breathtaking ambition.

"Aye, sons are a good thing to have." Godwine grabbed two of his nearest sons, one under each arm, squeezing their heads—Harold golden-haired and strong at twenty-two, Tostig handsomer, darker and slighter of build but a good six years younger. Godwine's hulking eldest son Swegn walked a few steps ahead, sodden and without the wit to put on a cloak in a storm. The oaf stopped to blow his nose into his fingers, then wiped the snot across the back of his wet shirt.

Leofric gritted his teeth and looked about for his own son, but Ælfgar seemed to have run off somewhere with Godwine's two younger boys; all three were more-or-less of an age, here to kneel and speak their first king's oaths as boys did after their twelfth year. Leofric had said his own oath some thirty-seven years ago before old King Æthelred, and now his son would kneel before Æthelred's son … as though the years of Danish raider-kings in between had never happened. It would be a proud day. He was only sorry it had to be in Winchester.

Young Harold asked, "Who'll be king now in Denmark with Harthacnut dead?"

"Word is Harthacnut swore an oath with King Magnus of Norweg in the *pax* they worked out to end their war," his father answered. "Whichever one outlived the other was to get both kingdoms."

"Aye," Siward agreed. "I heard the same. But Magnus is in Norweg, and there are others already in Denmark who might have other thoughts about sitting the kingseat themselves."

"Isn't there an aetheling?" Harold asked.

Godwine shook his head. "The Dane's kingly strain ended with Harthacnut. But there are some who stand near enough to make a bid. Your mother's own nephew Sveinn has a strong bid as the son of Cnut's sister. Whatever happens it will be a mess."

"Better them than us," Siward said, and they walked on without speaking for a time as the rain all at once came down even harder.

"Christ, I hate this place," Leofric broke the stillness at last. They'd done their best to wend their way up and down the straight lines of the town's rigid network of streets so as to bypass Tanner's Street which stank enough to make one's eyes tear. But Fleshmonger Street was little better, blood from the slaughtered cows pooling and running everywhere in the wet weather. And thanks to a westerly wind, they could still smell the hides as strongly as if they all swam in the piss baths together with them. When they crossed over the wide market street, carts and wayfarers from the East Gate fought against the cow herds being driven the other way. The result was an unending din of creaking wheels, angry yells, and deep lowing like horns before a fight, all against the underlying wonted roar of the market itself.

"And think," Siward said, "you can look forward to spending Easter here next year for the kingmaking."

Leofric spat into the mud. "Wonderful."

All England had chosen Eadward as king during the gathering of the *witenagemot* in London before the earls left for Winchester. As Eadward was King Æthelred's only living son by either of his two wives, it had been an easy thing to do even if Eadward had spent most of the past twenty years outcast in Normandy. But the crowning itself would not happen until the following year; Eadward was a holy man by all Leofric had heard, and the archbishop had also thought it appropriate to bide until Easter. The day of Christ's own rising from the dead was a fitting day on which to bring the old English bloodline back to the kingseat.

"I'd have thought he'd want to be crowned at Kingston," Leofric mused aloud, "sitting the stone like his father and forebears. Why Winchester?"

Godwine snorted. "Haven't you learned yet, man? When it comes to the wills of kings or archbishops, it's often best not to ask questions."

On that, if nothing else, they were of one mind, but Leofric wouldn't give Godwine the satisfaction of an answer.

Swegn spun around and smiled—a thing that only worked to make the young man's grim cast even uglier behind his matted hair. "You think Winchester's bad now? Come back next month on the ides. Saint Swithun's Day it's like a whore's cunt here. All the stinking misborn, sick and wounded lined up outside the church for the saint's blessing .... By the Blessed Mother's milky dugs, you'll be tripping over the crutches cast off by the lame!"

"I'll bear it in mind," Leofric answered, crossing himself at the foulness of Swegn's words when the lad looked away again.

"If anyone would be glad of all this wet," Swegn's brother Harold said, "I reckon it would be Saint Swithun. They say he liked the rain."

They all laughed, Leofric as heartily as the rest, glad enough for something to lift his mood. It had been nothing but wet since April—so much water the acres were drowning all over England, and widespread hunger was a growing likelihood in the months to come. The damp had even given some bloody flux to the herds; already more cows had died this year than in any other a man among them could bring to mind.

But for here, it seems, where the cows look to outnumber men two to one!

Leofric sidestepped a fresh dung clod, then said a thankful prayer when they left the herds behind at last, crossing from the market street into the wide minster grounds. Here the din was less, the mud gave over to turf and stands of trees and, not far ahead the old and new churches with their abbeys stood one alongside the other. The closer they got, the more Leofric thought maybe he did see why Eadward wanted to have his kingmaking in Winchester. The great, stone church that held Saint Swithun's shrine was as awesome a sight as one could look for—the biggest church in all England. Some said there was none bigger anywhere north of Rome, and Leofric could well believe it.

The king's hall sprawled nearby, and Eadward awaited them within.

Leofric steeled himself for the meeting, but when he came inside, there was at first no sight of Eadward. They spotted the king's Frankish nephew, Ralf, who'd come over to England with Eadward from Normandy. A brash young man of eighteen years, he was seldom far from Eadward and spoke only halting English. Earl Siward asked after the king.

Ralf closed his hands as if to show a man in prayer. "The king is .... He prays in his *sacraire*. He ask me .... You will be ... bide—"

"Aye," Godwine cut him off, "we'll wait here for him."

Nearly a dozen men and women milled about in the hall near a wide hearth.

Leofric was glad for the dry warmth, as he thought he felt a sickness coming on; his nose ran, his throat ached, and a nagging fever burned behind his eyes. First shaking the worst of the wet from himself, he made his way toward his wife, who stood speaking with Earl Godwine's wife Gytha and with Lady Emma, the Norman she-wolf who'd been queen first to Æthelred, then to Cnut, and who'd been mother to Harthacnut and now to Eadward. The kingseat could never shake Emma fully loose.

"You're wet, dear," Godgyfu said as he neared. "Is it raining outside?"

Leofric huffed. "You're a great laugh. See if I don't shake some of this water on you."

His wife gave an impish smile, but Leofric saw no mirth in her eyes; the day had likely been hard for her. He couldn't say which woman Godgyfu hated more, Emma who she deemed a traitor or Gytha who was sister to Godgyfu's own first husband Eilífr, about whom she seemed to keep few good memories. Lately Leofric often found himself thinking of what it might have looked like when that long-dead Dane would come of a night to a much younger Godgyfu and thrust himself inside her. *He'd have been a grim, hulking man, thick-limbed and hairy. Hard, rough-skinned hands against her soft flesh—*

Gytha clucked a tongue behind thin lips, cutting short his thoughts. "I thank you not to wet the wee *kogursveinn* with that rainwater," she said in Danish-hued English, casting knives at him with her eyes. Godwine's wife held a fat baby to her breast. Wulfnoth they'd named him, a good English name unlike the first four of their five elder sons; Godwine had seen which way the winds were blowing.

Damn, but that woman's like a broodmare! And Godwine foresees an earldom for each son. Leofric thought they had three daughters as well. They'd brought the eldest with them, a comely thing Godwine was shamelessly throwing at Eadward so that one day his grandchildren might sit the kingseat. *Christ help us all!* Leofric could hardly think whether it would be worse to kneel to Danes again or to the apples of Godwine's seed! He needed more sons of his own if he wanted to hold steady against that bloodline. He wondered if Godgyfu still had it in her to bear another child; maybe they could try later that night ....

Leofric glanced at his wife, at the way her clothing held her curves. He tried catching one of the other men stealing a look and thought Swegn might have been ogling the swell of a breast. *Does he want to grab it, take the nipple between his teeth?* He felt a stiffening between his legs and tried to push such thoughts aside. Now was not the time to let himself be drawn in by the unsettling musings that seemed ever to nettle him of late ....

"Lady Emma," he said, hoping the shrewish old woman's wrinkles would quench his fire, "I have not yet told you what a wondrous gift you gave today. The head of Saint Valentine the Martyr! I'm sure the new minster's monks are most thankful."

Emma sniffed. "It was the least I could do to give worth to our dead king's name, and I don't need the likes of you telling me of holy wonders."

Leofric set his mouth in a smile and bit his tongue. *And there's Emma boiled down to her pith! What's no wonder at all is why my wife can't abide you, you sagging heap of bones.* Godgyfu was not alone in her feelings; he'd heard even Eadward felt every bit as cold toward his mother. For that Leofric couldn't blame him. Even with Harthacnut dead, Emma seemed to hold him dearer than her living son.

"We should get the baby away from all this wet," Godgyfu said, freeing him from the awkwardness. "Come."

Gytha and Emma followed her from the hall, and Leofric could have kissed her for it.

"Lovely woman, Emma, no?" Earl Siward said, coming up alongside him.

Leofric turned and pretended to strike him in the gut, drawing a wheezing laugh from his old friend. The movement made his head swim, and he lifted a hand to his burning eyes, cooling them with the rainwater on his knuckles. His fever felt worse.

All at once a great upheaval arose at the hall's far end, and Eadward strode in ringed by a gaggle of holy men. The past months had been so busy, Leofric had only ever met twice with the man who was now the king, and both meetings had been brief. Today would be something altogether different. His stomach began to tie itself in knots again, the fear stalking him since Harthacnut's death looming large. The death itself had been a blessing for Leofric and all the English, but a man cast out by the Danish raiders under which Leofric had thrived now back to sit the kingseat ... How would that play out?

The men shadowing Eadward did nothing to better Leofric's mood. Eadsige, the Archbishop of Canterbury who'd come to say the death mass for Harthacnut, was the best of them—holy enough to seem worthy of his spot. The same could not be said for Bishop Ælfwine of Winchester, whispering in Eadward's ear; the man made Leofric's skin crawl. One of Cnut's priests, Ælfwine became one of the strongest men in the kingdom and held onto that strength under both Cnut's sons. The word was he and Earl Godwine had been the ones to put the idea into Harthacnut's head to bring Eadward back from Normandy as his heir, which likely went a long way toward smoothing over their pasts for Eadward. And there was much to smooth over, not the least being Godwine's bit in the blinding and murder of Eadward's brother.

But I'm the one who stands here wetting myself while these men already have Eadward's ear. Every time Godwine looks about to step in shite, the shite turns to gold. God damn him and Ælfwine both!

Worst of them all was Ælfric Puttoc, newly named Archbishop of York again after briefly losing his seat under Harthacnut. The little hawk-faced turd had met Leofric's gaze as soon as he'd come into the hall and hadn't looked away once. When Harthacnut's housecarls were murdered in Worcester, it had been under Puttoc's short-lived hold of the Worcester bishopric, a spot he'd bought with lies and worse. It was a good guess he had fanned the flames leading to the mad killings of the geld-men, but by the time Leofric came to overrun Worcester, Puttoc was no longer there to reap what he'd sown.

Devils! Leofric's head began to ache worse than his throat, and he rubbed at the tender scar over his right eyebrow.

The last thing he wanted on this day was a reminder of Worcester. But that's what Puttoc was—a walking reminder of it all! *The smoke, the blood ... the pale flesh.* It had been seven months since he'd come against the burh ... Seven months since he'd seen the girl prodded naked through the streets.

More than half a year, but still she burned as bright behind his eyelids as on that cursed day. The sight haunted him. *She* haunted him!

He'd sought her out during the four days of viking that followed the first, searched wildly among the dead, peered at every teary-eyed cast among those women the housecarls had bound for their play. But she'd melted away. Her father was dead, as Leofric had guessed, killed by Godwine and his men on the High Street. The girl had not even come to take the body.

In truth, Leofric wasn't even sure what he would have done had he found her. He half feared the answer. *Did I wish to soothe her, give her my cloak, make up for what my men had done to her? Or would I have made her strip again, made her walk with me through the town, taken her back to Coventry to show Godgyfu her nakedness ....*

He felt the blood rushing to his groin and tried to drive the thoughts from his mind. As ever, nothing worked.

Nothing. He'd tried making a thrall back in Coventry strip for him, but it hadn't been enough. Then there was the Welsh ceorl who lived down by the stream; she would bed down with a man for half a penny or a bit of bread and meat. Leofric had never before even thought of visiting her, but he'd paid her to let him tie her with a rope and fling mud at her naked body; try as he might, though, it never gave him the same thrill as having seen that chapman's daughter in Worcester. He wished he had the backbone to make some higher-born woman strip herself bare and show herself before him, maybe even before his gathered men .... All those eyes roaming her flesh.

I am an earl! There were women—even highborn women—who would have done his bidding, given in to his lordly sway ... *But what if they don't? What if instead they spurn me before the town—make known my inner devils? Could I bear the shame?*

"Earl Leofric!"

The intruding voice caused laughter.

Leofric blinked, dizzy. His fever definitely felt worse, a spike of pain driving sideways through his forehead. He'd forgotten for a time where he was.

King Eadward stood before him, spoke to him. The man's long, rippling beard was a creamy-yellow hue so pale as to be almost white. It flowed over his chest even as his thick hair hung down past his shoulders, wanting only for the crown that would come at his Easter kingmaking. If nothing else, Leofric had to grant Eadward *looked* like a king. Time would tell if he had the wit and strength to sit the kingseat better than his forerunners had done.

At least he's English, he kept minding himself. It was the Danes—Harthacnut's asking him to kill his own folk—that had led Leofric down the road to hell. *The kingseat's ours again, and by God may it never bear some outlander's arse again!*

"I welcome you back, my lord," Leofric mumbled and straightaway wanted to take the witless words back.

Eadward laughed. "It is I who welcome you all to my hall, though I must say you lot look half-drowned."

Leofric bowed his head. Although Eadward hid it far better than Ralf, the king's words were also somewhat brushed with a Norman lilt. "A little rain for once," Leofric answered, hoping to hide his earlier blunder with a laugh.

"No matter." Eadward waved a hand, "I'm afraid I must leave you all again for a time, as I've things to work out with the archbishop. Go dry yourselves and get warm, and be back here in two of the priests' hours."

The earls all bowed, and Leofric found himself being led from the hall by a king's houseman, outside along a covered walkway, then into a nearby outbuilding. He was glad enough for the help, as the ache in his head nearly blinded him now, and he might not have remembered the way to his rooms. His belly felt a bit queer as well, and he thought he should eat something, but what he needed more was a few winks of sleep.

When the houseman threw back the waycloth over the room's doorway, Leofric mumbled his thanks. He threw his sodden cloak to the floor and kicked off his muddy shoes for the man to gather, bidding him to come back and wake him after noon-meat.

He went within the room and was glad for the fire already burning in the little hearth. Its glow gave the only light, but it was enough for him to see Godgyfu's skirt from the burial mass, spread over two wooden chairs to dry. Atop it, she'd left a bright penny, glinting in the firelight, and Leofric knew what it meant: the heregeld.

Leofric had been stalling on his wife's plea to free Coventry from the geld. With Harthacnut dead, he'd hoped she'd drop the whole thing. Instead, Godgyfu worried anew that Eadward would seek to punish those earls who'd thrived under the Danes by milking them for every penny their lands earned. Then, contradicting herself, she'd whispered to him that morning during the death mass that this might be the good hap they'd been waiting for—a way to start fresh with a new king willing to strike down the woeful burden his forerunners had put upon the folk.

She's gone wholly off the furrow! He took up the penny, feeling how wet the skirt still was beneath it, and even sick as he felt, he found himself growing hard again. He closed his eyes against the headache and thought of his wife, the wet cloth clinging to her after they'd left the church, all the eyes that must have been on her .... He grabbed at his straining flesh through his clothes, opened his eyes ... and nearly fell down.

The room seemed bigger somehow, a great cave ... or was it a clearing in a wood? A long, narrow bridge, stretched away from him, dwindled into the mists.

Mists? Where am I? I was to meet with the king. He had to cross the bridge if he hoped to get back to the hall in time. He took a tentative step. Stone. It was one unbroken line of stone barely wider than his foot. Unbelievably far below, a wide stream rushed around gray, stone fingers. One misstep, and he'd shatter his bones; the water would swallow him ....

He took another step. And another.

He froze, staring down at the long fall, feeling the water's pull. It would be so much easier to let it take him, to slide into its flowing madness and rid himself of the world's woes. And yet … *What greater woes might await a man such as me in the hereafter?* He lifted a shaking foot, held it above the stoneway, but couldn't bring himself to set it down. Surely the stone would grow slick the farther out he went. *I will fall!*

"Fear not." The words came from the air, the stone, the mist. "You will cross the bridge."

He knew the speaker—and yet did not. The words held only truth.

Leofric set his foot down, blinked, and was all at once across. He turned back, and the stone line stretched forever and ever behind him.

A whisper of cloth drew his gaze forward again. A youth had come to show him the way. Again there was something in this youth he knew—a shock of black hair, pale skin, wide green eyes flecked with gold. *Where have I seen him before?* The youth walked off, and Leofric followed, unhesitating, for a long way. Indeed, for half the day they fared through white mists grown into a fog so thick it was as though they two were all alone in the world's wideness. It was a mild lonesomeness, restful, the wet air's brush soothing as soft bedclothes.

The fog went away, not slowly but all at once. They stood in a fair field brimming with the sweet smell of lavender. And they were not alone after all; a great throng was here as on the days after Easter when men would go forth in solemn gangs to make God look with mildheartedness upon his children. All were clothed in snowy rail, even as a deacon might wear when reading the gospel. Only one among the throng stood out—a man in a mass-priest's clothing. The man's face was a smooth mask of silver, nearly without mark, and where his eyes would have been he wore a white blindfold in the way of a blind beggar.

"Do you know what this is, Earl Leofric?"

Leofric shook his head. "No."

The youth nodded and swept an arm toward the mass-priest. "That is Saint Paul, who has said mass and now blesses these folk. Come." He made his way toward Christ's Apostle, and Leofric followed.

The others stepped aside before them until they came to a spot where the folk held their ground, making them stop. Six graybeards sat about on wooden stools, each more richly clothed than the last in furs and cloth of gold, bedecked in bright stones and wearing golden arm rings. One looked up, and upon seeing Leofric, hissed as though stung by some venomous wyrm. "Why must this worthless wretch be in our fellowship?"

Leofric was straightaway ashamed, sickened to his heart. He turned to leave, but another man leaned toward the first speaker and said, "He may be with us. He is newly christened through shrift, and he will come to us on his third birth into Paradise."

Leofric's happiness was so great he went to his knees, weeping. *It's alright! Everything will be alright!*

The ground broke beneath him, and he was falling still when he leapt up from the rushes in the spare room of Eadward's hall.

"Sweet Christ," he breathed, and he pushed out into the throughway.

The houseman from earlier lurked there, holding his shoes and his cloak folded neatly over an arm.

"Send word to the king," Leofric said. "I beg his forgiveness for not coming when he bid. Why did you not wake me?"

The man stood blinking like a lackwit.

"I was to meet with King Eadward," Leofric yelled. "Has my son yet knelt before him? Where is Godgyfu?"

"Forgive me, Earl Leofric, but … but I understood you wished to refresh yourself first with sleep."

"A brief rest, man, not for half the day!"

The man shook his head. "Half the day? Sorry, lord, but I don't ken your meaning. You only now bid me wake you after noon-meat, and … now here you are again in a wink. Do you wish me to come sooner than that?"

What? Leofric looked more closely at the cloak, still dripping with wet. The mud on the shoes had not been cleaned; it was still slick and fresh. *The man speaks true! All that I saw … It came in the barest twinkling. A vision from heaven!*

He dropped to his knees and crossed himself in wonder at God's workings.

FIVE

COVENTRY
25 JUNE 1042

Godgyfu stood outside the mean house on the Sherbourne's banks, steeling herself to knock. *I'm already late getting to Tova's. Maybe I should come back another day.* But at last she took a deep breath and put her knuckles to the crooked door, three short raps.

"Right, right," a voice within growled. "Bide a wink!" There was a great rustling, then the door flew open, and the woman stood squinting against the daylight as though she'd been roused from sleep. Her bright red curls fell wildly about her shoulders; her shift was wrinkled and not altogether clean. "Christ's teeth, it's barely noon, and you'd think—" She seemed to see Godgyfu for the first time, and her words cut off. She blinked once, twice, then made a flustered bow. "Godgyfu. I .... Welcome! I'd ask you in, but I fear the room's in ...." She glanced back over her shoulder into the darkness. "Well, I haven't yet had the time to give it a good Lenten cleaning."

The Welsh was thick on the woman's tongue, making it seem she chewed wool while she spoke. Godgyfu guessed at her age and deemed her not that much younger than herself; maybe six or seven years. No younger than twenty-five, though her cast was still fresh and clean, her skin unmarked. Godgyfu had known she was comely enough, but it was the first time she'd seen her up close, and she had always thought the girl's skin would be more pocked, bearing some mark of . . . of what she did.

"I'm not here to weigh your housekeeping skill," Godgyfu said, pushing her way past the woman and into the darkness. She set her basket down on a small table near the door, then crossed the room to open its only shutter, letting in some light before turning back. *Heavens, she wasn't lying! The place is a sty.* Godgyfu wrinkled her nose against the rotten smell and was glad for the fresher breath now wafting in from over the stream. "The rain's stopped, and we may see sun before long."

The woman nodded foggily, then raised her eyebrows when Godgyfu said nothing else.

"Oh," Godgyfu said, nodding toward the basket. "I brought those for you. Fresh baked this morning."

The woman peered into the basket at the honey cakes, still warm from the hearth. She looked up then at Godgyfu with something akin to fear. "Let me get my pennies. I will have no debt." She began casting about on the floor among filthy rushes that were in woeful need of sweeping out and replacing.

Godgyfu put out a hand and stilled her with a touch on her elbow. "No, dear . . . Blodeuwedd, do I have it right?"

Blodeuwedd nodded.

"The cakes are a gift. The basket too."

The woman blinked anew, and this time her cast hardened into a thin-lipped frown. "I thank you, but I'm no beggar. I have pennies."

Godgyfu well knew where those pennies had come from. Townsmen and wayfarers, likely even some of Leofric's own housecarls. Men who would stoop to paying a girl for bedgames. A shameful thing. "Friends may give and be given gifts. I don't call that begging."

"Are we friends, Godgyfu?" Her mouth twisted now into an unbelieving crook, her eyes flashing mirth.

Godgyfu felt like slapping the woman, but instead she smiled. "I hope we might be. I've been meaning to come see you since you came to Coventry."

"That was three years ago."

Three years? Godgyfu shook her head to hide being taken unawares. "I should have come long ere today. And there are other good women in Coventry who would befriend you as well. Abbess Tova, for one. I know she would welcome you should you think to troth yourself to Christ and go live among her sisters."

Blodeuwedd barked a laugh. "I'm not the nunly sort."

"Tomorrow is what you make of it." Godgyfu had known this wouldn't be easy. She withdrew her boon book from a sling under her cloak and opened to the leaf she'd earlier marked. "I came today because I heard mass this morning, and Father Cynric spoke of blessed Saint Lucia, who this day gives us her light."

"The one who wards the blind, no?" Blodeuwedd asked. "I can see well enough, thank you."

Again Godgyfu was taken aback—happily this time. "You know your saints. The blind do pray to her to be given back their sight, but that's not why I speak of her. Did you know Lucia was betrothed to a pagan as a young girl, a man who sought to have her make offerings to devils. But Lucia did not want to wed him, happy to keep on with God's work, which she had been doing for some years then—uplifting the lives of widows, soothing the wretched, helping foundling children. Lucia wished to keep herself a maiden, for the apostle said those who ward their cleanliness in this way may be God's own temple wherein the Holy Ghost will dwell."

Blodeuwedd laughed again. "I fear the Holy Ghost has long since found another dwelling than my own."

"Hardly so. When Lucia spurned the pagan man, he warned her he would call men to lead her off to a house of fallen women to lose her maidenhead tenfold, whether she willed it or not. It was his thought the Holy Ghost would then flee from her body. But listen here to what Lucia said to him." Godgyfu held the boon book up before her, and she read.

> *No befouling the body puts the soul in plight if the mind likes it not. Were you to lift my hand to your heathen idol and so make me offer against my will, I would still be sinless in the sight of God, whose doom is for the will and who knows all things. If now, against my will, you befoul me, a twofold cleanness will be wondrously given to me. You cannot bend my will to your own; whatsoever you do to my body, that cannot happen to me.*

The words fired Godgyfu, and she looked up after reading them, hopeful Blodeuwedd would feel their strength too.

"How dare you question my worth?" Blodeuwedd yelled. "Who are you to say what I like? I take bliss where and how and from whoever I may."

Godgyfu gasped. "Who am I, you ask?! You're rather bold! I don't question your worth! Altogether witherwise. Don't you see? After Lucia said these words, no man could move her from the spot where she stood. Even a team of oxen could not, for she was filled with the Holy Ghost and grew as heavy as a hundred great stones. Wayward men killed her for standing up to them, but her pagan betrothed was put to death as well when his own evil deeds became known. You have the same strength in you that Lucia had, but unlike her you do not have to die. Before God and all his saints, know I don't question your worth in the least!"

The words she spoke were bare truth. *Would that someone had opened my own eyes to such inner strength when I was but a girl.* Whatever fleshly things Blodeuwedd had done with the men who came to her, it could be no worse than what Godgyfu herself had done so long ago with Eilífr. No worse than what she did of a night in bed with Leofric grunting above her; he was her husband, but there was nothing of love in what she did, nothing more than an act of the flesh. Had someone come to her all those years ago in Eilífr's home and given her twelve-year-old self a way out, she'd have leapt at the offer. *And if someone came to me this day with a like offer?* She knew no good would come of whatever answer she gave herself; she was too far along on her life's path. But Blodeuwedd could still make herself anew.

The woman still looked unswayed, but her tongue had stilled, and Godgyfu filled the stillness. "It's those men who come to you whose worth I question. It saddens me to know how they mishandle you for their own selfish lusts."

"Who says I'm not brooking them for my own lusts?" the Welsh woman said. "If they're daft enough to pay me for it, then more's the worse for them."

"Damn you, woman!" Godgyfu shook. "How can you stand idle and let men do such things to you?!"

Blodeuwedd shrank back, squinting her eyes shut as if waiting for Godgyfu to strike her.

Godgyfu's sudden wrath melted away into shame. *I scold myself every bit as much as I scold her.* This was not at all how she had wanted the meeting to go. She sighed. "Forgive my anger, but If you must give yourself over to another's will, let it be the will of God and the Blessed Mother's mild heart. Wed yourself to Christ her son, and you will not rue it. With Abbess Tova, you can work in the herb gardens. Your days will be ones of restful prayer. Tova will teach you to read and write in the English tongue. A new world awaits."

Standing straight again, Blodeuwedd cast a wry, almost sad look at her. "Your books are very pretty with their gems and golden staff, but they're not for me. Thank you for the cakes and the many words, but your being here may well frighten off buyers."

"Buyers?" Godgyfu asked, then felt her cheeks grow warm as she kenned the woman's meaning. "I will go. But do think on what I've said."

Blodeuwedd smiled weakly, and Godgyu saw that was as good as she would get from her. *For now.*

Stepping outside, she turned away as the door closed and wandered northward along the stream bed. *I'll give it a fortnight, then come back.* She would not give up on the woman.

The grass was still wet and glistening from the morning's rain as Godgyfu made her way back toward the heart of Coventry and Tova, who would be wondering what had kept her from stopping by for their wonted morning chatter. Her passing left dark footprints in the narrow, open stretch between the water and the thick woods to the west. She stopped when she spotted a swath of purple blooms growing at the edge of the trees. Breaking off several long stems, she ran her hands through the three-horned leaves with their toothed edges and somewhat hairy skin. The blooms themselves clustered at the tops, and once she had an armload, she gripped them to her chest, breathing their scent as she walked.

"Buyers," she said aloud to herself. "That's one word for them." *All those things Blodeuwedd must get up to with the men in the darkness of her cot ....* Unbidden, thoughts of Thomas came, bothersome thoughts. A warmth filled her as it did all too often lately when her mind strayed to the young novice. Not that there had been any hint of that sort of thing from him! She'd gone near Christmas to the monks, looking for one who could teach her to read and write Latin, and she'd been happy enough when Thomas had put himself forth for the task. He'd been mild and careful with her, never lacking in forbearance when she was slow to learn.

Best of all, he'd been warm and open, keen to speak with her but never overweening or in any way lewd in word or bearing as so many men were wont to be. It was in truth the one thing about him she found most gripping. He seemed to like her fellowship only for herself rather than for any hidden ends of a more wanton sort. He was mindful of what she had to say about matters of the kingdom, about the Church, the building of the abbey, and anything else she cared to speak about.

He had even asked her once what she most wanted in all the world, something Godgyfu did not think anyone—man or woman—had ever asked her before. It had so startled her, she'd had to think for a stound. But only for a stound, and then it came to her bare as day: she wanted Coventry to be one of the great towns of England—good hap for its folk, great worth given its saint, God's blessing on its fields and flocks. She'd half foreseen Thomas laughing at her. But he had nodded in shared understanding and flashed his bright smile. "I'll pray for those things every day," he'd told her, his words soft and earnest. Thereafter, Godgyfu had felt herself slipping away, lost in thoughts of this young man who had worked his way, so unlooked for but now so needfully, into her life.

I could have kissed him then. Her breath quickened. *What if I had? What if I had done more, and he'd put his hands—* Godgyfu stopped, dead still, and sucked a breath, looking about dazedly as though rising from a walking sleep. She'd made her way into the middle of town, over the high street without any awareness of those around her, and stood now on the minster grounds' south slope. *What am I thinking! Blodeuwedd's brazenness has followed me.* She brushed at her cloak with one hand and clutched the stems tighter to her chest. Then she all but ran to Tova's house at the edge of the busy abbey workstead.

Young Sister Eawynn was sweeping the threshold as Godgyfu stepped within. "Blessings upon you, Godgyfu." The girl was no more than sixteen, newly taken in among the sisters from nearby Binley and almost the same age Godgyfu had been when she nearly died. Eawynn smiled at her, cheeks rosy and plump.

Dear God, was I ever once so young as that? "Upon you as well," Godgyfu answered, her thoughts settled now that she was in the house that had begun to feel like an extension of her home so often did she bide her time there with Tova. "How fares Sister Sigrida?"

"She lies abed today, croaking as ever about her old, aching bones. But in truth I think she's as well as you or I."

Godgyfu laughed. "I pray I'm as hale as Sigrida when I've seen seventy years. I've brought more of the betony she likes for her shoulders."

Eawynn took the blooms from her and put them on a board along the front wall. "She'll be glad of it. I'll set some brewing in ale over the fire when I'm done here. Abbess Tova awaits you in her *cella*."

Nodding her thanks, Godgyfu made her way within. A narrow stairway hugging the back wall led to the upper floor. There, doors to the sisters' rooms flanked a creaking hallway—two on each side. The last one on the left was Tova's. Godgyfu knocked, and her friend called out for her to come. The room was small, holding little more than a narrow bed, a shelf with a bowl for washing, and a table stacked with written leaves and a half-finished altar cloth Tova had been broiding with green crosses.

"For Saint Michael's?" Godgyfu asked, waving a finger toward the cloth.

Tova looked up, her cast ruddy against the tight, white ring of her wimple. She nodded and rose from the stool behind the table to put her arms around Godgyfu in greeting. "The church needs brightening." She sat back down, and Godgyfu took her wonted spot on the edge of the bed. "And I happen to know green is Father Bergulf's best-loved hue."

Godgyfu laughed. "Thinking to buy him now?"

"Whatever it takes to keep this house."

"You'll keep it," Godgyfu said. "I give you my word." Of the many things standing in the way of her word, Father Bergulf was only the latest. The monks themselves, seemingly wanting even more than the abbey Godgyfu was having built for them, sought to keep the nearby house empty as a building in which to guest high Churchmen when they came to Coventry. Even Leofric didn't think the nuns needed to live on minster grounds when it would be so much easier to find a lesser, outlying house; he couldn't get it through his thick head how nearness to the abbey would help stave off the very sort of witlessness the priest had now taken to spewing. Father Bergulf called it sinful for women to live together in a house in the middle of town without some man to oversee their soul-health. "Let Father Bergulf worry about his own arse roasting in hell."

Tova crossed herself and held back a grin.

But Godgyfu was no longer in a laughing mood. "I should have set forth you would get this house before I gifted the land to the abbey, only I never thought we'd meet such an answering thrust. I could kick myself."

"What's done is done," Tova said with a shrug, "and you of all folk are not to blame. In truth, Bergulf's only one bit of a wider plight. Even should we keep the house, it will be hard to call it a rightwise nunnery; such houses for women have grown few and far between."

"There are still plenty in Wessex. Though I reckon there it's mostly kin of the old Wessex kings keeping houses hallowed to sainted women from among their own forebears." Godgyfu took up an edge of the alter cloth and admired Tova's careful stitches. "If the Church still allowed men and women under the same abbey roof, you could have been abbess over your sisters and the monks both."

Tova rolled her eyes and reached for her broiding needle "No worth in looking backward, and I've enough on my hands overseeing Eawynn and the rest without having to play mother to a houseful of Benedictines. What we *should* do is find Father Bergulf a wife to hold his bridle."

Godgyfu shuddered, sickened at the thought of any woman having to crawl into bed alongside that heap of sagging skin. *Now, were Thomas a priest rather than a monk's novice ....*

"Godgyfu." Tova waved a hand to draw the eye. "Godgyfu!"

"Yes, sorry, my thoughts were elsewhere."

"I asked if you'd spoken to Leofric about the heregeld again. I know how it weighs on you."

"No new word there," Godgyfu said. "But I'll keep at him. Did you see the way so many of the townsfolk stared down the geld-men last month? It's bare as day they blame them for what happened to the Worcester folk. One wrong word, and there might have been bloodshed in Coventry's streets, and then ... Well, I worry what might follow. Are we to share Worcester's fate?"

Tova clucked her tongue. "Eadward is not Harthacnut."

Godgyfu released her grip on the cloth with a weary sigh. "No, he's not. But if there's one thing the past few years have shown .... Eadward is king now, but who knows what tomorrow will bring? Another Dane? Something worse? Until Coventry's freed by writ from the geld, the pennies might always be a bludgeon in the hands of any king who wishes to use them in such a way."

Tova gave no answer, stitching in quiet for a time.

"I went to see Blodeuwedd too," Godgyfu said, thinking to push the geld from her mind. "As I'd said I would."

"Ah yes, the Welsh girl. And?" Tova well knew the more nuns she had under her, the easier it would be to keep the house.

I mucked it up something awful, Godgyfu thought, but only said, "More work to be done. In the meanwhile, my Latin's coming along well enough."

"A glad thing." Tova started on a new green cross at the altar cloth's edge. "You'll have to teach *me* once you're through."

Godgyfu nodded, hoping it would be a good long while until Thomas was done teaching her.

"You're happy, then, with that novice? Thomas?"

Feeling Tova had somehow been aware of her wayward thoughts, Godgyfu twitched guiltily and found herself choking. "I .... We don't .... He ...." She rose and began pacing.

Tova leaned her head to one side. "Is there something wrong with the novice? I'm sure they could find you someone else."

"No, no. Thomas is wonderful."

"What's nettling you? You're twitchy as a rat among hounds."

"I should be going now. I told Leofric I'd meet him at Saint Marie's this afternoon. He brought a relic back after the death-mass in Winchester—a tattered feather said to be the one Paul used to write his pistle to the Galatians. The monks there put it into Leofric's keeping when they heard of the heavenly wonder he beheld at the king's hall, and we're having a shrine made for it in the church."

Tova crossed herself. "Father Cynric will be glad. The earl has been blessed."

Godgyfu said nothing. It was indeed a blessing, but what she truly hoped was that whatever Leófric had beheld would at last give her and her husband something over which a bond could be made—a stoking of the fire she'd once hoped there could be between them. Something to make her happy in her heart when she woke in the morning to find him lying beside her, rather than waking with but a listless willingness to see her wifely burden through for another day.

Something more like what she felt when she was with Thomas.

Godgyfu pushed the last thought aside. *God help me.* Then she rose to bid Tova a good day, and hurried from the would-be nunnery before her thoughts became too bare to hide.

SIX

COVENTRY
6 JULY 1042

THOMAS ALWAYS FOUND IT ODD being in her house while she was aware of him. It made him feel like an intruder. This was true notwithstanding Godgyfu's welcoming cast, the way she crafted reasons for stepping closer to him, the way she seemed to want to breathe him in. *What a long way things have come since that day on the High Street … scarcely more than half a year ago!* A bit of him rued having ever spoken to her on that day, forever spoiling the wonder of the bond he'd felt when all he had done was watch. Somehow, as always, watching folk from afar was far more intimate than speaking with them, or eating with them, or doing any number of worldly things with them. But he had been too weak to stop himself, and of course he had needed to get closer; more so now that the Danes no longer held the kingseat and the path to uprising was all but closed. He would now have to remake Godgyfu fully from within her own self rather than by shifting the world around her. *Once I do that, once my goddess is reborn, the world will follow.*

And truth be told, though he had broken the watcher's bond, his goddess had not been lessened. Godgyfu always kept her unmatched wondrousness, even through the many hours and days they had now wiled in shared fellowship.

On other days, Godgyfu had sent her handmaids off telling them she and Thomas needed to speak of the building work and the adornments Mannig made for the church. Sometimes that was even true now that Thomas had fastened himself a spot working with the goldsmiths under Mannig. Today she'd sent nosey old Beornflæd off so they could have stillness while Thomas began teaching her to blacken her ABCD's on leaf.

"Hold the feather nearer the tip," he hinted as she dipped into the blackhorn.

"Like this?" She held the feather toward him.

Thomas nodded as he reached over to run a finger along the lines of what he had written for her earlier. She made another go herself as he showed her the way—always with words and with his own leaf, never touching her long fingers with his own. Indeed he was most careful to keep his fingers otherwise busy. Now he went back to his work on the hunk of boxwood he held, shaving it with a sharp knife, making another of the likenesses he had been giving to his goddess as offerings. He thought it might be time to let her know what the likenesses could mean for them, what they could do ….

"My husband is not here." She kept saying that, as though it were worth telling him, as though Leofric meant anything. Thomas couldn't rightly say whether she said it to warn or beckon. *Both.*

Thus far he'd paid it no heed, but this time he thought to answer. "And where *is* Earl Leofric?"

Godgyfu looked up sharply, the morning sun through the narrow window striking her from behind so a glowing halo ringed her, dust motes sparkling over her shoulders. "Today is the Octave of Saints Peter and Paul. Leofric hears mass at Blessed Marie and will likely stay behind to pray."

"On Tiw's day?" Thomas scoffed. "Betimes your husband can't get himself up early enough to hear mass on the Lord's Day let alone on the eighth day after a saint's feast!"

"Yes, well that's no longer the same after Winchester," she said. "Now Leofric's become wholly taken with blessed Saint Paul. Do you know he wants …."

He's taken with more than that, Thomas thought. Godgyfu still spoke, but he only half listened, staring at the way the soft down along one earlobe caught the light as she tilted her long neck. He wondered what she'd say if he told her what her husband liked to do to the thralls when she wasn't looking. *Or what he gets up to with filthy Blodeuwedd down by the stream. That one breaks troth with all womankind!* But he held his tongue. He didn't want to turn her against Leofric. Thomas might yet need him too ....

That was the thing about waking a goddess—such a thing happened on its own lead. It could not be shaped in the way he shaped the wood with his knife, nor could it be rushed. The stars were not yet right and Godgyfu not yet ready for her awakening. She might not be ready for years. Maybe even decades. But in time the world would shift; he and his Lady would shift it away from the choking hold of kings and bishops and of the Heavenly Father and his only begotten Son, shift it toward something more life-giving, into the arms of a great queen whose coming would overshadow even the wonder of Christ's crucifixion, death, and rebirth.

In the meanwhile, Thomas would keep working to bring himself closer to Godgyfu. With every passing day he felt himself drawn more strongly to her, needing to be near her nearly all the time. He was hollow when she was out of his sight for too long, and when she had to leave Coventry as she did all too often in these times of newness and upheaval, he was like a dead thing barely able to rise from his bed. *It is the toll I must pay. One day, years from now, all will fall into place. The longer it takes, the stronger our bond will be when it is time to go over.*

Godgyfu would have to come to love him; that he knew. It was what he'd been working toward ever since the day near Christmas when Godgyfu had come to the brothers looking for someone to teach her to read and write Latin. Thomas had put himself forward for the task, and since then his every word, his every stirring had been carefully crafted to bring him her heart. For a long while she had been wary, ever formal and proper, never letting herself open up to him. At best she had seemed tickled by him, her eyes glinting with mirth at his witty talk. But soon he saw it—a softening of her eyes, a bewildered wonder that spoke of endearment, maybe even longing. And the more he worked to know her, the more he saw how to crack her open like a nut. Her inner self had already come under his spell; she was almost ready to acknowledge it, but she was not the sort merely to give away her heart without thought. *She's no whore like ... like ....* No—he didn't want to think of ... her.

"There." He put the last strokes to his carving and set it down atop one of Godgyfu's blackened leaves. It was a horse—a fine, high-stepping steed.

Her happy sigh was gratifying. "What other hidden skills are you keeping from me?"

Thomas only smiled back in answer and stared at her until a blush came to her cheeks. When she looked away at last, he said what he had been wanting to for months. "I'd like to carve one of you."

"What?" She laughed, a merry sound to outshine the sun. "No, no, no."

"Well, not you as such, but a likeness of the Maiden Marie cast after you. After all of you. I would have it be naked in the way the Romans made their carvings. I'd need you to pose like that for me."

The laughter stopped with a sharp drawn breath. "Na—" She couldn't bring herself to say the word. "Those Roman likenesses were of pagan gods. Not of Christ's mother!" She rose from her seat and turned away from him, stepping toward the window. He wondered if he had pushed things too fast. No, he saw it would be alright. Had he hinted at such a thing a year ago, she'd have had him run out of Coventry or set Leofric's housecarls on him to beat him for *blasphemia*. Now she may have been taken aback, but she had only walked a few steps away and stood listening to him still. That alone told him he had her. *Maybe not yet, not today, but I will have her in time.*

"She is a mother, true," he answered, mildly, as though it were a little thing. "But she is also a queen. Her strength outshines that of all the saints. And her motherhood is not only that toward her child. She is a mother to all men and women. I would carve a Marie likeness the fieldly folk will better understand—not some mother who's kept her maidenhead, but an earthly mother."

"What are you saying?" She turned again to look at him.

Thomas took a breath before he answered. He had to tread carefully now. What he said had to sway her, for they needed the carving to help her inner goddess come into the light. She had to be a part of its making, bared before the likeness as he shaped it, so that it would bind itself to her and she to it. Gold would work better than wood, but even wood would be better than nothing. "When the ceorls plant their rows, who do they pray to when they bury their loaves in the new-turned ground? Marie? Christ? No, they pray to Erce—the All-Wielder, Mother Earth, the Lord of All. These folk know still the strength of the old gods, the gods of our forebears, and do not follow blindly every whim of the closed-minded priests and bishops—"

"The folk of Coventry have faith in Christ," she almost shouted. "What sort of monk are you?"

"I am only a novice." It had become something of an ongoing jape between them. "And as for Christ, the folk have taken him into their hearts, but what is taken in can also be cast out, and of late the folk look for someone to blame for their woes. A lifetime of Danish devil-kings. Crushing gelds. What good is the Church doing us? The monks pray for us, but still we're enthralled to Danish raiders. Before, it was gelds to keep the Danish kings on our kingseat. Now we go back to the old way of paying to keep them away."

"We have an English king again," Godgyfu said, but she didn't sound as though she herself believed it.

"Eadward's blood is English, but he's more a Norman than an Englishman after living with them most of his life ... beholden more to the Pope than to his own thegns. There's holiness, and then there's holiness, and many folk think it's time for all of them to go. Many look now to the old gods in hiding. To Rhiannon. I know your great love for Marie, and I would as soon have them look to Marie too, who is but Rhiannon in another cast."

Godgyfu's mouth hung open, and she made little choking noises. He gave her some time to think about what he had said, and at last she spoke. "I would not have the folk of Coventry fall into heathen ways. If I may bring them to Marie, then I would. But how would some carving of yours do that?"

Thomas smiled. "A likeness such as that, one to mind them of the old ways, will bring more to follow the Blessed Maiden than ever you could with your golden-hued likenesses in gem-crusted books. What link could the folk feel to that? How many of them ever even see such books? They need a Marie who is of the world, of the earth, not some otherworldly wight."

"I think you always mean to stay a novice," she said as ever. "And I think you're more than half mad."

Thomas shrugged. "I mean to stay true to the old gods and the new, as do many in this town and the neighboring lands with whom I have met often enough to keep the old rites of a night. Even your man Mannig has crafted things for some folk hereabouts. He showed me a hammer charm he made for a Danishman, a bull of the Romanish god Mithras he made for some Yorkshire thegn's wife. Our Mannig is a hidden lover of the old ways—"

"Mannig is a craftsman and a worthy monk. His crafts are a kind of prayer."

Again Thomas shrugged. "Maybe you're right. Mannig may well be a true Christian and have no gods before the Father, Son and Holy Ghost, but all craftsmen pine in their hearts for the past—for the old gods and the days when great battles were fought, when the world was ruddier and bloodier. What crafter of likenesses would not want to breathe new life into such heartening things—sights to fire the soul! You should come with me some time to one of the gatherings."

"You know I cannot. Nor will I let you carve a likeness of my ... without any ...." She looked away again. "It will never happen."

Thomas bit back his words. *It must happen. You must be a part of its making.*

She moved back to her seat and settled herself with a sigh, though she seemed restless. Thomas reckoned her belly must have been cramping. She was having her monthly bleeding; just before coming here to meet with her, Thomas had hidden himself to watch her bathe in the river, a thing she sometimes did rather than bathe in her own rooms when her heaviest flow was upon her. She'd scrubbed herself between her legs and washed the old cloth she kept there after switching a fresh one for it. He still hadn't worked out a way to get his hands on one of her bloodcloths before she had a chance to clean it. *Now* there *would be a thing of might and life, a tool to call upon Rhiannon's wondercraft!* He could use it to make a charm to further bind Godgyfu to him. Somehow he would have to distract her, but for now he wanted only to take her mind from her aches.

"Do you know how I feel sometimes? I feel as though all my life, I've been seeking you without knowing who you were. Running ever faster to overtake you but finding you somehow farther and farther away the faster I ran until ... at last I stopped running and came to Coventry to settle down to the quiet life of a Benedictine and ... there you were. I don't see now how I could ever leave."

Thomas was glad when Godgyfu smiled. "Coventry is like that. Until I settled here I had never known a home—never known a mild or restful sort of happiness—not since I was a little girl. I can barely remember back so far anymore. It's like some gleeman's tale heard in the feasthall, only half-minded afterward through the haze of flowing mead." He didn't bother stopping her to say it was her and not the stead's paths and fields he'd been speaking of. She had a far-off look in her eyes, and he wanted to know where she went with this.

"We lived in Newark then," she went on, not quite whispering, but it was a close thing. "Maybe we were happy. Then my father had a mishap on the road while faring south to Rome with Archbishop Æthelnoth to get Æthelnoth's pallium from the Pope. I think he was thrown from his horse, but I never got the full tale from anyone. It was the year of our lord 1022, not long after my twelfth birthday, when word came. My mother didn't cry or wail, only went still and held me stiffly when I buried my face in her skirts. Later that same night I couldn't find her and went at last into the barn. She'd hung herself, the rope biting into her neck so that a great wash of blood had flowed down over one of our mares—a piebald named Morgensteorra on whose back I'd learned to ride. I was alone after that. Until I wed Eilífr the next year."

She went still then, looking at the far wall as though she saw through it.

"What is it, Lady?"

Godgyfu could not meet his gaze, but through the blur of her tears, he saw her eyes were pleading. "You asked me to stand bared for you to carve, but aside from anything else, it is because of my first husband Eilífr that I could never do such a thing."

He lifted an eyebrow and leaned nearer. "Tell me."

She wavered a heartbeat more, then drew a heavy breath. "I was so young the first time I wed, not yet fit for those things a wife owes her husband. After bedding me once, Eilífr gave his oath he would not take me again as a man takes a woman until I said I was ready for it. I guess I should have loved him for the kindness, but I never did. Thereafter he only had me strip before him so he could look upon me while he fought with his own spear in hand!"

Her cast all at once twisted into a dreadful grimace, loathing and sadness making her look young again, the frightened bride she must have been. "Sometimes he even asked one or another of his thralls to be with us, and those women would use their mouths on him while his eyes roamed my body. It was wretched. Their eyes looking upon me, all those eyes upon my most hidden spots, things they were not meant to see. It was the most awful thing that has ever happened to me … worse in some ways than finding my mother."

Blessed Marie! Thomas felt a cold dread creep into his chest. *This will never do.* "Dear Godgyfu," he whispered, "you cannot know what sorrow I feel that you were put in such a spot. I hope you know what I ask you to do has nothing to do with that Dane's awful sort of lust. I would never look to make you into such a low and shameful tool. Any carving I make would be a way to give you the worth you are due, to laud your strength and greatness … to worship you."

Godgyfu met Thomas's gaze at last, and she laughed, coming back from wherever she had been. "Don't be silly. I don't know why I told you all of that." She smiled, and a lone tear slid past a cheekbone. "I didn't even have to abide him that long. We weren't wedded two years when Eilífr had his falling out with Cnut and fled back to Denmark without me. He was back briefly a year later, but I never saw him, and then he was off again for good and all. All the way to Constantinopolis he ran, to the Greek lands, to take up with the Væringjar, warding some caesar a world away. I got word a year or two after that. He'd fallen under a heathen sword, leaving me a seventeen-year-old widow.

"As for the rest ... what happened between us in the bedroom ... I never speak of it. Not even Leofric's heard the tale. Not even Abbess Tova, and she's my dearest friend and closest advisor now that Æfic's dead. And in truth I never told him ...."

"Æfic?" Thomas leaned closer still, feeling a pull, something tugging at his thoughts.

She nodded. "Surely I've spoken to you of Æfic. He was Prior of the Abbey at Evesham. The kindest man I've ever known. He helped goad me to build the abbey here in Coventry. Now he's dead too. Buried in the church Leofric and I built in Evesham. I watched them put him in the grave."

Maybe she *had* spoken of him; such men were worth little to him, so he might not have been listening.

Godgyfu let out a little laugh. "Maybe it's something about you men in monks' robes that draws me to you. Although Æfic was more like an elderfather, whereas you ...."

"Yes? What am I?"

Now she leaned toward him. When she spoke, he could feel her breath on his cheeks, could smell the berries she'd eaten earlier. "You are something else. You are .... In truth, I don't know *what* you are. You never speak about yourself. Tell me more about Thomas. About your father and mother. You told me once they were outlanders."

Thomas stared at her for a long time without speaking. At last he made up his mind that she must know him, understand him, see the murky depths from which he had come and how one could rise above them. How even she could rise above her earthly body and become something more. Something bigger than the world around her. *The woes of yesterday need not stop you from reveling in today ....*

"It's alright," she said. "If you'd rather not, I—"

"You want to know about my kin? My father was Norman, as I said, but he also died when I was young. Younger even than you were, maybe two or three years old. At least that is what my mother told me. I have no memory of the man. For all I know she lied to me, maybe never even knew my father. Or maybe she knew him, and he left us. Either way, the time came when my mother could no longer keep us fed, and she began to sell herself to men so we could eat. Men are not gentle with women like that, and before long she was dead at the hands of one man rougher and more brutish than the rest. I watched him kill her. I was five. So that's who my mother was—a Welsh whore."

He'd said it all quickly, scarcely stopping to breathe between his words. Now that it was out, he felt lighter somehow, as though a bit of the heavy memory had shaken loose.

Godgyfu's eyes were wide. Tears pooled in them, and when she blinked, they spilled out. "Oh, Thomas, I have never truly loved Leofric, you know."

Thomas cocked his head to one side. *What an odd thing to say.* It was not at all the answer he had looked for, but it nonetheless gave him hope.

All at once he thought Godgyfu had fallen from her seat. She was leaning into him, arms going out to stop her fall. Her palms pressed against his chest, fingers gripping his robes. Her lips pressed against his, her tongue snaking out to taste him.

Thomas froze. He retreated as his throat began to gag. He thought he might wretch in her mouth. "What are you doing?!"

She looked as if she'd been slapped. Her cast reddened with shame, and the tears fell unchecked now. It hurt him to hurt her like this, but she had almost spoiled everything. *How could she touch me like that? With her hands? Her ... her lips!* His stomach heaved, and he spun on a heel, lurching for the door, mind awhirl.

"Never touch me again!"

He stormed out. For the first time since coming to Coventry, he needed to be away from her.

SEVEN

COVENTRY
7 JULY 1042

GODGYFU STOPPED ONLY LONG ENOUGH to throw a small stone into the water, then turned back. She wandered northward along the soggy bank, no more settled than when she'd set out. Her mind spun in more dizzying eddies than it had that morning. She'd followed the Sherbourne south from Coventry until it linked with the Sowe and then farther, all the way to where its waters became one with the Avon's flow just beyond Stoneleigh. It had taken the better bit of the day, and Godgyfu sweated through her clothes in the muggy heat, but she'd have kept going if not for the fear she wouldn't make it home before dark.

Thomas. There was no shape or meaning to her thoughts. Only a wild yearning. *Thomas.* She was under some spell, her mind stolen from her. *Thomas.*

Take hold of the bridle! she told herself and looked about for something to draw her thoughts away. All she saw was two cows, dead from whatever sickness had come with all the rain, rotting in the heat, bloated and covered in flies. It had been the same all along the way, a deathscape as bleak as what she felt in her heart.

Why did I let myself feel anything *for him?* She asked it over and again but had no good answer. She worried maybe she'd only felt flattered a handsome man a good ten years younger than her had seemed so drawn to her. *Could I truly be so weak, so willing to throw away my good name, to fall into sin?* Even worse was the thought that she might only have been lying to herself, seeing what she had wanted to see through some lustful dwimmer. Thomas could not have felt anything for her; else why had he taken it so badly when she'd kissed him?

What was I thinking to do such a thing! She had a good life, a worthy earl for a husband, wealth and sway beyond what few could dream of. But now she also had Thomas, thrown in the kettle to make everything overflow into the fire. She did not *want* to feel anything for the novice, did not *want* to break troth with Leofric. *So what if I don't love my husband? Maybe that sort of wedded love happens more often among ceorls, but for highborn women like myself* .... She gave an angry sigh and wondered all at once if Thomas could have some other hidden mark, if he led her on for his own ends. *No—where's the wit in that? Had he wanted to lead me on, what better way than to kiss me back as hotly as I wanted to kiss him?*

Worst of all was not knowing if she'd hurt him in some way. He was such a soft thing beneath all his bluster—wounded somehow—and she wanted to mend him as her husband might have mended one of his falcons with a broken wing. But it was more, she knew. More than only a mothering impulse. She burned for him as she had never before burned for any man.

And she wanted him to love her; it was a hunger deep in her belly. She wanted to feel a link with another soul, feel needed and loved and wanted and to know someone else saw her as a sundry thing, as someone worthy. She wanted what she had not felt since she was a small girl and her mother and father had yet lived. *To be loved for myself and not only as a ceorl or a thegn loves his lord, not only as the Benedictines love me for what I've given them. To be wanted not only as Leofric does or Eilífr did, as though I were no more than a milkmaid for their seed, a broodmare to give them children, a purse to give them gold.* Thomas's love and friendship asked nothing in kind; he had never touched her though she would have welcomed such a thing. He had asked nothing more than to be allowed to call her his goddess, to shower her with kind words, and, now, to make her likeness in one of his wooden carvings ....

Have all the men in my life suddenly taken leave of their wits? First Leofric with his talk of stone bridges and Saint Paul in a field, now Thomas with his naked carving ....

Or am I the witless one? She had wholly misunderstood what Thomas wanted;

there was nothing of lust in what he'd asked her to do. *God help me, why did I kiss him? I've wrecked everything!* Maybe she had likewise been wrong to cast aside Leofric's dream of the saint as little more than something brought on by fever and too much mead. She'd told herself Paul would never waste his time showing himself to such an oaf as her husband, but .... *Was it only ill will I felt that such a wonder would come to Leofric and not to me? Maybe I've been too prideful, too unkind.* She swore she would make it up to Leofric somehow, that she would speak to him again of what he had seen that day in Winchester.

A bit of her, a hidden bit she did not want to acknowledge, wanted to let Thomas look upon her for his carving. *But it's so wrong! How can I do such a thing?* It wasn't even that she found it sinful; in the end it was only her body, and only he would see. Moreover it would be her own choice, not something she was made to do against her will. But no matter how she recast it, the bare idea of it flitted too close to memories of Eilífr making her stand shivering in the cold before him as other women warmed him with their hands and mouths, of Eilífr's seed spurting onto the ground, onto her shins and bare feet. She did not think she was ready to live that time anew. Not even if she could believe Thomas's lackwit tales that such a carving might bring folk closer to Blessed Marie.

There are other ways to put a fire in the folk, to show them Marie's wonder and Christ's blessed healing strength!

And that was what she would do. That was how she would shove aside the unhealthy yearnings. She would throw herself fully into the last work on the abbey, push the builders to get it done as soon as could be. When folk came to pray to Saint Osburh and saw what a thing of wonder had been raised in God's name, they would need no heathen carvings to draw them back to Christ and His Heavenly Mother.

LEOFRIC KNELT BEFORE THE ALTAR in one of Holy Trinity's side chapels.

Not Holy Trinity, he minded himself, *Blessed Marie now.* He had never gotten used to the new name after the re-hallowing. *Would that we had hallowed it instead for Saint Paul!*

He took deep, steady breaths, willing himself calm. The woody smell of frankincense was sharp in his lungs. A gaggle of priests and monks stood whispering elsewhere in the church, the sound coming to him like the wash of the sea on sand. They were all awhir over the twofold news that King Magnus of Norweg had stormed Denmark to take its kingseat and that Abbot Ælfsige of Peterborough was dead. Lady Emma had long been one of the abbot's greatest backers and he one of her closest advisors. *Maybe the sun's setting at last on the days of that old Norman witch's sway ....*

Emma's days were the days of fire and sword, of deviltry in the name of bloodthirsty kings. Now they had Eadward, the witch's son but a godly man and true. England stood ready to cast off the old ways, to doff sin and madness.

Broken kingdoms could be recast, could be smithed anew in the fire. Even as men themselves could be. *Blessed Paul once wreaked bloody fire down upon Christ's early followers before the risen Lord saved him from himself, made him an apostle.* Staring up at the holy rood above the altar, he said the words to himself as though they were a prayer. And maybe they were—a prayer of thanksgiving for the wonders Christ had shown him in the king's hall. Christ had shown him he could still rise above what he had been made to do to his own folk in Worcester, to good Christian folk, to Englishmen.

He closed his eyes to pray in earnest, but behind his lids he saw only the girl from Worcester, naked, her pale skin glowing. She bent over before him, looking back over her shoulder with a filthy rag stuffed in her mouth and tears in her eyes. Her hair was muddy. Her arms reached backward, toward him; then she placed her hands upon her haunches and parted her hidden flesh, opening herself to him ....

"No!" he shouted against the sudden, splitting ache in his head. He opened his eyes and leaped up from where he knelt, throwing himself over the altar, gripping its cloth covering in shaking hands.

"Blessed Peter, show me the way to freedom," he whispered, his lips kissing the green crosses stitched at the edge of the cloth. "I am lost even as you were on the road to Damascus! My eyes themselves break troth with me, bring me wicked sights. Blind me to these sins! Take my sight if you must so that true sight might come back to me and I might better do your bidding, better follow God the Father and his only begotten Son. Save me. Please save me!" His body shook as his tears soaked into the altar cloth.

THOMAS SAT HIGH IN A yew tree overlooking Swan's Well. The pool had swollen over its banks with the heavy summer rains, leaving young Ælfgar sparkling wet stretches of greenery in which to stomp about as he worked with the new sword

Leofric and Godgyfu had given him. The earl's son twisted and leapt, roaring as he smote the evil wyrms and viking raiders he dreamed up. For a time the lad hacked over and again at a rotting stump, sending wood chips flying. His swordsmanship was as yet most awful, but Thomas reckoned he would grow better in time.

Picking at a bit of ruddy-gray bark hanging loose from the tree's trunk, Thomas looked long and hard at the boy from his needle-cloaked perch. Ælfgar had not yet reached his thirteenth year but was already built like Leofric must have been in his younger days—stout and strong—but with more of Godgyfu's cast than Leofric's. A lucky thing for the boy, as the earl resembled a frog or some bloated, flat-faced fish with patchy gray whiskers.

Maybe it's time to strike up a friendship with the boy. Godgyfu worshipped her son, and Thomas could think of few things that would help solidify his own bond with his goddess than to have her son think well of him. He thought it might be good for him and Godgyfu to have some time away from each other's fellowship—a few days at least, maybe a week. He didn't think he could go much longer than that. *They say a reaving strengthens bonds of the heart, but after a week I'll need to go back to her and put the whole ugly mishap behind us, take up where we left off and pray she doesn't try anything like that again. If I can even wait that long ....* After little more than a day without her, already he felt as though he were missing a limb. It was hard to think, hard to do anything, knowing she was so near but gone from his sight.

His heart brightened. *How witless of me! I can go back to watching her now as I did before approaching her!* Thinking of the wondrous, raw feelings she would likely now be showing made him shiver with keenness. *It's not every day one can see a goddess weep! If only there were some way to drink her tears as an elixir ....*

Ælfgar had splashed off out of sight, and Thomas leapt down, bough by bough, until his feet touched the spongy earth. Then he ran southward, over the two bridges, flying through the market and down the Warwickshire road. With the house in sight to the east, already he felt better; so long as Godgyfu didn't know he was there, he might even hold out for a fortnight before speaking to her again. He went a bit farther, beyond a stand of maple trees, then looped back, cutting through fields so it was less likely any would mark his coming.

EIGHT

COVENTRY
4 OCTOBER 1043

Fifteen months. It had taken her fifteen months—the coming and going of four seasons—from that fretful summer day striding among the dead cattle, but the day's vow had driven Godgyfu through the ensuing final stretch, the task consuming her, and she in turn had driven the builders, the artisans, and the churchmen. The day on which the new minster was at last christened brought a light rain with dawn. But by the time the sun rose fully above the eastern fields, it shone with heavenly brightness in a blue sky, chasing away long, gray wisps of clouds.

Standing in the church with Leofric at her side and their son Ælfgar alongside him, Godgyfu felt a happiness that came all too seldom of late. The building itself was wondrous, decked out for the day with ribbons and harvest wildflowers, Mannig's brightly hued likenesses making the stone walls come alive with saints and martyrs, angels and kings. The greater lot of her gold and silver store had been given over to Mannig's craftsmen, and it shone out at her now from every nook, worked into roods, into covers for the gospel books upon the altar, and even hammered into flat halos to adorn the stone- and wood-carved likenesses standing watch along the walls.

The great sea of folk themselves added another bright whirl with their best feast clothes. Afterward, the church would be given over for their own masses to the twenty-four Benedictines who were to live in the attached cloister, opened only on high holy days and to those pilgrims looking to make offerings and say prayers before Saint Osburh's shrine. But on this day, all Coventry's folk and many others besides came to hear Archbishop Eadsige and his priests say mass and hallow the church in the names of Saint Peter, Saint Osburh, All Saints, and Blessed Saint Marie, Ever Maiden. Godgyfu had insisted the Queen of Heaven's name be given to her church along with the others.

Not my church, the brothers' church, she minded herself. She'd put so much of herself into it—her heart, her sweat, her pennies—it felt like her own.

Godgyfu and Leofric had a worthy spot nearby the altar for the blessings. She looked out, through the clouds wafting from the priests' golden *thuribula*, over the hundreds who had gathered. Highborn thegns and fieldly ceorls with their wives, chapmen and mass priests and all Leofric's housecarls. Abbess Tova stood smiling alongside her few sister-nuns, Beornflæd nearby, her old eyes watering and looking as though she held back a sneeze against the woody-spicy frankincense smell. Leofric's nephew Æthelwine, hunched alongside the Mouse, fared much worse with the scent; snot streamed from his nose-slit and dripped over his lips, the only bit of ugliness to mar the day. Godgyfu was glad Leofric had at last told his brother he could leave Coventry, and she hoped it happened before winter set in. Grisly cast aside, there was something about Æthelwine that frightened her, something a bit wrong. She looked away.

Straight before her the monks themselves stood under Abbot Leofwin's watchful eye, voices raised in hymn.

Hec domus rite Tibi dedicata
Nascitur in qua populus sacratum
Corpus assumit bibit et beati
Sanguinis haustum.

Godgyfu listened and found herself inking the staff of the words in her mind, seeing Thomas's hand hovering over her own, his strong fingers sometimes brushing the feather. She looked for him again among the brothers, knowing she could not have missed seeing him earlier but bothered that he was not there. *Where can he be?*

It had been more than a year now since she'd kissed him, and she hadn't been bold enough to make another try. Indeed, for a few months she'd arranged always to have someone else in the room with them during their lessons, a watcher to put any thought of untowardness from their minds. But after a while that grew tedious, and they'd taken to meeting alone again. She tried praying for an hour before each meeting so as to push aside any devilish fire, and that helped somewhat ... but never enough. Godgyfu grew so vexed with Thomas's failure to meet her fire with his own that at one point she swayed herself that she hated him, ending their lessons altogether. After a fortnight of that, she grew so beset by thoughts of him it was hard to do anything else, and she relented.

Now the awkwardness seemed to have mostly passed, the fire of that far-off kiss having diminished to a glowing ember. They once again spent long stretches together, and Thomas had as yet given no sign he'd welcome anything more. Whenever she felt her need overtaking her, she did what she could to bury the ember deeper beneath the ashes and made herself see only his robes and not the man inside them. *He felt strong beneath my hands, hard with muscle ....*

Once, Godgyfu had wondered if her kiss so bothered him *because* of those robes—because of his ties to the Benedictines. But he was still a novice, not yet bound by the celibacy oath some monks kept more steadfastly than others. Moreover, Godgyfu had come to see Thomas never meant to say his oath and be raised to full brotherhood. How he'd worked out to have Abbot Leofwin let him stay on as a seeming postulate beyond the wonted year, much less let him have such freedom to come and go at will, was a bewildering knot, but maybe one easily untied; Thomas had a sundry charm that ever seemed to get him what he wanted.

And, too, Leofwin himself was not the most ... steadfast cleaver to the *Regula Benedicti*. It was widely known he kept a wife in a house north of Swan's Well, but Coventry's monks did their best to downplay this. Leofwin was well loved among the brethren, having been taken in by them as an orphan of ten, near the time of Godgyfu and Leofric's wedding. When she and Leofric settled in Coventry soon after, Leofric took a liking to the lad, and in many ways Leofwin had become like an older brother to their own Ælfgar. For a time it seemed Leofwin's wyrd to end up one of her husband's housecarls or even a shire reeve. He'd surprised them all by taking the oath of Benedict instead. And now ... abbot.

"Leofwin looks happy among the brothers," Godgyfu whispered, leaning toward her husband.

Leofric started as though she'd woken him from sleep. "Do you know," he whispered back, "when Ananias of Damascus gave back Saint Paul's sight, he called him Brother as the blinding shells cracked and fell from Paul's eyes?"

Godgyfu smiled and nodded, doing her best to push aside any lingering doubts over what Leofric had seen in Winchester. They prayed together often now, always to Saint Paul, and she thought that new bond had made Leofric happy. But of late, even when they were not in prayer, it seemed all Leofric wished to speak of was Christ's Apostle. At times she'd even caught him speaking to himself, and she didn't think those half-heard words were prayers. He seemed always on the verge of tears or wrath or ... dread? She knew no other word for the haunted look in his eyes.

When they were alone of a night, together as man and wife beneath the bedclothes, his groans when they made love also sounded like words, like frightened pleas .... She'd swear she was hurting him in some way or that his words were meant to chide her for some wrongdoing. More than once she'd asked what she could do to ease his mind, but he ever only snapped angrily at such questions or waved her off as if he knew not what she spoke of.

Godgyfu turned now to regard Leofric. A deep sadness dulled his eyes, and all at once she saw how old he'd become. Likely it had been happening for years, but maybe she saw it more now from all the time she spent in a younger, handsomer man's fellowship. *Damn, if he doesn't look like the world's weight has graven itself into the lines of his face.*

In all her bickering with her husband, all her wishing that he might have been another sort of man, she sometimes forgot how hard he'd had it under the Danes. Two brothers killed, a nephew maimed, and Leofric having to smile through it all. She all at once felt a warmness toward him, and she reached out, placing a hand around his own and squeezing.

His graying whiskers split in a wide grin that gave him something of the look of a wolfhound pup, the years slipping away so that for a heartbeat he seemed his happier, younger self. It was at times like this Godgyfu came closest to loving him. But she knew it was born more of pity than of affection ....

The church doors burst open, their hands fell apart, and the monks took up a stirring *Martyr Dei.*

Saint Osburh had come to her new home.

She rode from the sister church of Saint Marie in the new reliquary Mannig's goldworkers had crafted. Mannig himself was back in Coventry for its unshrouding, and he now led the way with the priests of Saint Marie's and Saint Michael's. All those gathered let out a great gasp and then dropped to their knees as one, in awe, Godgyfu along with them. The chest was indeed breathtaking—crafted of gold and copper in the likeness of a little church with a roof encrusted with gemstones. Golden plates were set into each side, most showing happenings from the saint's life and martyrdom and one, behind which Osburh's blessed head rested on a silk pillow, showing the martyr's cast, eyes upturned, lips smiling. Once, after Godgyfu came back from the death that had almost overtaken her in her youth, she'd been given a peek at the head itself under old Sister Eanfled's watchful eye. Death had not touched Osburh's flesh; she was ghostly pale but whole, her eyelids looking as though they'd merely closed for a wink of sleep. *One of God's wonderworks*, Godgyfu thought, and crossed herself as the golden house passed before her. She thanked God she'd lived long enough to fulfill her oath and blinked away tears.

The monks sang louder as those bearing the chest stepped up to the high altar, entering the thick clouds the Archbishop himself flicked from one of the *thuribula*. Then they had moved beyond and behind the altar and were lifting the blessed martyr toward the silver-plated beam that would ever after bear her shrine.

"*Deo Patri sit gloria*," the monks sang out, over and again as first Leofric and Godgyfu, then all the rest of those gathered stepped forward to bend the knee before Osburh.

Afterward, they wended their way from the church. The noonday sun was high overhead and the minster grounds at last empty of workbenches and carts, the piles of wood and stone, that had filled it for years.

"So the rites are over?" Ælfgar asked, barely hiding his eagerness.

Godgyfu smiled at her son, who like most fourteen-year-olds had little forbearance for anything that kept him indoors too long. "For the nonce. Later this afternoon there will be a reading out of the writ granting our lands to the abbey. Be here for that." It would be a lengthy reading—half of all her own lands in Coventry, everything north of the High Street, and twenty-five other good tithing lands she and Leofric owned throughout Warwickshire and in Worcestershire, Cheshire, Northamptonshire and Leicestershire too. In one stroke, they would make Coventry's abbey one of the wealthiest in all England.

Leofric grunted. "Aye, you won't want to miss hearing that! A goodly bit of what would've one day been your lands given away." Godgyfu clucked her tongue, thinking at first Leofric made light, but he went on in earnest. "Learn from it, boy. Whatsoever man may have in this life is nothing next to what awaits in the hereafter when the saints gather us up to be with Christ."

Ælfgar nodded and rubbed his nose with a knuckle as they strolled toward the far side of the abbey grounds to await the throngs who would now come to laud them for what they had built. "I thought cousin Leofric was going to be here."

Godgyfu shook her head. "I think your father's namesake is still wroth over not being named abbot."

"And well he should be," Leofric snapped. "I'd have seen him get the spot."

She held back a weary sigh. In a world of his own making, she knew Leofric would have rather had someone of his own blood named abbot; he'd even gone to the monks and asked them to choose the younger Leofric, son of his dead older brother Northman. That brother had been killed outright by Cnut after he took the kingseat—put to death as a sometimes friend of the traitor Eadric Streona. But from what she'd heard, Eadric had changed sides so often it would have been hard to find any man who hadn't been his friend at one time or another.

"You know it would have looked too self-serving," she reminded her husband as she had so many times in the past months.

"What if it did?"

Does he truly not call our words to mind, or is he only being childish? Lately it was hard for Godgyfu to tell what her husband remembered or didn't remember, most of his thoughts eaten up with the cursed dream in Winchester. *No, not a dream,* she minded herself, *a wonder from heaven.* "King Eadward must see the abbey's hallowing as an olive branch, not merely as a means for us to help our own. Leofwin was the best choice, as close to kin as one could be without being true kin." She only felt bad for Ringwaru, Leofwin's sweet wife, who now would have to hide herself away most of the time for the sake of seemliness; she hadn't even come to the hallowing. *Later I'll go see her and bring her some choice bits from the feast.*

Leofric spit on the ground, then Ælfgar did the same, ever looking to be like his father.

"Why should we have to kiss the king's arse," Ælfgar asked, "when our kin's suffered every bit as much as Eadward did from the Danes? Thomas says Eadward's no better than Harthacnut."

Had they not been standing in full sight of half the townsfolk, Godgyfu would have slapped her son to knock some wits into him. As it was she gave him a withering look and did her best not to blush at the mention of Thomas. *Where* is *Thomas?* "Don't ever let me hear you say such a thing again. Eadward is our king, an English king, and you knelt before him to give your oath! God willing he'll give you an earldom one day!"

"The lad's not wrong," Leofric said, rubbing his head above the Worcester scar and squinting against some inner ache. "Earl Godwine spent the past twenty-some years in bed with every one of Forkbeard's brood, and his kin never suffered under the Danes as ours did! But Eadward gives every sign he means to make Godwine's daughter his wife—his Christ-bleeding *queen*—while I still have to beg and bow and set myself aside from the Danes as though *I* was the one who'd been their faithful hound. More fair had it been the other way round."

"But life's not fair," Godgyfu said, more harshly than she meant it. She walked the marks of her forbearance with her husband and son both. "Think on it this way ... Osburh's old nunnery was burned by Cnut and Eadric Streona working together to bring down Eadward's own father when he sought to win back the kingseat. Now God's doom has put Cnut and his sons and Eadric in their graves, and the rightful English king's come back from over the sea. You are earl over the Mercians even as once Eadric was, and Eadward wears Cnut's old crown. Hallowing our abbey on the spot where Osburh's abbey burned can be a bright beacon, one of healing and a new friendship between the two men God raised up in place of the wicked. That can be your bond with Eadward. Surely you can see—" She cut herself off, for as if drawn by their talk, King Eadward's own men now neared. "Both of you fasten your lips."

Leofric gave no answer, cowed for the time being. Together he and Godgyfu donned their best smiles and awaited the three men Eadward had sent on his behalf. Each had come over with the king from Normandy. Young Ralf of Mantes walked a few steps ahead of Rodbert fitzWymarc, who was a round bear of a man, one of the king's dearest friends and his newest staller. Another Rodbert, this one the Abbot of Jumièges, visiting from Normandy, strode at his side, hands clasped within the wide sleeves of his robes; it was said Eadward was wooing him to settle in England with the prize of London's bishopric. Of them all, Godgyfu knew Leofric liked this last man the best, if for nothing else than for that Abbot Rodbert had once shamed Earl Godwine in the king's hall by bringing up the earl's lowborn forebears; Godwine's elderfather had been but a thegn and his father before him little more than a ceorl in the field.

But from the way Leofric all at once grew still and stiff, Godgyfu knew he looked not at any of these three men but at a fourth who swaggered along with them, laughing loudly. Swegn, eldest of Earl Godwine's sons, had been given an earldom of his own earlier that summer—an earldom over lands in the southwest Midlands hitherto under Leofric's oversight.

"At the rate my earldom keeps shrinking," Leofric had said only that morning before they rose from bed, "soon I'll be earl over little more than a few pigs and a goat." Outwardly, Swegn was here on behalf of his kin to acknowledge Coventry's new abbey, but Leofric was of a mind that he was truly here to rub it in their noses that the king had once again handed Godwine a win at Leofric's loss. Looking at the wide grin above Swegn's unkempt chin, Godgyfu found that maddeningly easy to believe.

"Earl Leofric," fitzWymarc was the first to speak, "and Godgyfu, the church is every bit as lovely as I'd been told." Almost nothing of the Normanish tongue overlaid his English. He took Leofric's hand between his own, then Godgyfu's, and Godgyfu allowed him to kiss her knuckles, as it seemed something all Normans liked to do. "The king regrets he could not be here in person."

"We are happy to have you good men here in his stead," Godgyfu answered.

A moment later, the oaf Swegn had taken her hand, perhaps to mock the Normans, and before she could withdraw it, he'd slobbered all over it with his wet lips. She fought to keep her smile bright, glad when Abbot Rodbert told Leofric some king's business needed talking over; now that Norweg's King Magnus had taken Denmark, he'd sent word to Eadward that Harthacnut's oath meant he was owed England's crown as well, and Magnus meant to make good on that oath.

"I'll leave you men to it," she said, snatching her hand back from Swegn and beckoning Ælfgar to follow her. "This hand will need washing," she said once they were out of hearing, and Ælfgar sniggered.

Before walking off with the other men, Leofric trotted up alongside Godgyfu and put a broad hand behind Ælfgar's neck to push his head forward so their foreheads touched. "Don't let these men get you down," he whispered to his son. "You're more worthy than the lot of them, and one day the king will see that even as I do."

Ælfgar made to pull away, too old now for such open shows of fatherly affection, but he couldn't stop himself from grinning and giving Leofric an awkward, pleased nod.

"Now I've got to go make nice with those turds," Leofric grumbled, rolling his eyes. He began to move away, but Godgyfu put a hand on his shoulder and squeezed, feeling kindly toward him for a second time in the same day, which she was quite sure had not happened in ten years or more. Leofric patted her fingers, then left them.

"Will Magnus truly come at England?" her son asked as he stared at his father's back. "With ships and spears?"

"Danes like to rattle their swords." She steered them away from the church toward the middle of town. "When Magnus and Harthacnut each trothed his kingdom to whichsoever one outlived the other, Harthacnut had not yet even taken England's kingseat. Even Magnus can't truly believe the oath touched upon England. King Eadward will set the Northmen straight." Then she was minded of Ælfgar's earlier words. "What else has Thomas said to you?" She did her best to make it sound like small talk. "Other than badmouthing the king?"

Ælfgar shrugged. "Lots of things."

Anything about me? she wanted to ask but didn't. Ælfgar had come to spend nearly as much time with Thomas as Godgyfu did herself, but she wouldn't stoop to pressing her son for his words about her. *What am I anyway, some lovesick young maiden with nothing better to do than pine after two soulful eyes and a dimple-cheeked smile?*

"Thank you," she said to a thegn and his wife who said something kind about the church. Men and women hailed her as she walked; she clasped some hands and gave smiling nods. All the while she eyed the crowd, hoping to spot Thomas. After a while she thought maybe it was just as well he was nowhere to be found. It had grown more and more awkward for them to be at ease together before others; their wont was to be far friendlier toward each other than seemliness allowed.

And when they were not before others ... gladly would she have given herself to him. *Only ... he never seems to want that.* Indeed he went out of his way to stand far enough away from her that there was little likelihood of even a stray touch. It had become maddening for Godgyfu, the utter lack of nearness driving her to want him all the more. Instead she had to make do with closing her eyes when Leofric took her and telling herself it was Thomas's strong, young body she felt beneath her hands ... *That he's putting himself inside me, deeper, so deep I can feel him in my belly .... If you ask me again, Thomas .... Should I let you see me naked for your carving? Would that make you burn for me ...?* She blinked, breathing hard, and stopped herself. *But, oh, this is a holy day! A day to think of Coventry, of Saint Osburh and the abbey, not of my own weak longings .... Forget Thomas!*

She stopped, put a hand out to grab Ælfgar's arm and steady herself, and looked back at the abbey church. The sun had now climbed far enough that its light fell straight upon the building's western fore, gleaming off the bright stones rising high over the minster grounds like some heavenly wonder. All the folk milling about were like many-hued ants alongside it. She dropped her eyes and—

Thomas stood right before her as though having risen up out of the ground. "My lady," he said, giving her a half smile.

She said nothing, but Ælfgar quickly filled the emptiness. "Thomas! We don't have to be back until later. Shall I get my bow?"

"If your mother wills it, then let it be so." He arched an eyebrow at her.

Godgyfu cast a sidelong look at Leofric, who still stood not far off with the king's men, having been waylaid by others who wanted his ear. She ever wondered if her husband guessed at anything of her feelings for this other man, but in this as with everything else of late, his thoughts seemed too drawn asunder to see what happened right before his eyes.

"Well, Mother? Can I go shoot with Thomas?"

She looked at the novice and imagined Thomas's muscled shoulders, strong enough to draw back a bowstring. "Yes, you may. Only be back for the reading!"

She shouted the last words at Ælfgar, as the boy was already running toward home to fetch his bow.

Thomas laughed. "He's a good lad. I'd best get down to Swan's Well to patch up our straw men for a new onslaught of shafts."

"Where were you?" Godgyfu asked, her words sharp. "How could you miss the hallowing?"

"Who says I missed it? I saw it better than any from where I perched, and it was stirring indeed. You've outdone yourself." As ever, Godgyfu's worries melted in the warmth of his smile.

"I looked for you inside." She swallowed and took a breath, making sure none were close enough to hear. "Shall we meet later?"

"As always," Thomas said with an overwrought bow. Then he was off without further ado, leaving Godgyfu to stare at his back. He turned, weaving into the crowd, and Godgyfu met Abbess Tova's gaze as her friend strode toward her through the spot Thomas had just left.

"I tell you that young man will bring you only hardship," Tova said as she drew closer. "What is this game you play?"

Godgyfu's cheeks grew warm, and she dropped her eyes, ashamed. Tova's mind was sharp, and in the end there had been no way for Godgyfu to hide her feelings about Thomas. Her friend did not think well of any of it, but she seemed at least to understand. And aside from that one brief kiss, nothing else had ever happened between Godgyfu and Thomas, so there was truly nothing as such to chide her for.

"God help me, I don't know," she answered.

Tova sighed. "I think you'd best work it out, my dear. But in the mean time, let me add my words to all the others you've already heard and say what a worthy thing you've done here this day. The abbey is a wonder, and I know Blessed Osburh is happy in heaven to look down on her body's new home."

Godgyfu smiled and nodded. "Thank you for saying so. I so wanted everything to be right. I can scarcely believe it's all done now."

"Come, eat with me back at the nun-house," Tova said. Some folk nearby had begun to get rowdy, and it grew harder to speak in the yard without shouting. A quiet bite with Tova, away from the crowds, was the very thing Godgyfu needed before the rest of the day's work and the feasting that would come with the night.

They crossed the yard, and Godgyfu soon found herself sitting at the little table in Tova's own bare room, Sister Eawynn setting down a bowl of the year's last pears, sliced and soaked in wine, and a round of brown bread with a sharp cheese. Godgyfu drizzled her pears with honey from the abbey's hives and sighed as the soft, sweet flesh broke between her teeth.

"I meant what I said about Thomas." Tova tore off a hunk of bread. "Whatever do you see in him anyway?"

Godgyfu thought for a moment as she chewed. "He is a man who's unlike anyone I've ever known. He doesn't look at me the way other men do, the way my husband does or my first husband did. Think what you will, but I tell you he is not a thrall to his lust. That's not his game, Tova. And he's smart and witty—"

"Let's not forget young and handsome," Tova cut her off, arching a scolding eyebrow.

Godgyfu laughed. "Yes, he's that too. But if I wanted a comely young thing, I could find any number of them willing to be with me. With Thomas I feel a … a closeness, a tenderness. I can be myself with him, share with him things I'd share with no other. When he sits with me and shows me how to hold the feather and make my words on leaf, it's … well, somehow we are like one, closer even than wer and wife."

Tova sighed. "From what you've told me the man is a pagan. You should have nothing more to do with him for fear of damning your soul even if you care nothing for your earthly body or the worth of your name."

Godgyfu waved a hand. "Come now, you know as well as I, scratch at half the men and women in England and you'll find a bit of the heathen showing through. It's in our blood, and it's all harmless—charms and folk healing and the like. Thomas knows much of herbs and blooms, more than any monk. He brews a draught like no other to soothe an aching head."

"But the man puts himself forth as a novice of the Benedictines! There is no place for pagan charms among their brethren."

"Think what you like," Godgyfu said with a shrug. "I grant he's not the most steadfast follower of the *Regula*, but he does love God and Christ in his own way, and he loves the Blessed Virgin as strongly as do you or I. And the saints! He knows more of the saints' lives than any priest I've ever met. I could listen to him speak of them for hours. In truth, I think he mostly finds the old ways charming. He looks back to the days of our forebears as a golden time, a time when men may have been without Christ but when they had more worth and were driven less by greed and shallow needs."

Tova snorted and reached for another bit of cheese.

Godgyfu gave her a hard stare. "You can't tell me you look well on everything the Church has done … putting an end to most of the nunneries, for one thing. Time was great nun-houses could be found far and wide across the kingdom, but now? Why should you and your sisters not have a house every bit as great as those of the Benedictines? There is no good answer other than that the Pope and the archbishops see it that way."

Tova said nothing, which from her wontedly outspoken friend, Godgyfu took as grudging acknowledgment.

Godgyfu helped herself to some bread and cheese, and for a time they ate in stillness.

"You look tired," Tova said at last.

She shrugged. "Everything I had to make ready for today, it—"

"You're finding it hard to sleep again, aren't you?"

Godgyfu laughed. "You know me too well. I've slept some, but last night whenever I slept, awful nightmares came to me. I spent half the night awake and cowering under the bedclothes like a little girl afraid of elves hiding in the shadows."

"Tell me what you dreamed. I find talking of mares robs them of their strength."

"It was awful." She stopped, calling it fully to mind, and shuddered. "I was giving birth to Ælfgar. In life, all went as well with his birth as such things can, but in this nightmare ... The midwives had fallen asleep, even as he was coming out of me, and when I cried out to wake them, they never stirred. Instead a great scaly hand began to wrap itself around me from behind, as though the bedding itself had come alive. And the wild thing with the great hand hungered. It was an empty hole that needed filling. Its hunger passed to me, and it became everything. I had to eat, something, anything, and in a mindless fever I ate my own child while his navel string still linked him to me."

"I swear your mind is bent. No wonder you're not sleeping."

Godgyfu shook her head. "There was still more. Only then did the midwives wake. They saw me all bloody from what I'd done, and they and Leofric and all the folk of Coventry cast me out. But somehow—and this bit is hard to understand—they cast me out not only from their fellowship but from mankind, so that I became instead a ... I guess I was some sort of horse that ever after men and women rode, their weight aching my back and their sharp heels cutting my flanks. Mother of God, I woke a sweaty mess, and I—"

She stopped to listen. The din from outside had suddenly become greater.

Tova heard it too, and she looked toward her narrow window. "What is—?"

The unmistakeable sound of steel on steel. Weapons had been drawn. *What in God's name?*

They both leapt to their feet, Godgyfu knocking her chair to the floor, and ran for the doorway, down the stairs and into the yard.

Outside, men and women shouted, and a great writhing and shoving went on along the abbey church's south wall. Over the din, she heard Leofric bellowing and felt herself grow cold.

"Stay here!" Godgyfu told her friend, and she lifted her skirts to run toward her husband.

By the time she reached him, men were holding him back, but he still bore his naked sword in hand, all but foamed at the mouth. Across from him, others held the great oaf Swegn Godwineson, who also had his sword out, roaring like some Danish *berserkr*.

"You dare to draw your blade at me?" Leofric shouted. "In my own town? After what you've done?"

"Come here," Swegn spat back. "By the Blessed Maiden's hairy slit, I'll shove this blade up your shit-stained arse, you flabby gray cunt!"

"Enough!" Godgyfu screamed. She strode toward Leofric and put her hand upon his sword arm.

Leofric's man Osmund was among those holding him, and he turned toward Godgyfu with a warning shake of his head. "I beg you, stay back Godgyfu. This is not—"

"This is *my* husband, and I will speak to him! What is the meaning of this?"

Leofric met her gaze, and his eyes held fire. "Osmund just got word from one of my men in Shropshire. Swegn's sent his hired swords in and taken lands that were my brother Eadwine's and which are now mine. It's not enough he's gotten a great swath of my earldom from the king to call his own, now he makes a bid to steal more!" He looked back toward Swegn. "Then you have the ballocks to come and sit in our church, eat at our table as though nothing were amiss, and when I learn of your treachery from another and call you on it, you bare steel at me?"

Swegn shrugged. "I didn't care for the way you said your words."

"You didn't ...." Leofric couldn't even finish whatever he had begun to say and ended up spitting like an angry cat. Then he made to leap forward, almost knocking Godgyfu to the ground, and his men had to hold him again.

"Husband, stop," she screamed. "*Stop!*"

At last he seemed to hear her, and he stopped straining. His men let go of his arms.

Godgyfu touched her own fingertips to the edge of his cloak. "Please, not on this day of all days. Not today."

The king's friend fitzWymarc came toward them. "Your lady wife has the right of it, lord. Put away your swords." He spared a glance for Swegn. "Both of you. You are Englishmen, not Danes. Somehow there has been some mistake over the reach of Swegn's lands, but it is something we can work out with words rather than bloodshed."

Grudgingly, Leofric slid Bloodwreak back in its sheath.

Swegn did the same with his weapon, laughing as he did so. "Well that was a bit of fun on an otherwise dull day."

"Enough, my lord earl," Ralf of Mantes warned, stepping forward, and Swegn lifted his hands as if to say he was done bickering. "Let us go and sit in the cloister, where we may speak in stillness."

It was agreeable to all, and Leofric and his men soon followed along behind the others, around to the far side of the church.

Godgyfu stayed where she stood, paying no mind to what those around her said, words meant to soothe her. She had no need of such words, for against all wit, she found herself smiling inside, glad to see her husband worked up about something … about *anything* other than Saint Paul for once. It was a fire she'd not seen in him since he was much younger.

Maybe some of that fire would work itself into more lively bedgames later that night. Godgyfu would find it easier to call Thomas to mind.

NINE

WINCHESTER
16 NOVEMBER 1043

THE HIGH WALLS OF WINCHESTER loomed before them. Leofric spurred his horse forward and came up alongside King Eadward, Earls Siward and Godwine doing the same. They'd left Gloucester before dawn and had been riding hard all day, first southeast along Ermin Street, then south when they reached the haunted ruins of the old Roman town near Reading. They'd stopped for fresh horses at the king's field house north of town and now rode toward Winchester itself as the sun crept fat and red toward the land's western eyemark. Already Leofric could smell the town's stink.

All the way along what was left of the old Roman roads, Eadward had kept away from his earls, speaking only with Abbot Rodbert within the ranks of the king's housecarls who rode in a tight ring around them. Leofric had kept to himself as well, brooding over what this faring to Winchester would mean, over why the king had asked him to bring his wife along, and over the wide smirk that seemed ever to cling to Godwine's chin. Godgyfu had done herself proud, keeping up with the hard pace the king set, but Leofric had shunned her fellowship too; the way she bounced up and down in the saddle set his thoughts racing down paths he didn't want to take. For the most part the apostle had helped him to keep the worst at bay, but there were still moments … smoke-clouded moments when the devils of Worcester clawed their way back in ….

Not now. Not today. I need to stay clear. Blessed Paul, blind me to the sins of my mind! Mostly he'd kept his mind busy by thinking on the ghosts of dead Romans who might still walk England's crumbling highways wondering where their once mighty reich had gone. *Faded into the mists.*

Now at last Eadward called his earls to his side, and the abbot fell back to ride alongside Godgyfu and the few handmaids she'd brought with her. The king leaned forward to give an apple to his steed as Leofric neared.

"A comely horse, Highness," Leofric said. "Looks to be bred for war."

Eadward smiled through his pale-yellow beard and patted the horse's neck. "Indeed. Tresseint here was my best-loved *destre* from among those I rode in my years overseas. I had him brought over from Normandy after my kingmaking. A good horse stays ever true, which is more than can be said for my mother."

Ah, here we come to it. Leofric cleared his throat, leaving it to the king to say more. When they'd come to Gloucester at the king's bidding, Eadward had been somewhat stingy with his words.

"Tell us more of this fox-craft you spoke of," Earl Siward said. "How is it you name Lady Emma traitor?"

Eadward shrugged as though it were a little thing, but his eyes had grown tight, his mouth set in a hard line. "I call her what she is," he answered after a time. "My housecarls got hold of a pistle my mother wrote, *leoms Dieux* before her man could bear it over the water."

"And to whom was this pistle written?" Godwine asked.

The king kept still for a long while more, staring ahead at the walls growing bigger before them. At last he spat onto the road and answered in what was nearly a hiss. "She wrote to King Magnus, bid him come against me with ships and men from Norweg and Denmark and trothed all the wealth of my kingdom to help him take my crown."

None of them knew what to say.

Siward found his tongue first. "But why, Highness? Why do such a thing to her own kin—the son of her own belly?"

Eadward gave a scoffing laugh. "Oh, she pushed me out, true enough, but she never did for me as she did for her other sons. She always liked Cnut and the boys he gave her better than her sons with the man Cnut overthrew. All I can think is she must now find putting some outlander she's never met on my kingseat easier to swallow than seeing me bring back the line of kings her dear Cnut and his sons spent the best years of their lives driving off."

"But it's madness," Godwine said. "Is there any way there's been some mistake, that the pistle meant something other than—"

"There's no mistake!" Eadward barked. Then he shook his head, seemingly finding it as hard as any to see wit in it. "Maybe she's just an unbearable she-wolf who thinks to bed down yet another king in the shape of Magnus, my own *membre* being something even she would balk at sticking back in the womb that helped grow it nearly forty years ago! Christ!"

Leofric dropped his eyes along with Godwine and Siward. In the short time they'd had to get to know Eadward, they already knew it was a sundry thing for the wontedly holy man to speak so openly of unholy things, let alone to take the Lord's name idly. Leofric wasn't sure if he was meant to laugh at the king's bawdy words and thought it better to keep still.

"Or maybe," Eadward went on, "my lady mother's at last grown so old her mind's addled, and it's time for her to be put out in the meadow like an old *destre* too weak to bear a rider."

Hearing these last words lightened Leofric's heart. When he'd heard what Emma had done, he'd begun to fear Eadward's highest earls had been called to come witness an old woman's hanging—not something he had much wish to see. *Maybe Eadward only means to bundle her off somewhere under careful watch now that she's grown old and feeble.* Then Leofric thought how Emma was only seven or eight years older than he himself, and he felt all at once wretched again.

"That's why you asked for my wife to come," Leofric said. "A highborn woman to lead Emma more softly out to the meadow."

Eadward nodded. "Whatever else she's done, she's my mother. I can't very well hand her over to my housecarls or even to my earls as though she were some thieving highwayman."

And Godgyfu's a better choice than Gytha, Leofric thought. *Emma bears as little love as I do for Godwine and his kin. The man murdered one of her sons, never mind it wasn't a son of Cnut.*

"Lady Emma doesn't know we're coming," Siward said. It wasn't a question.

The king sighed, a deep rumble in his broad chest. "By now she must have gotten word we're on the road. But no, that is why I bid you come to Gloucester in hiding. Why we've ridden hard and fast. I want this taken care of before my mother fully knows what's happening. And I also want this whole business with Magnus kept quiet. Tell no one."

They were skirting west around the town wall now, making for the King's Gate to the south which only opened for the king himself. Leofric was glad he rode with Eadward so they could miss having to fight through the cattle and throngs of folk they'd have met at one of the other gates. As it was, the south road was crowded enough with carts of food and drink streaming toward Winchester for the upcoming Saint Andrew feast.

Eadward's man had been sent on ahead, and the gates stood wide for them as they rode through—the king himself with a score of his housecarls heavily weaponed, the three earls and Godgyfu and her maids with Abbot Rodbert, and several other men besides from the earls' and abbot's households. From there a straight shot along a wide path brought them through the wooded lawns shared by the twin minsters and the king's hall with its linked outbuildings. The setting sun glinted bright and rosy off the waterways the saintly Æthelwold had built, back before the Danes came, to shunt water from the nearby stream in branching lines toward the monks' cloister, their *lavatorium* and *necessarium*, their gardens and sick house. It gave the evening a restful feel that hearkened nothing of the ugliness they all knew was to come.

All too soon they reached the inner gates leading to the grounds of the king's hall itself. They were thrown open, and Eadward spurred his steed through, the others fast behind. Since the Easter kingmaking, Emma had been markedly missing from the king's household as it made its way throughout the kingdom. She seemed to have made the Winchester hall into a lasting home for herself and her handmaids. Earl Godwine seemed bothered by this as the earls had spoken among themselves on the ride, but Leofric thought he understood; the woman was elderly and could no longer be expected to keep moving wherever the king sat his seat. What went unsaid in their talks was that it might have been best she'd settled down in one spot so Eadward was not seen to need his mother tailing along with him everywhere; it freed him from the shadow of the past.

"Welcome, Highness!" a door-ward said, bowing as Eadward alit before his hall. "Your mother the Queen has only just been given word of your coming and makes ready to welcome you. In the meanwhile, food and drink has been—"

Eadward grabbed the man's shirt and lifted him nearly off his feet. "She's ready now! Call her to the hall." He shoved the man back then onto his arse. Picking himself up, his cast grown gray as old oatmeal, the door-ward bowed low and hurried off without another word as Eadward strode within.

Once in the high hall, Eadward threw off his cloak, flung it to a housecarl, and climbed the step to his kingseat. He sat, uneasily, not leaning against the carved board but well forward on the seat's edge, back straight, the tip of his long beard hanging over his knees. His eyes were two burning embers.

Leofric, Siward, and Godwine stepped up too and stood behind and to either side of the kingseat, staring at the door through which the king's mother would soon come. They did not have to wait long.

"My son," Emma said, hobbling into the room. She had grown even more bent since Leofric saw her last. Her face looked pinched and bony within her wimple, lost behind a deep blue head cloth's hanging folds. "I only just got word of your coming! What a happy wonder …." She had been all smiles, but now she wavered. Her eyes met Leofric's and the other earls'. At last she saw the sternness of the king's own cast, and her smile withered.

"Mother," Eadward said, the word like cold iron. "What I have come to say will not take long. I and those who give me their wisdom have spoken of this, and I have deemed it unfit for you to behave yourself as though you were still some sort of queen. Your stead in this kingdom is not one of leadership, and it is long past time for you to acknowledge this. First and foremost, you have no business overseeing the kingdom's gold-house, and you shall hand over the keys forthwith."

Emma's mouth had shaped itself into a wordless ring, and her eyes now matched it, growing wider and wider as Eadward read off a tally—a long list of his mother's lands which he now took from her to do with as he saw fit. "But I don't leave you homeless," Eadward went on. "With no further need for you here, you'll quit the high hall, and I know the homelier softness of your own little house in town will be more to your liking—land I believe was given to you years ago by my own father. *Je me remembre mon pier. Vous?*"

Emma looked as though she wished to say something, but her mouth only opened and closed like that of a fish on the sand. Eadward leapt up from his seat and strode toward his mother. Leofric and the others walked with him, maybe in an unspoken understanding that they should stop the king if he sought to do his mother some bodily hurt. But there was none of that.

Eadward beckoned Godgyfu forward from where she had stood at the hall's far end, then turned back to his mother. "Earl Leofric's own dear wife has kindly come to help you make ready to leave and to see that you are well settled in your new home. You will surely not need the great gang of maids you've hitherto kept. You may keep a handmaid or two to see to your needs, but the rest shall stay here at the hall."

Again, Emma seemed ready to say something. There was even a spark of anger in her eyes, but as she looked about her from one stony cast to another she saw she had no friends left here and a fight would be worthless. The spark went out, and her back slumped even further. "As you say, Highness," she whispered and bowed her head. Then she reached beneath her wimple and withdrew the string on which dangled the ungainly keys to the king's gold-house.

As she passed the keys to Eadward, Leofric was close enough to hear the king whisper. "I have your pistle. You can forget any thought of Magnus. *Qi responez?*"

Emma said nothing to her son, only looking at him with something like befuddlement. For a heartbeat, Leofric wondered whether the story about her having written to Magnus was true or only something brewed up by Eadward, a half-truth to feed them and make them feel better about what they did. Whether even now he only said the words to his mother because he wanted his earls to hear them. In the end, it didn't matter. The king willed what the king willed, and his earls saw his will was done.

Eadward whirled the key string once about a long finger, then turned from his mother and made for the door. "I shall be leaving in the morning and may not have the time to speak with you again before I go." Just before he left, he turned back and said, as if an afterthought, "Oh, and Mother, should you wish to pray in your hour of need, I should tell you that even as we speak Stigand is being stripped of his see."

Leofric and the other earls traded sharp looks. This was something Eadward had not shared with them on the ride. Stigand was Emma's former priest and the newly appointed bishop of Elmham in East Anglia; he was among Emma's most trusted living friends. *What grounds has Eadward found to take down Stigand?* Though Eadward did not say it in so many words, he was warning his mother she'd find no help within the Church if she thought to raise a stink about her treatment on this day.

Then Eadward was gone, his housecarls' steps and those of Siward and Godwine loud on the stones behind him. Leofric stayed behind with his wife and the queen. *No, the queen no longer.*

Emma looked about, her eyes darting like a cornered mouse. She seemed so small. A lost thing.

Godgyfu stepped closer and bowed low, keeping her cast empty, carefully warded. "I have brought some of my own maids to help with your things, Lady. And two of my lord husband's housecarls will give you their backs for any heavy lifting. They are yours until you are well settled." She beckoned forward her girls and the two men and gave Emma their names. "If you have not yet eaten, it would gladden me to break bread with you in the rooms overlooking the gardens in a short while."

"Thank you, Godgyfu," Emma said, smiling weakly. "I would like that."

She nodded. "Then go now with these folk. Set them to whatever task seems best, and I will be along shortly to see that all's faring along as it should."

Emma let herself be led away by the maids.

When they were gone, Leofric reached over and gave his wife's hand a squeeze. "That was worthily done," he said. It could easily have gone quite another way. A lesser woman would have taken the chance to rub Emma's years of pridefully wielding her strength like a weapon back in her nose. But much as Leofric knew Godgyfu hated Emma for wedding herself to the Danes and for everything else the woman had done, he never saw her gloat even a little. In the end, she gave the old shrew nothing but gentle kindness. *I have a good wife, and I am a wretched sinner for all the sick thoughts I have about her ….* He pushed aside the things that ever lurked. *Stop!*

Godgyfu rubbed a hand over her mouth, and her eyes glistened. "She's old. I don't understand the things she's done, but I'm sure to her they seemed the best choices for herself and those she loved, and for a time there was none stronger than her, man or woman, in all the kingdom. Who am I to rob her of that in her last years? Let her hold onto it as long as she can. Her life is over now, and we still have ours to live. She knows it, and nothing I could say to her could possibly be more bitter than that."

Then she gave her arm to Leofric, and together they walked the hallways the king had taken earlier. When they reached the gold house, the heavy doors had been unlocked and thrown open, and the room was lit from within by firebrands on the walls. They stepped inside and gave twin gasps. Eadward, Godwine, and

Siward were almost lost among the heaps of riches. They stood laughing together, the king having draped himself with richly furred cloaks and gem-studded rings on every finger. Siward was fingering a gold-stitched scabbard while Godwine stood nearby letting pennies run through his hands back into a chest that overflowed with them. Here was the hoard Cnut had gathered and Harthacnut had added to—much of it likely from what had been taken from the raid on Worcester. In truth, much of this hoard was likely Emma's own … but no longer. Everywhere Leofric looked he saw gold and silver cups, sacks and boxes of pennies, rolls of silk, and tables stacked with books whose boards were thick with gems.

"Christ in Heaven," Leofric breathed.

"Leofric, Godgyfu, come come!" Eadward beckoned them. From his beaming smile it seemed his earlier dark mood had wholly gone. He snatched something up from a wall shelf and held it up for them to see. It was a golden box with a hinged handle. "The skull of Saint Ouen."

Leofric made the sign of the cross and dropped to a knee, paying no mind to the old ache in his bones.

"And who was he?" Earl Godwine asked.

Abbot Rodbert stepped out from behind a mound of woven rugs that looked to have come from the Saracen lands. He clucked his tongue at Godwine; the two were not fond of each other. "He was Bishop of Rouen four centuries ago," the abbot said, his English hard to understand, thick with the sound of Normandy. "Ouen brought many pagans to Christ. Before Jumièges, I myself was Prior of Ouen's abbey in Rouen."

Godwine rolled his eyes. "How lovely for you. And when do you go back to Jumièges?"

Rodbert bristled, but Eadward cut off further bickering. "Enough, Godwine. I hope Rodbert will choose to stay in England. And I'm bringing the relic to London for the abbey." Eadward was rebuilding Saint Peter's Abbey on Thorney Island in the Norman way; likely he wanted a minster of his own making in which to be buried one day. "And there is what I trothed to you, Leofric, for all you and your wife have done." He thrust a finger toward a silver chest sitting near to where the skull had been. "My gift to you in sorrow over having had to miss your own abbey's hallowing."

Leofric walked toward the table and put his hands upon the chest. The silver hummed beneath his fingers. Godgyfu had bidden him ask Eadward for this thing—an arm of Saint Augustine of Hippo himself—and the king had agreed to let them have it. He lifted it up, arms shaking, and bore it over to his wife. Looking almost afraid to take it from him, she drew a deep breath, then gathered it into her arms as though it were a babe in swaddling. Tears fell freely down her cheeks.

"My father died bringing this back to England with Æthelnoth," she said, a whisper, so that it seemed she merely spoke her thoughts aloud. Why the relic had been gathering dust in the king's gold-house was a riddle with no good answer, but now it would be given over to their abbey in Coventry, which seemed most fitting. It gladdened Leofric to see Godgyfu so happy.

"I fear I'll drop it," she breathed, and she bent forward to set it atop a bundle of silks.

In his mind, Leofric saw himself stepping up behind, lifting her skirts and thrusting himself inside her ... taking her like a steed takes a mare in the barnyard while the king and the others watched and burned for her.

Blessed Paul, help me. Make it stop!

His head began to pound, and he felt a wetness on his own cheeks, tears having nothing whatsoever to do with happiness.

TEN

COVENTRY
3 APRIL 1044

THUNDER WHISPERED IN THE DISTANCE, but the clouds fled eastward in a bluing sky. Godgyfu thought the rain would miss them altogether.

Two years had come and gone since first she'd knocked at Blodeuwedd's door, and in all that time Godgyfu had only made her way there twice more, each faring no more fruitful than the last. She'd kept telling herself she would go again but somehow never found the time. Drawing closer now to where the cot nestled in a muddy, woods-shrouded crook of the stream, she sighed. *Truth be told, all too much of the last six months has been given over to Thomas.* Nearly until Christmas, Godgyfu was away with her husband and the king in Winchester in the wake of Emma's downfall. After that she'd come back to Coventry and, whenever she could work out a way to do so outside Leofric's awareness, had whiled many long, fire-warmed stretches in Thomas's fellowship. It was one of the happiest winters Godgyfu remembered; the bond between her and Thomas had strengthened, and almost she thought she saw a new warmth kindling in his eyes, a love to twin her own. *And I do love him!* It was hopeless to deny it any longer, and she knew he must feel the same. There were even times she could have sworn the man was ready to lean forward and put his lips to hers, but maybe that had been but a dwimmer of the warmed, spiced wine and good Christmas mead.

With winter's thaw and Eastertide's coming, Godgyfu thought it time at last to go back to Blodeuwedd's and make a new beginning. Leofric had unwittingly set her mind to the task by pawing at her more often in the night of late. Men, like bulls and steeds, were ever lustier with the coming of warmer weather, and if Godgyfu could sway Blodeuwedd toward the nunnery, she might well spare her the wretchedness of the many who would otherwise darken her doorway over the weeks and months to come.

This time, Godgyfu brought Tova with her, hoping her friend might make happen what she alone could not. They'd earlier spent the morning together doing what they could to soothe young Gytha, who had been married to Alric the miller. Gytha was strong, and they had left her knowing she'd be well again soon once the sharp edge of her newfound widowhood wore off. Now she and Tova wended southward along the Sherbourne to the out-of-the-way spot Blodeuwedd had chosen to live because it was far from the town's streets and unwanted eyes.

"I was at Ringwaru's house last night," Godgyfu said, and then she nearly stumbled from a sudden onrush of lightheadedness the day's Lenten fasting brought on.

Tova put out a hand to steady her. "How fares she?"

Godgyfu drew a deep breath. "Well. And glad enough to live softly where she is, it seems. It's a comely enough spot in truth, overlooking Swan's Well. You can see the water from her front window. Have you been there?"

"Yes, once. There are worse spots to have to be hidden away." Tova cast a stern look at the mud before them and did what she could to skirt the worst.

"At least Ringwaru has a husband, even if he must now make believe otherwise. She wants to help with the nunnery. She'll work what sway she has over Abbot Leofwin, and she tells me that sway is more than slight. I think the abbot will give in and bestow you the house, though he'll likely tell you it was brotherly Christian love that led him to do so."

Tova laughed. "Let him tell himself what he must so long as he does what we want. You'll get the house for us yet."

"I know I've made much of it while nunneries are fading elsewhere in the kingdom, but to make Coventry a truly great town, it should have one as well. Folk will know ours is a good and holy stead."

"They know it already," Tova said, "from the abbey and from all you and Leofric have given to the Church." She lifted an arm. "Is that Blodeuwedd's house?"

Godgyfu nodded. "A sorry thing, no?"

They walked without speaking the rest of the way. Tova stood back a few steps while Godgyfu stepped up to the crooked door. She'd nearly put her knuckles to the wood when it swung open.

"Godgyfu!" Blodeuwedd yelped. "Abbess Tova? We .... This is an unforeseen thing."

"That's plain enough," Tova said, her words all at once cold when the shape behind Blodeuwedd stepped into the light.

Godgyfu let out a sound that was half growl, half whimper. "You! *Here?*"

"Good day to you, my lady," Thomas said. "And my lady abbess."

Godgyfu felt her mind breaking to bits, cold fingers squeezing her chest. "So this is what you do! This is why you never want .... Why I can't ...."

Thomas's eyebrows rose, his lips opened, and he made to say something.

"She's a whore, Thomas! An unclean—"

"Now then," Tova warned, a hand on Godgyfu's shoulder.

"Yes, *Lady* Godgyfu," Blodeuwedd said, adding the queenly word to her name with a smirk, "I'm a whore, although it does make me wonder to hear you say it, as ever before you seemed to be of the mind I was some holy maid being gamed by evil men. But I dare say Thomas is no worse a sort than your own self!"

"Will you let a woman like this speak for you?" Godgyfu was lightheaded again and couldn't stop herself from yelling. "Let her ward your good name?" *How could I have believed he was anything other than what all men are?*

Thomas laughed, the bright and easy laugh she'd so grown to love but which now seemed nettlesome, fiendish. "I am in no need of warding. Whatever else you think you've come upon at this house, I am here on God's work and have been coming for as long as you've known me, though I never spoke of it for the sake of Blodeuwedd, who did not wish it known. Each Sunday I bring the holy bread of Christ's body, for she is too ashamed to go and have it from Father Bergulf's hand at Saint Michael's." As he spoke, he unfolded a linen cloth, and within it was a loaf of the rood-marked bread the monks baked and the priests hallowed for mass. A bit of it was missing, torn away, given to Blodeuwedd.

"True enough," the woman said. "The looks I get from folk at mass are not ones I care to gather."

Godgyfu gaped at Blodeuwedd, then lowered her head in shame. Those looks would have held the selfsame gall Godgyfu had only then been spewing at her. *Whore! Unclean woman!*

"I come to spare her being among such folk," Thomas went on. "None of the other monks want to do it given all the mud."

Staring at his shoes, which were indeed decked in drying, brown filth, Godgyfu found she could not lift her eyes back up to meet Thomas's gaze. Or Blodeuwedd's. *What have I done? What have I said!*

"Blodeuwedd, forgive me," she whispered at last, still not looking up. "I spoke in anger at … that …." What could she say? She couldn't acknowledge to this woman what was between her and Thomas. "Anger that one who would troth himself to God might have been …." She faltered.

"You see there," Blodeuwedd said. "You've shed light on the root of why, even if I wanted to, I can't never be no nun. Put my hair up, cover it with a wimple, and would folks see a nun? No. All who knew me would still forever see Blodeuwedd the whore. Even the other nuns would see me that way, and I don't much like the thought of having to look at their snotty stares for the rest of my days. I am what I am, and there's nothing you nor anyone else can do to shift that."

Godgyfu felt herself quaking. Was Blodeuwedd right? Could folk never be made anew? Did the sins of yesterday ever haunt this world even unto the world hereafter? *Surely not if one casts aside those sins, if those sins were never truly one's own to begin with, if there was ever a will to be something better, something more.* "Maybe I should leave. Tova, you stay and speak with Blodeuwedd. I fear my being here will only hinder things further."

"Now there's the first wit I've heard from you since we got here," Tova answered.

When Godgyfu turned back to look at her, Tova's sickened cast was like a blow to the gut. *I have let her down.* Worse, Godgyfu knew she'd let Blodeuwedd down; her work with the woman undone in a twinkling through her own foolishness, her own selfish weakness.

"Tova," she said softly. "I'm so sorry."

"Shush. We'll talk later."

Thomas stepped fully from the doorway into the unkempt front yard. "I will walk you back to town, lady."

Godgyfu nodded, still not meeting his gaze.

Tova did spare him a glance, then looked back, and Godgyfu could see her friend was of two minds. "I would fain stay for a spell, but are you sure ...?" She left the rest unsaid, her eyes chiding Godgyfu as loudly as words.

"We'll be ... all will be well." Before Tova could say anything else, Godgyfu fled northward, Thomas falling in alongside her.

For a while, neither spoke. Around a bend, their faring startled a red fox drinking at the stream bank with four brown kits; the mother coughed at them, then herded her children off into the woods. Godgyfu watched them melt away among the trees and wished she could follow. At last, once she and Thomas had gone far enough the cot could no longer be seen through the trees behind them, she stopped walking and turned to him.

"I am so sorry for having thought the worst of you. Can you forgive me?"

He waved a hand as though it were but a small thing. "You of all folk should know that woman has nothing to offer me with her waywardness. My needs are not of that sort."

"I should have been more trusting." *What was I thinking?*

Thomas lifted a hand and held it alongside her face, seeming to want to stroke her cheek. After a long while, he dropped it with a heavy sigh. "As I said, I wanted to spare Blodeuwedd shame, but I nonetheless should not have kept it from you. Nothing should be hidden between us."

A lightness flooded her soul, the tight knot in her belly unwinding. He smiled, and the wind ruffled the gold-brown tuft of hair ever threatening to fall over his wide calf's eyes. "My sweet Thomas." She took a step forward, bridging the narrow gap between them. Before she could stop herself, her arms went about him and drew him near. She waited for him to hop back as if from a fire, to push her away in loathing as he had done before.

For a wonder, this time he did not. He stood—woodenly, it was true—but he stood and let her hold him, let her press herself against his broad chest. The smell of incense, of clean sweat, of the herbs with which he brewed his healing draughts ... all of it filled her and nearly made her drunk with bliss.

I will never doubt you again.

ELEVEN

COVENTRY
1 FEBRUARY 1045

The old ceorl Hrolf stood before Leofric, nose dripping from the cold. The hall's pit fire warmed Leofric's back but still hadn't reached his frozen bones. "And the boughs are all cut back?" Leofric asked.

Hrolf nodded, rubbing his hands together. "Aye, on Saint Vincentius's day. Furrowed the rows on Plough Monday. Buried a good cake in each acre and said my prayers."

"Good," Leofric said. "Let's hope the wheatcorn does better this year than last. You've done well."

"Thank ye, lord." The ceorl bowed and sidled slowly toward the doorway, loath to go back into the weather.

"Oh, and have Peada slaughter two sheep," Leofric called out as an afterthought.

"Aye, lord." An icy draft danced in under the door's overbeam as he left.

Leofric turned back to the fire and refilled his cup with spiced wine from the warming pot. "Christ, but the road was cold," he told his man Osmund, who sat at one of the long feast boards with Ælfgar. His son's cheeks were ruddy as the fire took away the chill from their long ride back to Coventry. All three sipped thankfully from steaming cups. Saint Paul was there too—among them; Leofric could feel the holy fullness within the hall. He lifted his cup toward the deeper shadows at the hall's far end and took a drink in the saint's blessed name. *Why won't you speak to me any more? Show me new wonders, Brother. Tell me what I must do.*

"How *was* the wedding?" Osmund leaned back against a knot-carved roof staff. "Did the king troth himself in Norman or English?"

Leofric laughed and whirled back toward his friend. "In English, though there were many Frankishmen at the feast, true enough. And Christ, but I've seen enough Godwine kin for ten lifetimes."

"Well, you could hardly think Earl Godwine would have his daughter christened queen without every far-flung cousin there to see!" Osmund groaned. "God in heaven, wedded father to the king! We'll never hear the end of it! Did they truly give her a crown of her own?"

Leofric nodded. "Even Emma never got that. But that wasn't wedding gift enough, seems. Eadward named Godwine's son Harold earl in East Anglia and gave Godwine's wife's nephew Beorn an earldom over Thuri's old lands in the southeast Midlands." He slammed his cup down against the board, sloshing wine over his fingers. "Other than me and Siward, the whole bleeding kingdom has become one big sweetmeat for Godwine and his kin!"

The wedding itself didn't bother Leofric half so much as the earldoms. After all, Eadgyth was one of only a small handful of maidens of wifely years from among Eadward's high men's daughters. There was little else Eadward could have done. *He might have looked overseas for a bride as his father did with Emma ....* In his mind, he said the words to Paul. *But then ... that ended up a goat's breakfast. Emma's steadfastness toward England was ... well, what you'd foresee from an outlander!* He supposed it was better Eadward went back to the long-standing way of his forebears and took a wife born and bred in the kingdom. In truth, Eadgyth seemed worthy of her new crown, taught by the nuns at Wilton, sharp enough to be a good help, meet for the king. Leofric quaffed the dross of his wine, then dipped again into the pot and made up his mind to get good and drunk. His damned head was beginning to ache again, and the wine helped dull the sharper edges of the knife behind his eyes.

"Maybe Ælfgar here's not yet old enough to have gotten one of those earldoms," he said after taking three big gulps, "but could Eadward not have found someone else! Even his nephew Ralf or another of his Norman friends would have been better! Things are skewed too far Godwine's way now. It upsets the scales."

Osmund nodded but waved a hand. "Young Harold as earl does seem a bit much. But as for Beorn, mind you he's not only Gytha's nephew, he's this Danish Sveinn's brother, and with King Magnus having taken Denmark, Sveinn's in a grim fight to wrest it back. It's good to keep Sveinn thinking we English are his friends and might even give him spears and men some day. As long as Sveinn and Magnus keep tugging two ends of a rope, Magnus can't make his bid against us."

Leofric sighed. "Maybe not, but Eadward still wants to gather a fleet this Eastertide just in case Magnus makes good on his threat." *Which means Eadward will need an even greater heregeld this year, and Godgyfu will start in on me again to get Coventry out from under it.* He turned back to the wine pot.

Behind him, he heard Osmund get up and clap Ælfgar on the shoulder. "What of you, lad? Weren't you to have met your own trothed bride while you were gone south?"

"Aye," Ælfgar answered. "Not in Winchester, but I saw Ælfgifu in London at the Christmas foregathering before we went to the king's wedding."

"I still don't see the wit in not having just held both things in Winchester," Osmund said.

Leofric blew a breath through his teeth. "Eadward wanted everyone in London first because he was keen to show off the plot for his new abbey on Thorney. Gathered us all there, then herded us like sheep along the road to Winchester. As for young Ælfgifu ... Do you know I was worried some years back we'd made a mistake linking ourselves to Cnut's first wife's kin rather than to Emma's?" He laughed. "Now with the Danes gone and Emma fallen from her heights, I reckon it's all worked out for the best, eh?"

"I'd heard Emma's been taken back into the fold," Osmund said.

Leofric shrugged. Little more than a year had passed since Eadward breasted his mother so harshly at Winchester, and now Leofric couldn't help but look back on the whole thing as some over-stuffed show. "Kings are fickle things. But he can give his mother back her lands, give Stigand back his bishopric, and Emma's still never going to be what she was. More so now we've a new queen."

"So lad, how was she?" Osmund asked.

Ælfgar looked up from his cup. "Who?"

"*Who*, he says!" Osmund laughed. "Grendel's mother! Who? Your bride-to-be!"

"Oh." Ælfgar blushed overtop his newly-thick, black beard. "Ælfgifu was a sweet-spoken maid. And godly. She looks forward to our wedding this summer."

"Sweet-spoken!" Osmund wrapped his arms around Ælfgar's shoulders and squeezed his chest with both hands. "Well and good, but how were her tits?"

Ælfgar choked on his wine, and Leofric and Osmund both roared.

"She was but a wisp of a thing," Leofric answered for Ælfgar, wiping his mouth with the back of a hand. "Thin as a whip, but comely and fair." Then he felt bad for having laughed and came over to rub a hand through his son's wild hair. "You pay no mind to Osmund, son. A godly woman is a thing to hold dear. Be good to her, and you'll find happiness together."

Ælfgar gave him a grateful nod.

"I'll drink to that," Osmund said, gathering all three of their cups for another round.

GODGYFU WAS GIDDY DESPITE THE shepherd's cot being freezing cold. Thomas started a fire on the floor, and its warmth began to fill the little stone room. Outside a wet snow blew about in whorls over the meadow, none of it sticking. It had likely been enough, though, to keep any prying eyes from spotting their coming together in this lonely spot.

She drank Thomas in with her eyes, greedily, the ache of missing him fading. A month and a half away from Coventry had been harder than she ever remembered it being, every day filled with bitter woe and longing. *I never even felt this way about Leofric back when I was young and thought I loved him.*

They stood close—leastwise as close as Thomas would allow. The one time they had been closer—that awful, wonderful, day near Blodeuwedd's now nearly a year gone—had not happened again. Even to share their bodies' warmth, Thomas would not let her break through that unseen shield he wore all around him. Godgyfu was almost mad with the need to be near him, to touch him, to let their bodies mirror the link they felt in their hearts, to put thought into deed in whatever way they could.

"You've come home on a worthy day," he said, standing up from where he'd been stoking the firepit. "The feast of Saint Brigid, well loved by the Scots. A pagan for a father and a thrall for a mother, and now Christians everywhere pray to her as one of Christ's blessed."

Godgyfu crossed herself. "A worthy woman."

"Brigid set up more than one abbey in her day—even as you've done. But she never forgot her roots, never forgot the small folk and the poor. You must not either."

His words took her aback. "I forget no one." She drew her cloak tighter about her. "I've not stopped looking to sway my husband to have Eadward free Coventry from the heregeld, and—"

Thomas cut her off with a laugh. "Good hap with that! With Magnus looking to storm our shores, the king will need to pay for ships and boatcarls. But there are other ways to see to the well-being of your folk having nothing to do with pennies. What of their soul-health? I tell you they still turn from the Church, still look to the old ways. More and more every day."

Godgyfu frowned; his words had begun to sting. "Why should that bother *you*? You seem well glad with either the old gods or with Christ and His saints—I dare say it's all the same to you." *It's true! What am I even doing with a man like this?*

"You know me too well," he said with the crooked smile she loved. "But I also know you, my lady, and I know how strongly you cleave to the Blessed Virgin. As you lose more of your folk to the old gods, Marie loses them as well. They break their troth with the Queen of Heaven, a traitorous faithlessness of the highest kind. But if they see how much you love Marie—"

"Did I not show my love for Marie by having the abbey hallowed in her name?"

Thomas shrugged. "Abbeys and incense and archbishops in golden robes—what do your ceorls know of such things? None of that touches their lives. Show yourself to me. Let me carve you in a likeness of Marie in all her naked might, freed from the awful clothes priests bind her in, and—"

Now Godgyfu scoffed loudly. "What witless rot. Why must I do such a thing? What have I to do with your carving? Craft your pagan Marie goddess from a worthy bit of wood and be done with it!"

"But you are the spark that gives me the fire I need—the fire to do it as it should be done. You are my *Musa* even as the bygone craftsmen of Grikaland had theirs. Without you, my carving will seem a dull thing. Only you can breathe it to life in my hands."

"Then put your hands on me," she said, stepping closer to him. In the back of her mind, she heard Tova warning her to have nothing more to do with him, but she pushed those words aside. "You know how it is for me with … with what happened before with Eilífr. Why only look? Feel me in the flesh. What better spark than that?"

Thomas looked at her askance. She closed her eyes and for a heartbeat thought she would at last feel him take her in his arms. Instead, his next words were steady and low, lacking any hint of fire. "You know, in four days, it will be another saint's feast—Saint Agatha."

Godgyfu opened her eyes, spread her hands. "What?"

"Agatha died to ward her maidenhead, keep herself clean and holy."

"I'm already dirty," she answered. "This is no maiden before you. I've had two husbands, and I've a grown son soon to wed himself. I know as much as you about Blessed Agatha. Did she not also speak against pagan carvings—*idololatria*?"

Thomas shook his head. "I want to make a carving of Marie—Christ's mother."

Godgyfu had to laugh. "But you want to make it like one of those pagan carvings."

"Only to help bring your folk to Marie, and thus to her son Christ and God the Father. And, true, also because I know that would make you happy. A martyr dies to ward the Christian faith, not to cling blindly to some thought with no grounding in the world. Even Agatha might have given worth to pagan carvings if they led to the greater wonder of God."

She gave him a hard stare. "Maybe she would even have given in to the lusts of the flesh for God's greater wonder." She felt wicked as she said the words, but she was angry now.

Thomas laughed, a loud, clear sound she seldom heard from him. It minded her of how young he was. "Truly you have the wisdom of Rhiannon. Which is why I love you."

The words sent a thrill through her. It was the first time he had spoken them. "Oh, my sweet, I love you, I love you. A thousand times, I love you." She reached out to him but stopped herself with her hands bare inches from him. "But this dance grows tiresome. I've waited for you, because you do seem somewhere beneath all your witless words to love me, but I can't keep doing this forever. You know I'm not happy with Leofric, and I thought it might bring me some happiness to be with a man like you, someone with a fire in him, someone who doesn't always stink of mead, someone with a knowledge of saints and tales and the wisdom of our forebears. Someone with whom I can speak of something other than earls and swords and horses."

"Speak to me. I'm listening."

She dropped her hands and found herself yelling. "Talking is no longer enough. I burn for you as men and women are meant to burn for each other. I understand you find it hard to … to touch me. To touch any woman. Maybe it's because of what you saw happen to your mother. But God damn you, Thomas, I'm not your mother! And I'm not some Welsh goddess! I am flesh and blood, and I burn for you! If you cannot help quench that fire, then I fear there is nothing more for us. Why gamble with my good name, much less my soul, over this? Why gamble Coventry's good name? We should not see each other any more. I should put you from my mind, go back and play the worthy wife for Leofric, and do what I may to help my folk in the best way I can!" Her last words came in a whisper. "Maybe you should leave Coventry."

A little quake shook him. "I've been unfair. But you *are* a goddess—my Rhiannon. I give you my troth, the time will come when our bodies should be linked even as you ask of me. It may be the only way you can find the goddess dwelling within you."

He raised one hand toward her, brushed the back of a finger down the side of her neck. In more than three years since she had known him now, it was the only time he had ever willingly touched her. The spot on her neck burned like a brand. A shivering delight traveled down from her throat to her breasts then into her stomach and farther to the folds between her legs. Everything blurred and turned white for a heartbeat. Two.

Nothing had ever thrilled her as that lone touch now did, and in a flash of awareness it suddenly came to her why that was so. *God help me, it's because he's doing it to please me!* It felt good—more than good. And Godgyfu wanted more of the same.

But Thomas snatched his hand away. "But that time is not now. Not yet." He left her, abandoned her for the swirling snow. She was alone, breathless and shaking on her knees beside the fire.

TWELVE

COVENTRY
31 MAY 1045

Thomas rode north with Ælfgar. They let their horses walk as they would over blossom-decked meadowland, among newly shorn sheep who bleated happily at them in their newfound nakedness. Soon they'd be back in Coventry, where Thomas could sit again at the altar of his goddess.

Each man bore a longbow before him, a bag of arrows over a shoulder. They'd spent the morning shooting before heading off on the daylong ride home. The past two days had been all Thomas had hoped they'd be. Ælfgar was awed indeed by Rollandriht and its ring of mossy stones on a scarp in the rolling wolds near to where they'd slept under the stars. Thomas had Godgyfu's son half believing the old tale that the ring and another nearby stone were all that was left of some bygone Mercian king and his housecarls cursed by a Welsh witch-wife. Better yet, Ælfgar had felt the true strength of the spot—the goddess-might that rose from the ground beneath the stones. It was good for him to soak it up, to make it part of him. He'd bring Ælfgar back there again some day soon for one of the gatherings of the folk who betimes met there on the nights of the old pagan feast days.

"You shot well today, Pryderi," Thomas said. "By summer's end, you'll be as good as me."

"Ha," Ælfgar bellowed. "I'm already better than you." He pulled his horse closer to Thomas's own and reached over to punch him in the arm. Thomas took it without flinching, but the blow hurt. Ælfgar had become an ox of a man, seemingly overnight, bulking up like his father. *Mutton-headed dimwits, both*, he thought to himself.

"Why must you always call me Pryderi?" Ælfgar asked. "I've told you it's bothersome."

Because Pryderi was Rhiannon's son, he might have answered. *And your mother is Rhiannon born again. Leastwise she will be soon.* "It's a good nickname. An aetheling's name. It fits you."

Ælfgar laughed. "I'm no aetheling."

"No, you're not. With the addled blood that sits the kingseat, be glad of it."

"But one day soon, I'll be an earl," Ælfgar said. "And father's wrong. I'm old enough to have been given the earldom that went to Godwine's son Harold."

Thomas shrugged. "Maybe, but he is nearly ten years older. How would he have felt if the earldom went to you?"

"What do I care how he'd feel? He can go sheathe himself in a sheep for all I care."

"Lovely," Thomas said with an overdone sigh. "Where'd you hear that, from one of your father's men?"

Ælfgar gave his customary oafish smile. "What about Beorn? Osmund says making him an earl helps keep Sveinn fighting Magnus over in Denmark, which keeps Magnus away from England."

Thomas nodded as though he gave deep thought to the words. "I'm sure your father's men are wise in the ways of war."

"And yet King Eadward's still gathered a great fleet. Father's leaving for Sandwich straightaway after my wedding. Why? If Magnus isn't coming?"

"Better safe today than sorry tomorrow." *I'm just glad we'll have your shit-lick of a father gone for the summer. Maybe he'll fall overboard and drown in the Wantsum Pipe.*

Between the boles of a maple thicket, Coventry's southernmost outlying houses came into view. Thomas was glad he'd soon be rid of Ælfgar's whining. Rather than make for the earl's house, Thomas led them east toward the curve of the Sherbourne.

Ælfgar seemed to remember where they headed—the little cot by the water where Blodeuwedd lived and where she gave herself to men for pennies. It looked maddeningly like the mean house in which Thomas had once lived with his own mother, and he ever hated going there. But he'd needed to. And at least Blodeuwedd had been quick-witted enough to go along with the answer he crafted when Godgyfu came upon them that day a year ago. It was well he'd had the bit of bread he'd snatched from the kitchen before leaving the abbey that morning; it helped put truth to his lie, the lie he'd had to tell his goddess for her own good and the good of all mankind. *As if either the Welsh whore or I have any need for the bleating priests' holy bread!* No, if Blodeuwedd kept true to anything it was to the old gods, and though she hadn't needed much swaying to agree to help Thomas with Ælfgar when the time came, Godgyfu's outburst swayed her more than any words Thomas himself had said.

"Must I do this?" Ælfgar asked, the earlier bluster gone from his speech.

Thomas put on a wounded cast. "It's my wedding gift to you. You can't spurn a gift."

"But I'm to be wedded in a fortnight. Ælfgifu and her kin are coming in a few days to help make things ready."

"All the more why you must do this." Thomas alit and tied his horse to a tree. He beckoned Ælfgar to do the same. "A man should not come to his wedding bed still a fledgling."

Ælfgar leapt down and looked away to hide his reddening cheeks. "I know what a man and woman do in bed."

Thomas laughed, louder than he needed to; shame could work wonders on a man-boy like Ælfgar. "You know what you've been told, but hearing and doing are two sundry things. If someone had merely told you about the bow, how to sight it and draw back and shoot, would you have been able to take one up, nock an arrow, and send it through a straw-man's eye on your first go? Never. Like anything, it takes working at it, coming to know the feel of the bow, the touch of the wind, the hundred other things your body does when you let fly, until the time comes when you no longer even think about it. It becomes something you do without even knowing you do it. The same's true with a woman."

"It is?" Ælfgar stood gaping at him like a bludgeoned calf.

Thomas nodded. "Unless you want to be fumbling about on your wedding night, shooting your seed all over dear Ælfgifu before you've worked out how best to hit the mark, you'd best get yourself over to Blodeuwedd's." He lifted a hand. "Look, there she is now."

The Welsh whore had indeed stepped out onto her threshold, all but falling from her thin shift. The setting sun turned her red hair nearly to fire and gave her skin a rosy hue. Ælfgar looked at Thomas, then plodded toward the house like a man walking to his own hanging. When he came within Blodeuwedd's reach, she wrapped one arm around him and led him inside. Before they melted into the darkness, Ælfgar looked back once more over his shoulder, almost pleadingly.

Thomas waved. "I'll bring Widfaren back to the horse stall for you! See you in the morning!"

That's that. Ælfgar would soon be lost to her wiles. Once he got the smack of her on his lips, he'd be back to this little house again during the fortnight before the wedding and likely beyond if Ælfgar was as weak as his pig of a father. Thomas had heard a boy's first lover had a kind of sway over him, one Blodeuwedd could use to drive him far more toward the old ways than Thomas ever could have done with words alone. He'd had long talks with Blodeuwedd, not about everything but about enough, and she knew what to do. *If I had one, I'd wager a sack of gold he'll stumble out of there in two weeks as enthralled to Rhiannon as the holy halfwit King Eadward is to Christ.*

Ælfgar's now well out of the way for the night. Nothing should keep me from my night's errand.

Thomas looked westward. The sun was almost fully below the fields. He'd have to hurry to get to his spot before it was too late.

THOMAS LAY HIDDEN IN THE dark. The roof over the oldest wing of Godgyfu's house was likely a hundred years old, the thatch grown to a truly great thickness as newer and newer layers had been added on over the old. Weeks of careful work had allowed Thomas to hollow out a burrow, just long enough for him to lay within, a hidden spot all his own inside the oldest layers. Once he climbed up onto the roof and slid in, he could pull a bit of thatch over the opening so nobody passing by outside would ever mark it. The thatch held him tight all around, like a womb, a sturdy wooden roof beam right under his thighs to help bear his weight.

Thomas had laid there, still as death, for a long, long while, waiting for his goddess to come to her bed. Now at last he heard talking, saw the glow of a lone candle, and he worked his fingers carefully to part the thatch enough so he could peer through a slim opening.

Godgyfu and Leofric moved about in the room below. Leofric was mumbling drunkenly about something, though the thatch made it hard to hear and the man spoke barely above a whisper. Like as not he growled again about Earl Godwine or the king. Or else he spouted more of his blather about Saint Paul. Thomas paid it no mind, letting all his awareness dwell upon his goddess, who stood at the bed's foot and let her clothing slide down to puddle among the rushes on the floor. She drew her shift over her head and stood waiting for Leofric to see her.

When at last the oaf shut up long enough to do so, he let out a throaty sigh. Thomas heard him swallowing the last of what was likely mead, the gulps loud and awful in the night's stillness. Then the cup banged to the floor, and Leofric threw himself at his wife like some rutting boar. He pawed at her, kissed and licked her neck and breasts.

"Have you thought of what I said earlier?" Godgyfu asked, this time loud enough that Thomas could hear. "After Ælfgar's wedding, ask the king about the heregeld."

Leofric mumbled something, then half fell with Godgyfu down onto the bed. She must have been gritting her teeth as she drew her husband up atop her, and Thomas nearly had to look away when Leofric's fat white arse came into view, cursedly well-lit by the bedside candle.

"I mean it, Leofric. You must ask Eadward. For once, think of Coventry, which has been so good to us, rather than of your own selfish yearnings and kissing the king's ring." *Good for her*, Thomas thought.

"Enough, woman! I'll ask. I'll ask." Leofric's breathing grew heavier as he began pumping atop her. All at once the earl broke wind, and Thomas nearly laughed aloud, which would have been wretched indeed—an end to all his carefully hidden work. *Christ in heaven, how can she stand to be under him?*

Thomas waited for Leofric's writhing to hasten as he neared the end of his work, but instead the earl pumped more and more slowly. At last he stopped altogether. *Has he fallen asleep?*

Leofric rolled off his wife with a grunt. "I've lost it again." Thomas saw what he meant; the earl's snake was slick with Godgyfu's wetness but it had shriveled to wormlike limpness.

Ever the worthy wife, Godgyfu reached a long, white arm across his body and grabbed him between his legs. "Let me help."

After a long while, Thomas wanted to scream. *How tiresome this grows.*

At last, the earl gained back some stiffness, and Godgyfu climbed on top of him, spreading her legs to straddle him like a man on a horse. *This is what I came to see!* He dared to open the thatch a bit more, getting a better view as Godgyfu worked her long, lean legs to lift herself up and down, Leofric again inside her. Her hair was fully unbound, a dark spill that covered her back and buttocks. Soon she made little mewling sounds, lustful whimpers. She had told him once that she often thought of him when she was in bed with Leofric. *I wonder if she's thinking of me now?*

Thomas took great heed of her every move. He needed to see how she liked it—how fast, how hard—so when the time came for him to awaken the goddess in her, to go with her into the holy stead between the worlds, he would know how best to handle her and bring her to the heights of bliss they would need.

It became hard to keep his thoughts together when Leofric reached around and began slapping his wife hard on her flanks. Thankfully, it was not long after that Leofric made a din like a calving cow and shuddered mightily. *He's spent his rotten seed in Rhiannon's womb. I wish I could kill him for it.*

Thomas's mood brightened a heartbeat later when Godgyfu herself let out a squeak and arched her back. *There it is! Her goddess strength showing through—her womanly might, wild and free from all the world's bindings, following naught but her body's own need.* It seemed a holy, blessed thing to him. The muscles in her legs locked tight around her husband's flabby thighs, and she fell over his chest with a sigh. *At least she can find some bliss in all that mess.*

There was some more whispering Thomas couldn't hear, then they snuffed the candle.

In full darkness again, Thomas knew he dared not slip away until they both woke in the morning and left the room. Else he'd make far too great a rustling in the thatch; he'd be found out, and there'd be no way to make Godgyfu understand why he was there. Leofric would likely look to kill him. All his years of work would have been for naught. Instead, he drew upon a lifetime of working out how best to handle the long watch: one had to let the mind go elsewhere to help the dull stretches go faster.

His bladder was full to bursting, and there was no way he could hold his water until morning. He pissed himself, but he'd worn two sets of woolen hose to help soak it up, and felt much better afterward. He shifted ever so slightly, settling in for the night.

THIRTEEN

COVENTRY
21 APRIL 1047

Leofric knelt in one of the abbey church's side chapels, the noonday sun bright through high windows overhead. Abbot Leofwin allowed him to come to this chapel at will, and Leofric had made of it his own harbor, a spot to flee life's many storms. Closed in by its holy walls, he found himself warded—sundered from the world's rotting sway, from the maddening pulse of the passing weeks and days and hours.

Today he came because he had awakened, head pounding from a night's drinking but with a sudden clarity as if the sleep he brushed off was one of months rather than mere hours. Whatever trick time had played upon him, it felt as if two years had gone by in a sudden blur, leaving him little more than scattered, unhinged memories that rose to the fore like bubbles in a thick pottage over a cookfire. Godgyfu smiling at him. *She does love me. I know she does, though I've hardly earned such a gift*. Earl Godwine laughing and gloating, teeth flashing behind his plump lips. *Prideful bastard.* Christmas feasts and summer hawking. Ælfgar's easy laugh as he held his firstborn .... *My son. A man grown, and now to be a father again ....*

That was why he'd come. He'd let too much slip past him, take him unawares, the days tumbling past in a meaningless blur of mead and headaches and wretched dreams of pale flesh. *Buttocks, breasts, bared in the sunlight before God and man and* .... No! Not today. He would not let himself come under their sway.

Today, he had come to pray. To speak with Blessed Paul while, back at the house, his son's wife gave birth to her second babe in as many years.

"Let him be healthy and strong," Leofric whispered, sure in his heart it would be another boy child, a brother to little Eadwine. Yes, that was his name, sweet child.

He looked up, awaiting Paul's answer. Blossoms ringed the altar, still fresh from the Easter Sunday mass two days before. Most of the blossoms would be gathered soon so folk could bear them forth in the upcoming days when Coventry's folk would make their way through the streets to beseech the Heavenly Father to look upon them with a mild heart in the coming year. *Then the bright petals will all wilt and die* ....

Leofric wondered if Paul kept silent because he went about this in the wrong way. Rather than beg another boon, he should have been thanking God for all his good hap of late. Another memory—recent—rose to the fore, and Leofric nearly laughed with gladness. Godwine's son Swegn was to be cast out from England, at last having showed himself fully the wretch Leofric always knew him as. When the eldest of the Godwinesons went over to Wales to lend his sword and his men to King Gruffydd—the Welshman who'd killed Leofric's own brother—no one apart from Leofric had seemed to care. Everyone bent over backward to talk it away—Swegn was only helping Gruffyd to storm another bit of Welsh land in Deheubarth—never mind that the raid helped strengthen a sworn enemy of England!

But then Swegn went too far, taking and holding the Abbess of Leominster in some half-mad bid to wed her and gain Leominster's wide lands for himself. It had taken threats from Archbishop Eadsige and Bishop Lyfing to sway the oaf into letting the poor woman go at last, but not before he'd had his way with her, treating her like some penny-whore. *The Abbess of Leominster!*

It was something Leofric himself might have done in one of his darkest dreams. *Think of the shocked look on her face when Swegn tore the nun's rail from her body!* But ... no! Those are *not* my dreams. They are someone else's. Why must they haunt me?

Leofric closed his eyes and crossed himself. *But for Paul's strength, a path I might have followed* .... He prayed his thanks to God—for taking his foe's eldest away from him. It was the start, maybe, of a new day ... of Godwine's waning hap and the waxing of Leofric's own. Maybe that was why he felt an awakening. It was too late for him to match Godwine in sons of his loins, but today Godwine himself had one less boy, and before the day was through Leofric would have another squalling grandson. It was a race he still might win.

"*Ask the king to give Ælfgar the empty earldom,*" Paul's voice spoke in his head.

Leofric looked up, into the bright shafts of sunlight. "Blessed Paul, the king's already split Swegn's shires among Swegn's brother Harold and his kinsman Beorn."

He waited, but Paul said no more in answer. "I will do as you ask. Ælfgar's old enough now—husband and father, why not earl?"

"*Go home.*"

Leofric rose, grunting at the sharp ache in his knee, and left the church. One of the Benedictines said something to him as he went down the church steps, but Leofric paid it no mind. Paul told him to go home; the new babe must have been born!

The market was maddeningly crowded as always, and Leofric shoved his way through, pushing aside any who got in his way. His hip caught a stall's corner, upsetting the board and spilling a flurry of early radishes over the ground.

"Christ," he shouted, rubbing his hip. Someone bent to sort the mess, begging Leofric's forgiveness. Leofric waved a hand and hurried on, over the high street, then down the wooded road to his house.

Ælfgar saw him coming and stepped out from the neighboring cot where he and Ælfgifu had been living until they built a bigger house of their own. He held one-year-old Eadwine in the crook of an arm, and a wide grin split his beard nearly in two.

"The babe?" Leofric asked.

Ælfgar crushed him in a hug with his free arm and laughed. "Another strong lad, Father! We've named him Morcere after Ælfgifu's father."

Leofric laughed with him and looked down at Eadwine. The boy played with a small wooden horse Ælfgar wore on a string about his neck—one of the many carvings Thomas the monk had given them. Something about those carvings bothered Leofric; they were almost too lifelike, so unlike other crafted likenesses he'd seen. "You hear that, Eadwine? You've a brother now! Brother Morcere!"

Eadwine cooed and dropped the horse to tug on the tip of Leofric's gray beard. He'd grown his whiskers a bit longer of late after the king's own wonted way, though they were still nowhere near as long as the king's. "Elda!" Eadwine shouted, his cast reddening with the strength of his bellow. It was the best his wee tongue could do to call Leofric elderfather.

How could I have forgotten this! My little boy's strong boy!

Leofric clapped Ælfgar between his shoulder blades. "I want to see our new wee harrier."

He followed Leofric into the house, through to the back room where Ælfgifu lay resting on a nest of bedclothes among the rushes. A midwife sat on a bench nearby and rose when she saw them. The woman bore a wrapped bundle over to Leofric, and he took it from her, doing his best to be gentle. Tucked within the swaddling's folds, a little red elf looked out at him through half-closed lids. A thick shock of dark hair sprouted on top, even as Eadwine and Ælfgar himself had had at birth. Then the babe's eyes opened wide, bright and blue, fixing Leofric with a fierce gaze.

"Morcere," Leofric breathed. The baby pushed his lips out then drew them back into a kind of grimace. "Oh, a harrier indeed," Leofric said through happy tears. "Give him a shield to chew on."

"I think he'd better like some milk," Ælfgifu's soft voice came from the floor, and Leofric nodded, handing the bundle back to the midwife who brought it to Ælfgifu.

Leofric nodded proudly at his son, then looked about for Godgyfu. "Where's your mother?"

"Went down to the stream to wash off," Ælfgar answered. "You know her—two midwives on hand, and she was still up to her elbows in birth blood."

Leofric wanted to be with her, to share the day's happiness, the happiness of another little bit of themselves passed down through Ælfgar into a new life. He left Ælfgar with his resting wife and wandered off south and east toward a spot he knew Godgyfu sometimes liked to go. As he walked, he whistled a cradlesong she often sang for little Eadwine when she helped put the boy to sleep—something about bright stars chasing dark shadows. The land sloped down toward the Sherbourne's banks here, wet and fresh from a straight week of rain before Easter. It was as bright and golden a day as one could look for. He thought later he'd see if Ælfgar wanted to do some hunting. Maybe they'd even have a go with the new hawks he'd bought from a Danish chapman.

He caught a stirring up ahead in the greenery and took it to be his wife. Then he saw it was someone else, a man crouched low near the water in a stand of cherry trees still mostly covered in their white blossoms. Fearing it was some highwayman, Leofric dropped into a crouch himself and looped around to the north until he reached the bank farther upstream. Wishing he had his sword with him, he crept back and peered out from the shadows under a leafy bough. *That's Thomas! What in heaven's name is he doing?*

All at once, he glimpsed something beyond the would-be monk, a white shape splashing in the shallows. It was Godgyfu, naked in the sun-flecked water, scrubbing her limbs roughly to wash away Ælfgifu's birth-blood. Her pale breasts heaved in the brightness as she straightened from her washing.

Thomas saw it all.

All Leofric's happy thoughts came crashing down around him in a twinkling. A stabbing pain worked its way into his forehead, and the other thoughts, those darker things he'd been keeping at bay with Paul's help flowed back in as though a weir had burst in his mind. The girl from Worcester, goaded before his men … the thralls he'd made strip for him … Blodeuwedd naked and smeared with cow dung. He saw again all the madness of his dreams, each more awful than the last. Godgyfu with arms and legs spread wide upon the abbey church's altar, all the folk gathered for mass walking past her, peering at every inch of those hidden spots only Leofric had ever seen. His wife's friend, the Abbess Tova walking through Coventry's market with her heavy, sagging tits bared. Young Queen Eadgyth bent over before Leofric so that he took her like a horse takes a mare while her father—thrice-cursed Godwine—was made to watch and King Eadward sat nearby on his kingseat, burning with lust as he witnessed his wife's shaming.

Now here was Godgyfu, bare in the light of day—one of his dreams sprung to full-blooded life. Leofric found he shook; his arms trembled, teeth chattered. His manhood was so stiff it ached. He had to free it from his breeches. It stood straight like a longship's mast, harder than it had been since Leofric was a much younger man.

What in Christ's name is Thomas doing? It's my wife! His earl's wife! He should not be seeing this!

Done with her washing, Godgyfu rose from the water to dry herself on the bank. The dark mound of fur beneath her plump belly glistened until she passed a cloth between her legs. Then she patted herself all over, from neck to toe, turning this way and that so there was no side of her Leofric and Thomas could not see in the bright sunshine.

I will have him flayed!

Even as he had this thought, Leofric's knees nearly buckled. He looked down and saw his hand wrapped around his own flesh, his seed spurting from the tip in long ropes onto the ground.

Christ in heaven! He put his hands to the sides of his head as the pain behind his eyes was all at once blinding, an aching burst.

For a short while, he lost all thought of who or where he was. When he came back to himself, the ache had gone, and he hurriedly straightened his breeches. Godgyfu was fully dressed, striding away from the water. Thomas kept himself hidden, waiting until she was well out of sight, then he spun on a heel and would have followed her back toward Coventry.

"Ho," Leofric called out. "You!"

Thomas turned with a start and lifted his hands as a shield when he saw Leofric running toward him. Leofric didn't stop but put his driving bulk behind the fist he mashed into Thomas's chin. The wretch stumbled back a step and fell over, landing on his arse. For a wonder, he began laughing.

"You laugh," Leofric yelled. "After what you did here, you laugh? I'll kill you." He crouched over Thomas, lifted him by the shoulders, and mashed him down against the earth, hoping to break his head on a rock.

Thomas grunted, then wriggled and got one shoulder free, surprising Leofric with his strength. "So, I'm found out at last. In truth I can't believe you never spotted me sooner."

Leofric looked down at the man and shook his head. "What do you mean sooner?"

"Oh, my good earl, I've been watching your wife for years now. I've seen her naked more times than I can count. Seen her bathing and sleeping and shitting. I've seen you dip your sorry bit of meat into her, seen you kiss her tits and slap her arse. I've seen you dribble your weak old seed on her belly, even on her lovely pink tongue. So you see, what I did here today was nothing."

Leofric's mind spun. He worked to find wit in Thomas's words. "Have you gone mad, man? I'll kill you for what you say."

"Do shut up, Leofric," Thomas said, squirming out from Leofric's slackening grip. He pushed himself to his feet and brushed off the monk's robes he still wore without ever having been raised to brotherhood.

"What did you say?!"

Thomas sniffed. "You heard me. Shut your fat hole. You're not going to kill me, and here's why. I've not only spent my time watching Godgyfu, but a fair lot of it watching you, so I know all about your games with the thralls. About your mud-flinging with Blodeuwedd, and Blodeuwedd told me the sorry tale you gave her about the girl in Worcester. I've seen how you find ways to make a show of your wife's flesh. More than once you stole her clothes from where she leaves them outside her bath so she had to go find old Beornflæd, naked as a babe, to bring her fresh rail. That and so many other sick little games you play, so, you see, I know it's your deepest wish for others to see your wife even as I saw her just now in the stream. You want to make her into that girl in Worcester. It's the only thing that gets you hard so—"

"Liar!" Leofric yelled. *Am I still asleep after all? Is all this some wretched nightmare come to me in my bed? How can he know all this? Blessed Paul, how?*

"I'm a liar, am I?" Thomas answered through a smug grin. "So then if we were to wander over to the bank where earlier you stood watching both me and your wife, we wouldn't find you'd watered the flowers there with your seed? There'd be no pearly gift you've left for the worms?"

Though he fought not to, Leofric couldn't help but let his eyes drift back to the spot beneath the bough. His cheeks grew warm with shame.

Thomas sighed. "Were you truly standing so close? I must be slipping. I should have heard you."

Leofric had nothing else to say. What could he say to this devil grinning before him. He'd left the soft sun of Eastertide behind and stepped into a sort of hellscape, a dark world of his own making. He felt himself breathing harder and feared his heart might give out on him. *Then will I be in hell for good and true.*

"Earl, be at ease," Thomas said. "God's truth, you look as though you're about to be sick, and I think the blooms have had enough of your watering for one day. Please don't retch on them now."

"What ...?" Leofric struggled to find his tongue. "You can't tell Godgyfu."

"My friend, my friend"—Thomas walked over and patted Leofric on the shoulder—"goodness no, we won't tell her anything. Your wife is a lady whose worth is far greater than yours or mine. She is my goddess made flesh, and I would not see her wounded over the knowledge of what an evil shitlick she has for a husband. Christ, no wonder you pray so earnestly to Saint Paul. I'd pray too were I as twisted as you."

"I ..." Leofric stopped. He heard the man's words, but for the life of him he had no idea what they meant. "Your goddess ... made flesh?" All at once a thought came like a cold stab in his guts. He spun and grabbed Thomas by his robes and shook him. "Tell me you haven't bedded her, man, for if you have I'll break your chicken's neck right now."

Thomas laughed again. "In Christ's name, I've never set a finger on her. That is not the way my need lies. But I do want to keep watching her, and the way I see it this is something we should both be happy for. I've a little spot in your roof, where I can see right down on you where you sleep. Tell me it won't strengthen your bedgames next time if you know I'm there to see it."

Leofric let go his hold on the man and stepped back. *A spot in the roof?* His mind whirled. *Let him watch us. Let him see Godgyfu.*

"Your body answers for you, earl," Thomas said, dropping his gaze.

Leofric looked down and saw the bulge in his breeches bright as day. *Hard again so soon?* He mumbled some answer but wasn't sure what he said.

"And let me tell you this: for the nonce, Godgyfu doesn't know she's being watched. How much better would it be for you were I to sway her to knowingly show herself to me. Sway her to play the wanton—the wife of an earl baring herself to a Benedictine novice like some Welsh whore? You'd like that, no?"

Yes, yes. He had to stop himself from reaching down to grab himself. "She'll never do it," he said in a ragged whisper.

"I think she will. Give it time, and I might find a way to do even more. What if a whole crowd of folk could see her naked?"

Leofric shook his head. "Her folk love her. They'd never do that against her will, and she'd never be willing."

"Not Coventry folk. But others. From towns to the south. If you and I keep our troth, I swear to you it will happen."

Leofric wanted to punch this man again. To beat him until he spit teeth and choked to death on his own blood. Leastwise some of him wanted to. A larger bit couldn't stop thinking about whether the man spoke true. He couldn't push aside the thought of his wife naked, eyes roaming her. Thomas's eyes. Other eyes. All the eyes in the world.

"Give me your word you'll never touch her," he found himself saying, and he knew he was lost, damned beyond redemption. "I'll not be given horns."

Thomas dropped to a knee and crossed himself. "Before God and all his saints, I swear I will never touch her in any unseemly way."

Leofric gave a short nod, then looked away. *Christ help me.*

"Wonderful." Thomas rose and gave an overwrought bow. "I bid you make merry in the rest of the day's warming Eastertide sun! Go be with your kinfolk and give the new babe a pinch for me."

Then he was gone.

Leofric stared up at the sky, but the bright blueness was gone; he saw only black. The sun was stained with blood, and its touch burned him. *"You've made troth with the devil,"* Paul's voice came.

He dropped to his knees, then slumped onto one side and wept. "Go away! Go away, and never speak to me! I am a sinner, and you cast away your words with me. You know! You know there's no hope! That's why you send me no more wonders to look upon. I'm lost now." He took a deep breath, then another. He waited until his tears stopped. Again he saw Godgyfu naked, scrubbing herself in the water. "Lost where nobody can find me. God help me, I don't want to be found." He lurched to his feet and stumbled homeward.

FOURTEEN

FOLESHILL
28 APRIL 1047

THOMAS SAT WAITING IN GODGYFU'S small house in Foleshill, listening to the wind soughing in the trees overhead. The room swam in the smell of the little blended bags of dried blossoms and spices Godgyfu had stowed throughout. The house itself was well hidden, away from the prying eyes of any of Godgyfu's landmen who lived and worked the fields beyond the woods and, more the better, away from Leofric who since that day a week ago by the water tended to watch his wife's comings and goings like a hawk after a mouse. Then again, it was near enough—a short ride north—that they could be back to Coventry after meeting here before either of them was missed.

It also gave Thomas a good way to keep the fire burning in some of the neighboring folk he'd swayed onto Rhiannon's path. Straightaway before coming to the house, he'd met with a handful of them in a nearby field, and he thought he'd calmed their growing lack of forbearance. The old ceorl, Alfkil, was the worst, likely because he was old and thought he hadn't much longer left to live. But even some of the younger folk like Culfre and her brother Coenwulf, who'd walked over that morning to Foleshill from Allesley, had grumbled over how the king's gelds were still too high, how Leofric did nothing to help them, how only the churchmen seemed to keep growing fatter while others starved. Mostly they were all worried that Thomas had not yet gotten more folk to come over to stand with them, to pray with them to the old gods.

"You've not met all the folk I've swayed," he'd told them. "There are more of us every day."

"What good's another two or three here and there?" Coenwulf had asked. "Still too few to make any matter."

"We must have faith," Thomas said. "Even Christ began with only his twelve disciples, and now look at the Church and the might it wields over all the world. Keep in mind too that Christ lived more than thirty years before dying on the rood to be reborn. Only when the time was right did God let his son be given up, and then the sun itself hid from sight at the wonder of what unfolded under heaven. We too must wait for our time, for the stars to be right so the way between worlds is open to let a new goddess be reborn."

Thomas sighed happily in the stillness of the little house. His words had soothed the folk, and they'd gone off with a renewed eagerness for what was to come.

And there's my goddess now. The soft tread of hoofs on the wood's rich loam drifted through the broided cloth over the room's only window. Not long after, the door rattled and swung open, letting in a heady waft of spring.

Godgyfu stood in the doorway as her eyes grew settled to the room's darkness. Then she rushed in all at once and threw herself into Thomas's arms. Pushing back the lingering upheaval such nearness still brought to his belly, Thomas instead let himself be driven by the newer feelings that drew him to her in kind. When her body pressed against his, it almost soothed him, made him want to burrow in even closer, to crawl under her skin and become one with her. *In time. In time.* The greatest wonder of all were those brief flashes in which his breath quickened, his limbs yearned to hold her in the way she held him .... A bit of him—a small bit—had come to want her in a way he'd never thought he'd want another soul ... to want her in the way men had once wanted his own whore of a mother.

"No, don't let go yet," she whispered when he would have pulled away.

"My Rhiannon," he said, choking back the bile in his throat and letting himself be held a while longer.

"Must you go tomorrow? With Leofric gone, we would have so much more freedom to be with each other."

He sighed. Leofric would leave in the morning for Canterbury, called there by the king over some new threat from Magnus in Denmark. And Thomas would go too—Leofric had demanded it, as he no longer seemed to trust him alone in Coventry with Godgyfu. *A wise man for once.* Thomas had needed to come up with some other mark for his going—something to tell Godgyfu. "It won't be for long," he answered her. "A month or two at most. The Archbishop is pushing to rebuild Christchurch Abbey, which is long overdue. The abbey's lay in ruins since the Danes raided it back ... well, I should think shortly after you were born, Godgyfu. There will be a great lot of goldworkers there, the best in the kingdom, and I've gotten a letter from Mannig—I should say Abbot Mannig now—naming me to them. It will be good for me to spend some time among them, hone my skills, skills I might some day put to good use here in your own abbey. Abbot Leofwin's already given me his leave, so yes, I must go. I'll share the road with your husband and his men."

She looked sad, but she nodded. "Maybe it will be good. Lately I have been most ... that is, my thoughts have been most drawn asunder by our being together. I've been putting Coventry aside, but there are things I should do here. Now that the nun-house is well and truly in Abbess Tova's hands, she wants to make it bigger for her sisters, maybe add a wall around its yard and gardens. I will help hire the workers and oversee the work. Only ... I *will* miss you."

Thomas knew he shouldn't wonder at the stronger new feelings they both had. It was the way their link had been growing for a year or more; a greater and greater need to be with each other. He had at last worked out a way to steal one of Godgyfu's monthly blood-cloths and had made a charm from its burnt ashes. They were bound to each other now in body as well as with those bonds of the soul that made them one since time out of mind ....

Moreover, whenever it seemed she began to drift away from him, or if her forbearance waned and she need more bodily closeness, he would touch her again. Briefly. A little more each time. Now he leaned forward and breathed into her ear, letting his lips brush her skin, his tongue taste the salt of her body as he spoke sweet words to her. "My beloved goddess."

Then he drew back; he never let things go too far. Only enough to keep pulling her along in her need. And she *did* need him now, his touch, his words, his nearness .... It was like some men grew to need mead or wine, craving it, living for it. He noticed she'd even begun to shake at times, ever so slightly, another thing he had seen in those for whom drink had become lord and king. Only, for Godgyfu, Thomas himself was her drink, and he doled himself out in forsakingly small draughts.

She shook again now, but this was something else. Tears filled her eyes—eyes that had come to be ever ringed with darkness like deep bruises.

"What is it?"

Godgyfu sniffed and wiped the tears with an angry flick of the wrist. "More of the same. I saw some folk as I left town. Sigrida and her husband Acca. They're starving."

"The God damned heregeld," he said, nodding. "With Magnus ready to bring spears against us, the king's left them nothing."

"Yes, but ... their little one died over the winter. I didn't even know it, did you?"

He shrugged. "I did hear something."

"Sweet Christ, they should have come to me. I'd do anything for Coventry and its folk. I'd have given them whatever they needed. It breaks my heart." The last words came out as a sob.

"Godgyfu," he said, lifting a hand toward her, then dropping it. "You know Acca's a proud man and only lately raised up to be a thegn. He'd never have come begging. And you can't save every ceorl and upstart thegn who happens to live on your lands. Not even with all your pennies. Men die. Children too. It's the way of the world. Only their souls can be truly saved, but with the king taking what little they have, is it any wonder folk like Acca and Sigrida spurn Eadward and his Frankish friends, spurn the Church for growing fat while they starve? They need to come back to Christ's light. To Blessed Marie. Let me carve you."

Her sigh was deep and tired. "By God, you've been asking me to do this for, what? Five years now? Don't you ever give up?"

"How long have you been asking Leofric to get the heregeld lifted? Still you keep asking."

"If I wouldn't do it for you then, why ever would I want to now that I'm growing so old and wrinkled and awful. How could the sight of my sagging flesh fire you to carve anything worthy?"

"Have you still not learned? All who have faith are fair in the eye of God. Only sin is ugly."

She looked sharply at him. "Where … where did you hear that said?"

"An old monk I once knew. Brother Beocc."

Her eyes went wide, and Thomas was glad to see she'd held onto the words all these many years. "You," she breathed, almost frightened. "It was you—the little boy in my room when I lay dying."

Thomas smiled. "I wondered when you'd see it. Brother Beocc cared for me in those first years after my mother died. He was one of those wandering sort of monks. We were on our way back to Wales and had only stopped for a night's rest in Coventry with the brothers and sisters of Benedict—few though they were here in those days. I was helping Father Offa with some chores when he was called to come give you the holy chrism. I remember even then—even through the wretchedness your sickness had brought to you—thinking what a shining wonder you were. I saw the goddess smiling out from behind your gritted teeth, though then I still did not know what I saw. It was only later I came to know Rhiannon and knew she was the one I'd seen that day in the darkness of your bedcove. In truth I never thought I'd see you again, but then my life's wending way brought me back to Coventry, and I knew I'd come home."

"But it …. It's all …." She stared at him, gasping. "I thought there was to be nothing hidden between us. You said as much that day after I found you at Blodeuwedd's. Why did you never tell me?"

"It never seemed to matter. I'm no longer that boy any more than you're the broken thing I saw curled naked in those soaking bedclothes." *No more than this fleshly shape you hold bears any link to what I'll one day help you become once I've stripped the flesh away.* Thomas cocked his head, seeing the questions in her eyes, and deemed it as good a time as any to tell her more.

"Soon after I went to Wales," he went on, "I first heard the tales of Rhiannon, and the more I heard the more I knew I'd found my goddess, a beacon to show all the world how much better it could be, to show kings and lords what true lordship is. I made it my life's path to help that beacon shine, but I now know I wasted years wandering lost, never finding the rich, life-giving ground I needed for a seed to take root. Then I came again to Coventry and saw you, saw that you already followed Rhiannon's lead in your love for Marie, Queen of Heaven, who is but Rhiannon in another cast. You give of yourself for the betterment of your folk rather than for your own selfish ends. It is something only a woman—only one who holds in her own flesh the means of making life—could ever truly be, and you yourself are the utmost shape of womanhood. You have grown into your godhead. You are a queen every bit as shining as Marie, and your strength has flowed into the land about you so even the folk hereabouts are open to the thought of a better world. I would take hold of some bit of that shining fairness within you and put it into a shape to draw others even as it draws me."

"You're quite mad," Godgyfu said through a dazed half-smile. "Hue your words however you will, they still come down to *blasphemia*. I am no goddess, no queen. I am but a woman."

Thomas spread his hands. "What greater thing is there to be? I love you, Godgyfu, with a love greater than even the holiest of priests has for his God. To me you are nothing short of a queen." He stopped himself from saying more, hoping he hadn't already gone too far. *I must tread with care now lest I spook her.*

"God in Heaven." Godgyfu shook her head slowly, her breath heavy in the room's stillness. "That was you! I can't believe that little boy was *you*! But, yes, I see it. You still have the same eyes—wide and blue. I saw those eyes over and again in my fever dreams as Saint Osburh asked Christ to heal me, to bring me back from death. I always wondered who he had been and where he might have gone."

"Will you let me carve you? Let me look upon you naked again as I did all those many years ago?"

She laughed, loud and merry. "You truly don't give up, do you?"

No, my lady, he thought, doing his best to keep a mild cast. *You must agree to this.* Without her willingly giving herself over to let him carve her, he would have no way to bind her to the wood. He knew every curve of her body from having watched her for years, and he could have carved her with his eyes closed whether she stood for him or not, but that was not enough. She had to be present, baring herself before the wood so as to put herself into it as his knife pared away the dross. Elsewise, the rite would not work; he would never bring her to that stead between the worlds and find the goddess within her.

"What do you say? For Marie if not for me?"

"Here is what I say: You think the folk need a Marie like one of the goddesses of old—naked and open, carved from wood that has drunk from the earth. I say they need something else—a great queen, Marie crowned and mighty. A queen who is better than Godwine's daughter, more godly even than holy King Eadward. She should be made all of copper and gold with gemstones set in her crown and in her flowing robes. You can call upon some of those skills you'll be honing in

Canterbury and work with Abbot Mannig on the best way to show her as queen. And the day you give enough pennies to the abbey to pay for Mannig to craft such a wonderwork, then will I do as you've asked and let you make your pagan carving as well."

Thomas spread his hands again, wider than before. "You know I can't ever hope to pay for such a thing! It would need a great hoard of pennies, a hoard dug up from where some wyrm had been sitting upon it, warding it in a dark cave." He sought to make his cast look stricken, but inwardly he laughed. *I have her now! Oh, and this will bring an added bit of wonder to the rite. A cunning twist worthy of a gleeman's saga! I should have thought of it myself!* "I beg of you, set me some other mark. One I have at least the hope of reaching!"

She crossed her arms over her chest. "Those are my words. Take it or leave it."

"Then swear it to me, my lady. Swear to me that if I do as you ask, you will let me carve you. Naked. Freed from the clothes with which men bind you." He went to her and took her hands between his own. "Kneel and swear it before God and Blessed Marie and all the Saints."

Godgyfu knelt. "With God and His mother the Queen of Heaven and all the Blessed Saints as my witnesses, I swear that if you do as I've asked, I'll bare myself to you, and you may make your carving. You have my holy oath." She gave him a smug smile, thinking she had him where she wanted him, that she'd tied him in a knot.

No, my lady. I have you.

He knelt with her, pulled her close so their bodies touched. Then he let go her hands and reached down to cup a breast through her clothes; it was the farthest he had ever dared to go, but he felt as though he were flying now, lifted high by the unlooked for turn of good hap. She shuddered, and he leaned in, kissing her ear, biting the soft lobe. Her nipple hardened beneath his hand. *Yes, burn for me. Burn.* In another few heartbeats, he would stand and leave her there in the house. Leave her wanting more. "Something to think of while I'm gone," he whispered. "My Godgyfu. My goddess. My Rhiannon. My love."

FIFTEEN

CANTERBURY
5 MAY 1047

Leofric shifted on the bench. *I've overeaten.* He leaned back against the wall of the feasthall in which the king sat at board with his men. A belch rose in his throat, and he rubbed his gut.

"More mead, Leofric?" Thomas asked, waving for another cup for himself. "Helps settle the belly."

Leofric shook his head. Unlike most in the hall, who seemed hellbent on drowning themselves in drink, Leofric had been milking the same cup for most of the night. He was happy enough to be in the fellowship of men getting good and drunk, but mead only made things worse for him of late—fired his devilish lust and brought … darker thoughts. He turned toward Thomas, who smirked beneath those wide eyes. Eyes that had seen what no man but Leofric himself should have seen. *Christ! In my own roof, like some hell-spawned rat nesting in the straw. The gall of him!* His arms twitched, and almost he reached out to grab the man's throat, squeeze until his eyes bulged and his tongue hung swollen. *I should kill you!*

He set his cup on the board and looked away with a low snarl. The dull ache boring its way through his head made him want to lift it again. *No more mead. Not tonight.*

The worst of it was he knew his fear was not so much of what he might do to Thomas in a drunken fit but of what Thomas's death would mean: no more watching the man look at his wife, no more baring Godgyfu's flesh to him, unbeknownst to her, in their own bedroom's stillness. Twice more before leaving for Canterbury, Thomas had worked out ways of having Leofric see him slink about to look upon Godgyfu unclothed—once while she was in the shit-house and once more down by the water. Nearly every night during the last week in Coventry, Leofric's bedgames with his wife's had been witnessed by Thomas. *God damn him, but the wretch was right! I haven't worked my spear like that since I was a man of twenty.* Even Godgyfu had wondered at his sudden boundless strength.

And damn me if I don't want more of the same.

"There's a thing I've been wanting to speak of," Thomas said, leaning toward him.

Leofric twitched as though Thomas had snuck up on him from behind. "What? What thing?" He reached for the mead but left his hand hovering over it. Never mind his own dark thoughts, he needed to stay clearheaded for the talks happening on the morrow. The Danish Sveinn had asked for England to send ships to aid his crumbling bid to drive Magnus from Denmark. Earl Godwine thought they should do it, which was enough in itself for Leofric to stand against it even were it not mad to send even one ship into that mess. Earl Siward stood firmly with Leofric, and he hoped King Eadward would heed the wit in their words. Surely they were only here meeting in Canterbury so Eadward could oversee some of the new work on Christ Church and not owing to its nearness to Sandwich and the likeliest spot from which to send ships. *Keep telling yourself that* .... His fingers traced the rim of the cup.

"Land," Thomas answered.

Leofric only half heard him. He turned his gaze toward Eadward, who smiled nearby at the board's end, ringed by his wonted gang of Normans. Eadward laughed loudly, and his pale beard glistened with meat drippings in the dim light of two nearby fire-pits. But Eadward's golden cup sat all but untouched before him; Leofric knew the king also drank little. Now and then Eadward's bright eyes turned chidingly upon the loud merry-making of young Earl Harold who sat at another table with his three even younger brothers and his men. All Godwine's sons were well in their cups, which seemed to bother Eadward. *Another goad not to drink too much this night; keep on Eadward's good side.*

"Leofric," Thomas said.

"Aye, I heard you. Land." Leofric made himself look at the freakish monk. "What land?"

"In Herefordshire—mostly church lands, some abbey lands. The gelds are long overdue on them, and as you know, should someone else pay the gelds …."

"The lands pass to the one who pays," Leofric finished. "A bit of bloodless reaving."

"I want to pay them," Thomas said, "but I haven't the pennies. You could lend them to me, and with what I can earn from having the lands worked, you'll get your pennies back and then some."

Leofric grunted. "How much?"

Thomas reached into a sleeve of his robes and withdrew a folded leaf that he opened and pushed across the table. Leofric snatched it up and looked over the careful tally Thomas had blackened on it. He gave a low whistle. "No small thing. Why should I lend you so much?" He squinted at the man. "If you think to hold any of our …. understanding over my head, know that I'll kill you before I let you try to wrest a mint from me with some threat of blackening my name."

Thomas sighed and put a hand to his heart. "You wound me, earl. Our dealings are holy to me. I'd never dirty them. I ask this of you because I know it will also make you happy. You see, nearly all the lands are in one way or another linked back to Swegn Godwineson or to his trothed men. One bit even owes fieldwork to Earl Godwine himself. Likely it's owing to the upheaval over Swegn's being cast out that the gelds have gone so long ungathered. I thought it might gladden you to see those folk lose something."

Failing to hide a smile, Leofric glanced across the wide table at Earl Godwine, who was going on at length about something to a bored looking Earl Siward. "Gladden me it would," he said, speaking low while keeping one eye fixed on Godwine. "But why shouldn't I pay the gelds myself and take the lands for my own? How did you learn of these unpaid gelds anyway?"

"I have my ways," Thomas said, winking. "If there's one thing Benedictines love to do it's gossip; you'd wonder at the things I hear! Yes, you could reave these lands yourself, but then you risk an open clash with Godwine's house, which could be a messy thing. Better to keep your name out of it. Let me dirty my fingers. I get the land, and you get the glee of knowing you've hurt your foes."

Looking at this man sitting before him, Leofric had to grant him grudging worth. *He's a slippery eel, a wretched little devilish shit but no dimwit. Far from it.* "All right," he said, making up his mind to loan him what he needed. "But there's still the knot of my wife. She'll never let me reave church lands, Godwine's or no. I tried it once before and never heard the end of it. She keeps our riches well under lock and key."

"Not all of them. There's the hoard you brought back from Worcester."

Christ, is there anything this man doesn't know about me? Leofric nodded. "You'll have your pennies when we get back to Coventry." About to grab for his cup again, Leofric stopped. "What does a monk want with lands anyway?"

"No monk, only a novice." Thomas gave one of his maddening grins. "And I have to think of the days to come. I won't stay in Coventry forever."

Leofric looked sharply at him. "Why? Where are you going?" He said it before he thought and straightaway rued having spoken. He didn't know what was worse, that he might have sounded too eager to get rid of Thomas or that he sounded afraid of losing him … of losing the sole means by which to give life to his sick dreams.

But Thomas couldn't answer anyway, for a stillness all at once fell throughout the hall as a stooped graybeard stepped up toward the king's seat. "A wandering gleeman," Thomas whispered. "A Danishman, but his father was Icelandic, come to tell a tale for the king. I spoke with him earlier."

Somewhere else in the wide hall, a bone pipe took up a low trill as a drum marked a steady beat. The gleeman turned in a wide ring, staring into the hall's four corners before he began. "Gather now and hearken!" he said in a rich, deep voice that belied his stooped shape. "I am Ulf Gunnarsson, and I tell the life of King Ragnar Bear-Breeches, grim harrier of old …."

Before long, Leofric had fallen under the old man's spell, whisked back two hundred years to the days when Ragnar's longships were dreaded far and wide for their viking. Leofric had heard many of Ragnar's deeds before, but this gleeman had a silver tongue, and Leofric felt fire in his blood as he was there with Ragnar, wading into the spear-storm in a bid to take the kingseats of both Denmark and Sweden. Later, Ragnar made Frankish streams into the highways on which he rode to bring fire and sword, even as deep inland as Paris. Leofric laughed at the great silver geld Ragnar wrested from the Frankish King Carl so his longships would go away. He knew the stories, and hearing them again was like coming together with old friends.

Then came a bit Leofric did not know—something he'd never heard before. The gleeman spoke of the great harrier Sigurd and the shieldmaiden Brynhildr who was one of the *valkyrja*, the Northman's choosers of the slain. A girl child was born to them, and they named her Aslaug, leaving her to be raised by Sigurd's foster-father Heimer. When Sigurd and Brynhildr died soon after, Heimer feared for Aslaug's safety and so crafted a harp big enough to hide the girl within. He took to the road, putting himself forth as a lowly harpist and bearing the girl along with him inside the harp. In time they came to the house of one Ake and his wife Gríma on Norweg's southern tip. Thinking they saw riches hidden inside the harp, the man and wife killed the harpist in his sleep. When instead of riches they found the little girl, Ake and Gríma kept her and raised her as their own, calling her Kráka, the Northman word for a crow. To hide her highborn blood, they kept her always dirty and gave her filthy rags to walk in.

Like the girl in Worcester, Leofric thought. He closed his eyes and saw the mud and cow shit his men had spattered on her ....

Then came a day when Ragnar and his storied longships came to the south of Norweg. Some of his men went ashore to bake bread, and they happened upon Aslaug bathing in what she thought was a hidden spot. So struck were they by her great fairness that they let all the forgotten bread burn. Ragnar was wroth with them and bid them tell how such a thing had happened, and when he learned of the comely maiden, he sent for her to be brought before him. But he wanted to know whether she had wits to match her fairness, and so he had his men tell her she must come neither clothed nor unclothed, neither hungry nor full, and neither alone nor in fellowship.

Thomas nudged Leofric in his ribs, breaking the word-spell. "You'll like this next bit, Earl."

Leofric batted the man's hands away, angry that his thoughts were now scattered. He wanted to know how Aslaug would untie this riddle, hanging on every word the gleeman spoke.

Aslaug said to Gríma, who thought it could not be done.
"I'll first make new my rail:
You've a woven trout-shroud, which I'll wrap about me,
And the golden wheat of my brow there through I'll wend,
My skin nowise to be seen by Ragnar's gleaming brow-stones.
I will but put my tongue to earth's tearful root,

So it lays upon my breath though I've eaten naught.
Your steadfast tail-wagger shall go with me,
And so I will not go alone
Though no son of Ask nor daughter of Embla be at my side."
And Gríma thought Aslaug had great cunning.

A cold rush ran through Leofric's body. *She will go all but naked, then, in naught but a fish net? Before the grim raider king?* He looked uncomfortably toward Thomas; the man wore an irksome smirk.

Then, in bright, bold words, Ulf Gunnarsson told how the maiden Aslaug did indeed go before Ragnar and his spearmen, a scruffy hound at her side, her breath smelling of onion-leek, and covered by nothing more than her own long hair, which hung down to her ankles and which she had woven through a fishing net.

Leofric's heart thudded against his ribs. The room's fire-lit dimness swam before his eyes, and the ache in his head throbbed stronger.

Why does he tell this *tale? To mock me? How can they know my mind?* He cast his gaze about the hall, looking to see who might be watching him. Who might see his rising lust, the hellfire scorching him within.

The gleeman told how Ragnar saw Aslaug's worth and wedded her and how she gave him many sons.

But all his men had seen her naked! Leofric's thoughts whirled, and the blood-rush in his ears was so loud he only caught the rest of the tale in broken bits. There were the wonted verses about Ragnar's further raiding. In time Ragnar came against England, before there even was an England as such. But he had not heeded Aslaug's warnings that his ships were in need of mending, and when a storm struck, he and his men were shipwrecked. King Ælla of Northumbria took Ragnar in hand and for his many misdeeds had him killed by throwing him into a pit of writhing adders ....

Leofric only half listened, still seeing Aslaug coming naked before Ragnar, and instead of Aslaug, it was Godgyfu. *Godgyfu called before my housecarls with naught to clothe her but her long locks, unbound like a maiden's and wrapped about her!* He grabbed the cup before him, drained it, then shoved it toward a passing girl who ladled more for him with a sieve spoon. He downed that as well. It smacked of ashes in his mouth, but it helped some with his head. *So hot in here!* He couldn't breathe. But he couldn't get up either, not until the tale-telling was done.

He looked toward Eadward, who sat grinning impishly behind his whiskers, wrapped up in the words, merry over the way the old king raked over the Northman raider. *Or is he laughing at me? Was all this set up to mock me? Do they know? God help me! Has Thomas told them?* He sweated now, reached up to wipe his dripping brow.

When at last the gleeman ended his tale and bowed, Leofric rose as the rest of the hall clapped and banged and shouted. Thomas grabbed him. "Some tale, no?"

Leofric shoved him away, driving him back down onto the bench. He made for the far door, but the room was crowded now, everyone having gotten up to find more mead, to talk of Ragnar and Ælla. Thralls bore in still more food—great wooden boards piled high with cow and lamb and spitted hens. Leofric's belly heaved. *Christ! No more!*

He needed air. Then prayer. He'd bidden the lad Oswig to linger and be ready for him to light his way to nearby Christ's Church where the warden had said he'd wait in the *sacristarium* to let him in to pray once the feasting was done, but the young man was nowhere to be seen ....

Then Leofric found himself in the last spot he wanted to be—wedged between Earl Godwine and his sons on one side and Godwine's wife's nephew, bald-headed Earl Beorn, on the other. "What did you think of the gleeman, Leofric?" Godwine asked. "A gift sent over with Sveinn's errand men from Denmark."

Leofric barely managed a grunt. Instead Earl Beorn laughed and rubbed a hand back over his shining head. "I say the skald did well to leave out the last bit ... how Ragnar's sons got even by coming back to treat King Ælla to the blood-eagle. Pulled his broken ribs out through his back like wings. Ha!"

Godwine clucked his tongue. "Whyever would he want to spread such lies? The skald was sent to mind King Eadward how we English bring wrath down on the heads of Northmen who overstep their bounds."

Leofric began to think it might have been good he'd gotten wrapped up in this talk. He was growing angry at Godwine, and that anger pushed aside much of his earlier lust and fear. "Forget it, Godwine. The king will never agree to send ships to your nephew. Why stick our necks out when it's likely Magnus will keep the kingseat anyway. By helping Sveinn, we'd only make it more likely Magnus would chose to raid England in a year or two. Leave well enough alone, and after months fighting off Sveinn, Magnus might have had enough for a while—a long enough while that he'll forget his mad bid altogether."

"Sveinn could yet come out on top," Godwine's son Harold said, wiping mead from his golden whiskers, and holding out his cup for a thrall to come and fill. "What then?"

"Then he's done our work for us, my young earl," Leofric said. "We won't have lost any of our ships or men, we'd not have bled our thegns with a higher heregeld, and Sveinn has no claim on Eadward's kingseat—not even one as moon-mad as Magnus's."

"A gutless mouse's way," Harold said, and Leofric's anger burned brighter. The young earl surely only said what he'd heard his father say before.

"You're young, Harold," he answered, "leastwise younger than me, and I can still call to mind how youth makes one careless with words. So I'll tell myself you didn't truly mean what you said. I'm wearing new shoes, and I'd hate to dirty them with your blood."

All the men around them laughed at that, and Leofric turned to go. He felt a hand on his shoulder and looked back to find Harold's younger brother Tostig thrusting his chest out at him like some half-grown barnyard rooster. "My brother can knock you on your fat arse any time he wants to if you'd care to do more than boast, old man."

"Does anyone else hear the buzz of a fly?" Leofric mocked, and the laughter came again, even louder.

Tostig alone didn't find mirth in Leofric's words. He threw his cup to the floor and stormed off, nearly spitting.

God save me from Godwine's dimwitted kin. Before he got pulled into further foolishness, Leofric shoved his way through the smoke haze and nearer to the door, stepping around a man bent over to retch a surfeit of mead. *Christ, get me out of here!* Rough shoving broke out all around him, mead-born fights that would likely lead to at least one broken bone before all was done. It wouldn't be long now until even the stoutest drinkers would begin dropping their heads into their arms atop the boards or falling off the benches to sleep with the hounds among the rushes. That was not for him. Not this night. *Time to leave.*

Outside at last, the night air was a cool blessing on his cheeks. He breathed deep, seeking to rid himself of the lingering thoughts of Aslaug, of Godgyfu, of the Worcester maiden.

The half-moon had fallen low among the stars, and he deemed it almost midnight.

"Earl Leofric?" a small voice came.

He turned and saw Oswig, his man Osmund's young son, who he'd taken on as a houseman, waiting as Leofric had bidden him. "Steadfast lad," he said. "Light your lamp."

In the flame's brightness, Leofric saw how bleary-eyed and wobbly the boy looked—likely half-drunk himself, but Leofric didn't chide him for it. *Who am I to chide anyone, man or boy, unworthy wretch that I am. A thrall to the devil, and to Thomas who is surely the devil's own archbishop.*

They walked northward along the east bank of the Stour, which wended its way through Canterbury. Before long the bones of the old Roman theater opened up like a wound in the ground to their right. Leofric thought of Godgyfu there, ringed about by a throng of seated folk on the benches rising up and away from her. Naked but for her hair, unbound like an unwed maid's, wrapped about her but barely hiding her breasts, her wide hips and round buttocks … "Stop!" he said aloud.

"Lord?" Oswig asked, tripping over a stone in the path.

"Nothing. Watch your step." They went on in stillness through the night until they came to the Burh Street, and then Canterbury's great church loomed before them, its two middle towers rising into the night, the more northerly one of the monk's cloister still a burnt husk from Danish fire. Leofric led them instead to the more southerly tower named for Saint Gregory and into the open porch beneath it. Once inside, Leofric stepped up to the heavy South Door—locked at this late hour—and rapped with his knuckles. Awaiting the tell-tale rattle of the key within, he stamped his feet eagerly. "Cold tonight, eh?"

Oswig nodded, but the ruddiness in his cheeks looked more from the drink than the weather; likely he didn't even feel the cold. *Ah, to be young ….*

After a while, the lad gave the doors a searching glance, and Leofric laughed. "Sleeping." He stepped up to the doors and knocked again, longer and with a heavier fist. Still there was no answer. "I bid the warden to expect me!" he growled, the smoldering glow of his earlier anger rekindled. He took hold of the great iron door ring then, dangling from the mouth of an iron lion, and pounded it against the knock plate fully twelve times.

"Earl Leofric, listen!" Oswig hissed, leaning toward the door, letting his arm fall so his lamp hung crooked.

"Watch what you do, lest we burn the church down again like the filthy Danes!" Then Leofric heard it too: a noise like a hog choking on its own mash. Drunken snoring. "Curse him! He must be right on the other side of this door. If my knocking didn't wake him already, we're never getting in."

"Maybe'n morning," Oswig said, slurring his words, then barely holding back a yawn. He turned to go.

Leofric stopped him with a hand on his arm. "Wait a stound, lad. This is still a church, and we're somewhat out of the weather under here. God will hear my prayers well enough on this doorstep." *If He still hears them at all from one such as me.* He felt like weeping; all he had wanted was to pray in God's house, to drive out the devils dancing in his skull, the naked devils with his wife's own cast. *God's will, that's what it is. He welcomes me no longer in His hall.*

Leofric knelt upon the stone step and crossed himself. Spreading his hands before his chest, he closed his eyes and began with a paternoster.

But having gotten no farther than asking God to give them their daily loaf, a loud crack suddenly broke the night's stillness. Leofric stopped and opened his eyes to see the heavy door swing wide. He rose and stepped within, the lamp quickly following him in Oswig's hands.

The dancing light drew Leofric's eyes first to the shadows that swallowed it under the church's soaring roof. Then he dropped his gaze to the narrow opening to his right in which the mead-weary warden slumped against the bottom of the steps leading up into the tower. An upset flask lay on the floor between the warden's spread legs, and his shirt was a mess of spilt drink and the leavings of a round of cheese. Had things stood otherwise, Leofric might have kicked the wretched man to wake him and upbraid him for his loathsomeness. But it came to him that the door had seemingly opened of its own will.

"Wondrous weird." He stepped over the warden, climbing the steps until he came out into the wide room over the porch which held the altar hallowed to Saint Gregory the Great. Again, Oswig followed him, his flickering light chasing more of the shadows away here than it had done in the vastness of the wider church.

Leofric stepped up to the altar and raised his arms again to finish his prayer. "Forgive us our sins," he whispered to the silver rood propped upon the altar cloth, "as we forgive those who sin against us. Lead us not into the cunning ways of the flesh, but free us from evil ..."

The light looked to be fading, and Leofric's words faltered. He turned back toward Oswig and saw that he'd sunk back into a corner of the tower, cowering. The boy shook so that it seemed he must drop the lamp at any time now.

"What ever has gotten into you?" Leofric asked, his voice echoing hollowly, over and again, in the flickering darkness.

It struck him that Oswig's eyes were fixed fast on Leofric himself. He looked down, and his breath caught.

The clothes he had worn earlier had become something else—a priest's mass-robes. Over his shoulders and hanging down his body between his upraised arms, a woven, green hackle shone brightly, as though the threads themselves held their own light.

"Christ in heaven!" It was another wonder given by Paul. The blessed saint had come back to him.

I was lost, but I am found.

He spun, dropped to his knees, and took hold of the altar cloth's edge. Heavy, shaking sobs overtook him. "Forgive me, a sinner! Forgive me! My Lord Christ and all the saints, forgive me!"

SIXTEEN

FOLESHILL
3 NOVEMBER 1047

Outside the house, the wind whipped up, rattling a flurry of brown and yellow leaves against the shutters. Godgyfu was glad for the hearth-fire's warmth, and she pulled her stool closer. She thought it might soon rain, but she hoped any storm was short lived. Otherwise she'd be soaked by the time she got back to Coventry. *I'd have earned it by coming here!*

Thomas's whistle drifted in from outside, and Godgyfu leapt up to unbolt the door.

"Leofric's back for good now?" he asked, sweeping within as Godgyfu shut the door fast behind him. "Looks like we'll be spending more time here again."

Leofric had been wending his way back and forth between Canterbury, Winchester, and London for most of the year. He was home in July, but only for two days before going off again on king's business. Godgyfu had spent the summer and harvest-tide among the folk of Coventry, helping where and when she could as the town and all the kingdom was taken in the grip of some wretched sickness. She herself had not fallen ill, but many others had; eleven townsfolk had grown weaker and weaker, bone tired and shaking from fevered chills until death took them.

Most who died were ceorls, which also made the harvest a harder thing. Godgyfu had bidden Ælfgar go out with the men to reap, had even sweated herself for a few days to help bring the wheat to the mill for grinding. She would not let the town suffer through another hungry winter. The one bit of bliss throughout it all was the happy time she'd whiled with Ælfgar's little babes, growing bigger by the day; those two angels had been the only things sure to keep her mind from straying to Thomas and to how much she missed him.

Thomas had at last come back to Coventry near the ides of October, giving them a few happy weeks on their own.

Now Leofric was back too.

"Yes," she said. "He's been rather keen to be with me since he's gotten back. Talking and talking of how he's stuck it to Godwine, about the king withholding the ships from Sveinn even over Godwine's urgings, about Sveinn's crumbled uprising and the Danes taking Magnus well and good as their king … God in Heaven, I've heard it all now more times than I can say, and Leofric's only been back a day!"

Thomas laughed. "Yes, well, I'd guess most of your husband's happiness comes with this newest word of Magnus's sudden death! A lucky thing for Leofric, as it looked for a while as if there was a good likelihood Magnus would come against England before the winter. Had that happened, I think Eadward might have looked less well on your husband's wisdom in holding back the ships. But I've heard it said God wards dimwits, and Leofric is nothing if not that."

Godgyfu frowned and turned away from him. "He's no dimwit, Thomas. I may not love him, but he's no dimwit. Maybe *I'm* the dimwit—a woman breaking troth with her husband for a man who won't even bed her."

"You don't think him dimwitted?" he asked, paying no heed to her thorny mocking. "Then you believe all his drivel about Saint Paul, about the holy wonders he's seen?"

"Why not?" she asked, sitting on the little bed fast against the south wall. She reached toward the table at the bedside and grabbed a handful of hazelnuts and the nutcracker from alongside the bowl. "He wouldn't be the first to see the like." She wanted to believe such wonders could happen, but Leofric had seemed so addled of late, his thoughts so scattered, it was hard to know. She'd asked Osmund's son Oswig about what he'd seen in Canterbury, but the boy knew nothing. He told her it was late and he'd been tired—which from his blush likely meant drunk. He said he'd crawled into a corner to sleep while Leofric prayed and then found Leofric looming over him, going on about the glowing mass-robes.

Maybe Oswig was frightened by the holy wonder ... or so drunk he couldn't call it to mind the next day. Do the saints truly speak to Leofric? Saint Paul himself? She almost needed it to be true, wanted something to strengthen her own faith which had been so shaken lately by her dealings with Thomas ... her head muddled with all his talk of pagan gods. Some of what he said called out to her, to something inside her, maybe some ghostly echo of her bygone pagan forebears. *I am Christian! But if the saints have chosen my husband who I myself forsake, what does that make me?*

"Is Godwine's kinsman king now in Denmark?" she asked, grasping for anything to take her mind from such darkness. She chewed a hazelnut, but its woody smack seemed slightly off to her, and she put the others aside.

Thomas lit two beeswax candles at the hearth. "Looks that way." He set the candles down by the nutbowl. "Leofric's men say there's a new king in Norweg too—Haraldr Sigurdsson—half-brother to Saint Olaf, newly come home from years fighting as a Væringjar in Constantinopolis."

"What *is* it all these Northmen see in Grikaland?" Godgyfu wondered if the man had known her Eilífr. *No, don't think of him either.* "Will this Haraldr be a good king?"

Thomas shrugged. "Time will tell, but at least neither he nor Sveinn seem to have any thought of coming against England. More likely they'll end up fighting each other. Leofric told me Sveinn still wants ships."

"I know. Leofric won't shut up about that either. Godwine wants to send them, but Leofric says he's winning the war of words. If I had a penny for every time I've heard that—"

"Oh, that reminds me," Thomas said, all at once taking her arm and steering her toward the door. It was still such an unwonted thing for Thomas to touch her, even in so light a way, that her breath caught, and she let herself be led.

Only once they were outside and she had to close her eyes against the wind did she find her tongue. "Where are we going? It's going to rain!"

"No, it's not," Thomas said. "And we're only going to see the horses."

Thomas brought her around to the side of the house where a rickety stall was built against one wall. They stepped inside, and their horses nickered and shook their manes. It was dim, but enough light leaked in between the wallboards that Godgyfu could see two heavily laden bags hung behind Thomas's saddle.

"What have you brought?" she asked, patting a bag. It shifted with a loud clinking. She looked sharply at Thomas, who untied the drawstrings and pulled open the sacks to let her peer within. Silver pennies filled them to overflowing—a vast, sparkling hoard. There were even some bits of gold, an armband or two and other rings and gewgaws. "What is … where did you …?" She was at a loss.

Laughing, Thomas grabbed a handful of pennies and thrust them at her. "For your golden Marie. Or did you think I'd forgotten our understanding?"

"Our understanding? It's so much. *Too* much!"

"Not too much. It's what's needed for a golden likeness such as you want. As for how, you and Leofric are well liked throughout the kingdom. I spent most of my time away honing my goldcraft, but whenever I wasn't working I fared where I would, speaking of the wonders of your gift to Coventry. I told everyone what a happy thing it would be to give a gift back in kind, a great golden Marie, crowned and decked in stones, to adorn your abbey church. Many highborn women, more so than the men, were most willing to give what they could for such a thing. You're not alone in your love for the Blessed Maiden; here in Mercia folk might be looking to the old gods, but elsewhere in the kingdom Marie's following grows deeper and wider by the day. The pennies came flowing in."

She stared at him. They were blithe words, but she knew there weren't enough highborn ladies in Canterbury for all that he'd brought. *There's something he's not telling me.* "You've been home for weeks. Why do you only bring me this now?"

He smiled. "You're loved hereabout too, my lady. Before I gave you this gift I wanted to grow it as much as I could. I made my way to all the neighboring steads—last week while you were busy with Abbess Tova making ready for All Saints. That's why I wasn't here for the feastday."

Godgyfu frowned. She was quite sure Thomas had missed the holy day because he had been off somewhere with the fieldly folk making merry the night before—the night of the old pagan harvest feast. Tova had told her as much, had named Thomas a silver-tongued liar. *But I doubted him once before and rued it afterward. He does have the pennies, which means the church will have its golden Marie. And, too, it also means ….* A bright shudder ran through her.

"All this is for me?" she asked. "For the church?" She leaned toward him, sure now that at last she would have him. *The carving is but his clumsy way of thinking to get me naked and in his arms, though I could hardly have made it more clear such games aren't needed! What fools men are.*

"I'll bring the pennies to Abbot Mannig in Evesham on the morrow," he said, turning away from her to tie up the bags. "It's been too long since I've been to see him anyway. I'll let him know what you want, even sketch some likenesses to show him, and you can give me a pistle in your own hand to bring him, bidding him let me work with his goldsmiths to see that all's done to your wishes.

"Thomas," she reached out but stopped before her hands touched his back. It was still so hard to know how much closeness he would bear. She didn't want to spoil the happiness that now ran between them.

When the bags were fastened, he turned back toward her, a knife in one hand and a block of wood in the other. He gave a half smile. "I believe all that's left now is for you to hold up your end. Shall we go back in the house so I can begin my carving?"

"What?" She had known this was coming, but still she backed a half step away from him, heart thudding.

"Well, I'd hardly think you'd want to strip off your clothes here in the stall? Much warmer inside by the fire."

"You … you want me to do that here? Now?" She felt herself sweating beneath her clothes notwithstanding the chill. *Where might this lead?* She had a guess, and she hoped she was right.

"What better time? I've my wood and my knife, and you have Rhiannon's beauty and wonder to show me, a beauty I'll put into my own small but loving likeness of Marie. You *did* give your holy oath …."

Again, she found herself being led, this time back into the warm house, her steps wooden and without thought. The room was lit only by clouded sunlight leaking around the edges of one shuttered window and by the golden glow of the hearth-fire and the candles. Thomas fed another log to the hearth, then sat on the bed and looked up at Godgyfu, waiting.

Can I do this? She stood in the middle of the room, breathing hard. There was the bit of her that had always wanted to bare herself for him—for her own selfish, lustful ends. As sundry a soul as Thomas was, he was still a man, and Godgyfu knew men well enough to guess no man could withstand his own lust in full sight of a woman unclothed. Maybe he would at last come to her, drawn by her nakedness into her arms. And even if he did not, at least it would be a way to share themselves in the flesh even as they shared their thoughts and their hearts. It was not *all* that she wanted, but it was something to bring them closer ….

But …Eilífr …. She couldn't help but think of how her first husband had made her do something so like this. How would this be anything but the same? *No, it's not the same. This time I do it also of my own will, and for Blessed Marie! For the golden likeness that will shine forth in my church.* She reached up and slipped off the ribboned headcloth. *Women young and old will have her to look up to—the Queen of Heaven.* She unhooked her belt, and it thudded to the floor, weighted down by the keys to her penny chests. *If Thomas is right, and the folk look to the old gods for such strength as this, then I will do what I may to give Marie back her crown. My own shame is nothing alongside that.*

She drew her arms up and into the shorter sleeves of her brown, woolen outer-rail. Thomas sat still, staring. His wide blue eyes caught the nearby candles' glint and threw it back at her. *Oh, to hell with all the rest! I'll have his eyes on me and, God willing, his hands too.*

"I'll do it!"

Thomas almost seemed startled, but he covered it with a grin. "There, you see how easy that was to say?"

She wriggled beneath the wool. Thomas rose and went back to the fire. From a pouch at his belt, he drew forth a fat wad of sprigs and leaves, which he threw among the embers at the base of the hearth.

Godgyfu lost sight of him for a heartbeat as she pulled, skirts and all, up and over her head. She let the heavy wool drop to the rushes, then quickly undid the clasps at the cuffs of her long-sleeved, blue silk tunic and drew her arms inside. When it was off, she dropped it atop the woolen rail and she stood in her linen shift, shivering but not from the cold.

Thomas was mumbling something now—something in Welsh she didn't understand, but it sounded like a prayer by the careful way he meted his words. The room began to fill with a sweet, cloying smell from the burning wort. It was a spicy, outland smell, not unlike what the priests burned in church but with a wilder waft.

Any time now, he will turn back toward me. Before she lost her backbone, Godgyfu yanked the shift up and over her head, tearing it in her haste. Her breasts hung free. The warm air stroked her belly, her hips, between her legs.

Thomas rose, and when he looked, she was naked but for her red-dyed leather shoes and the stockings wound tightly with long, linen strips to mid-thigh.

It was deeply fulfilling when she heard the breath catch in his throat. "My Rhiannon," he whispered, and he stepped toward her, walked all around her, drinking her in with his eyes. She reached behind her and pulled out the clip holding her hair; it tumbled down in a long, loose braid. She felt Thomas step up behind her, run his fingers through the braid to draw it asunder, loosen her hair so that it hung down over her back as though she were still an unwed maiden.

Godgyfu turned her head this way and that, watching for something from him she could take as lust. If it was there, he hid it well. "Put your hands on me. Do it, or I'll put my clothes back on and damn myself as an oathbreaker. See if I don't."

"Such fire. All right. You've earned this." He put one hand out, set it flat against her belly, and then he froze.

She could feel him shaking, saw how hard it was for him to do this. *God damn him, I don't care. Just touch me!* She had hold of the bridle now, and she would bend his will to her own. The mere thought of it lit a fire in her that drove her mad. "More!"

He flinched, began to move his hand up toward her breasts, then he made a choking noise and drew away as though he'd been scalded. She reached out and took him by the wrist, tugged his hand back toward her and pressed it flat against her left nipple. *Yes. This is what I want, and for once in my life I'm going to take it!* She quaked with the fire now, and tried to spot something of the same in Thomas. But his eyes were flat behind a teary wetness, his hand as still and lifeless on her chest as a dead fish on the shore.

"I beg of you—not yet! I'm not ready. Soon, my love, I swear to you we will be together soon. But not yet. For now I only ask that you let me carve you."

She let go his hand, then dropped her eyes as he withdrew it, all at once highly aware of her wide hips, the sag of her breasts. *He must wish I were a younger maid.* "I'm too old for you."

"What do you speak of!" he answered. "You're all I could hope for and more. A goddess in truth. Do you have the slightest knowledge what strength there is in you?" He stopped, knelt so his eyes were straight before the dark mound of hair beneath her belly, and he breathed deeply through his nose. "I can smell it—the wonder of your godhead."

"Thomas," she said, dizzy with the thought of what they did, with the smoke's heady sharpness, with a need that grew ever stronger in her. "Kiss me. Put your lips on my body. Taste me."

"I .... Godgyfu ..." He swallowed, his words lost, but he came no closer.

There! She saw it—a fire in him. *He wants me too.*

Thomas took a deep breath, and it was gone, shoved away again. But it had been there; she would swear her life on it. *You're mine. We will be together!*

He shifted, and Godgyfu thought at last he would take hold of her. Instead he leapt for the bed. He took up the wood and put the blade to it, shaping it bit by bit. Godgyfu watched him, looking to see if his hands shook, if his breath quickened, if he grew hard beneath his breeches. Whatever she had seen had passed; nothing about him spoke of lust, leastwise not of the sort Godgyfu herself felt.

She closed her eyes and for a while lost any awareness of where she was, of how long she stood there.

A new sound woke her. Thomas had set aside the wood and was scratching madly with a bit of charcoal on a clean leaf of the sort one might find in a book. "What're you doing now?" she asked, and her voice sounded far away to her, as though her own words came to her from the sky above a deep lake in which she lay on the muddy bottom.

"I'm drawing you, catching your wonder," he said. "I'll never get the carving done in what little time we have to ourselves, so I'll need these drawings to work on it when I am alone. Take off your hose."

Godgyfu bent forward, untucked one of her wrappings, and began to unwind it from her leg. She blinked, and for the length of two breaths, she saw the ribbon unwinding by itself ... a long, pale snake with a flicking blue tongue. "What've you put on the fire?" she asked, lifting her head through air grown thick as honey to stare at the smoke haze round about her.

"Leaves and blossoms. Their god-kindness will help you see truth."

She shook her head to clear it and went back to unwinding what was once again only cloth. *His blossoms.* When she reached her ankle, she slipped her foot from her shoe and let the loosened stocking slide down and off. Then she did the same with the other. *Blossoms. Blooming like spring ....*

"What pale and comely legs," Thomas said. "See how the bindings leave marks! You should never keep yourself chained up like that. A goddess must be free."

"Yes," a voice said, not quite her own. "Free. Blossoms." Nothing stood now between her and Thomas but her own skin. Skin that burned her as though afire. A wetness grew between her legs, a deep yearning.

"It is your godhead that makes your husband earl, that gives him the strength to lead, but you are the true leader. Forget Eadgyth! It is you who are queen. With your great love and wisdom, you should be lord over the kingdom, over all the world! Your son and his children are aethelings, and should one day be kings and queens themselves. All of this flows from you—the king-maker! My one and only God!"

Godgyfu closed her eyes again. This was nothing like how it had been with Eilífr. *A wild Dane, half a beast, stalking me.* But now, here, she showed herself of her own will. *We're in love.* Such wicked happiness filled her! She wanted to cast off all bonds of seemliness and make merry in the trembling bliss of her nakedness. *Burning among the blossoms.*

"My goddess!" he said again

She felt a line of wetness drip down the inside of her right leg. She was falling inward, down into her own belly so she became one with the yearning, flowing out with the wetness like warm, lovely rain. *Dew on honeysuckle. Burning!*

When she and Leofric played at bedgames, she always made as though she took bliss from what they did; once or twice she had even known the last and greatest bliss that came with such things. But that had ever been a thing wholly of the body, her skin answering much in the same way she might get gooseflesh when it was cold or feel soothed when she scratched an itch. What she felt now, though, in this little room where she stood before Thomas, was something else altogether, a feeling coming not from without but from within. Some bit of her that had ever slept had awakened, come alive.

Yes, make him look at me. I beg it, God and Blessed Marie, Saint Osburh and all the Saints, let him look! Let him feel the fire! Make him come to me, take me among the blossoms .... It is meant to be .... It will *be!*

His charcoal scratched against the leaf, and she felt every stroke, her own skin one with the drawing.

"My goddess," he said again.

Godgyfu's head swam. She shimmered all over. Fiery blossoms. *This is another world.*

"Yes," she called out to him. "I am your goddess. Your Rhiannon! Now and always!"

SEVENTEEN

NEAR COVENTRY
14 JULY 1048

THOMAS PUT ASIDE THE HEAVY book he'd borrowed from Evesham Abbey, thinking on the words he'd been reading as Godgyfu began to doff her clothing. Eight months had passed since that first time she'd bared herself to him in Foleshill, and it had now become almost a rite for them, with all the weightiness of a christening or holy shrift. Thomas would sit back and watch as she stripped, speaking lightly of other things. He'd seen how that fired her lust—the way in which her nakedness slipped in unlooked-for where it would not wontedly be.

Thomas laughed to himself. *In time she might become nearly as twisted as the earl.* He cocked his head in thought. *No—never that bad.* But these showings, which had begun with the need to make the carving, also helped put her ever more at ease in her skin. Foremost before him. In time, before others, as needs must happen ....

They were in one of Leofric's many hunting houses now, another good spot they'd found in a wooded heath an hour's easy ride to the southwest of Coventry. It helped break the dreariness of always having to slog up the road to Foleshill.

The room held nothing more than a narrow bed, a wooden folding stool and a side table. It was enough for their needs.

"What is that book?" Godgyfu asked, sitting on the bed and unwinding the hose from her legs. She still wore a linen shift, but nothing else.

"Verses. Eadward's forebear, the great King Alfred, had them cast in English from the Latin of Boethius's *Consolatio Philosophiae*. I dearly love the way in which they've put the faring of the stars across the heavens into words. There's some skald-worthy bits here." It helped him to think of the stars as Alfred's wordsmiths did when he stared at the night sky, working out when the heavens would be as he needed.

Godgyfu smiled, looking into his eyes as she drew her shift up and over her head. "Read it to me."

He shrugged and opened the boards again, finding the right leaf.

It is with like ease upward or downward
For this earth to fare at will.
This is most like unto an egg, wherein lies
The yolk in the middle, and the shell glides
About the outside. So stands the world
Still in its stead, the streams about it,
The whirling floods, the loft and stars,
While the shining shell round all slides
Each day, and long has done so.

When he looked up, she stood naked before his stool, her legs straddling his bent knees. He put aside the book and sat forward, wrapping his arms around her waist, one hand clasping the other above the curve of her buttocks.

"Are you ready yet?" she asked, the words coming in a husky breath.

"Maybe. I'll try."

He rose then, his fingers moving up along her spine then drawing apart so he could hold and knead her shoulders. She pressed herself up against him, bare flesh against his roughspun robes. Her cheeks flushed, and her eyes were bright and merry as she drew in to kiss him—first on the neck.

Thomas felt the old queasiness in his belly, but he had learned to push it aside, to keep himself thinking of where this would in time lead them rather than on what they did. Godgyfu's kisses came harder, her lips opening so she could taste the skin at his throat, behind his ear. Thomas craned his neck to look over his shoulder at the knothole in the wallboard to his left. *Still safe*. He put one hand out and allowed himself a single brush of his fingers along her left thigh's sweaty curve.

Without warning, she snaked an arm between them and grabbed his chin, roughly, yanking his face forward so their lips met. Her tongue lapped greedily into his mouth, and he could not lie to himself: he had grown to like the smack of her—a blend of the leeks she loved to eat and the mint she wontedly chewed before coming to him. He let his tongue answer hers, two slippery fish dancing in a dark pool. It took him aback when he felt a stirring beneath his own robes, a yearning in his flesh.

Her breaths grew louder at the edges of their kiss, nearly groans. *Soon I will have to stop this*. He allowed things to go a little farther each time, but he feared they were now going too far, too fast. The stars did not yet call to him, and he would not betray them. When she made to grab him between his legs, tugging at his robes, he broke their kiss and drew away from her.

"No, Godgyfu, I can't—"

She hooked a hand into his belt and pulled him back to her. "You would light this fire in me, then have me snuff it? Give me what I need!"

"Not yet. I—" His words cut off, his head ringing, and he realized she had struck him with the back of a closed fist. Now she grabbed a handful of his hair and tugged him forward, their mouths meeting again with such force that his upper lip was pinched between their teeth, and he tasted his own blood.

He reached back and pried her fingers open—no easy thing—then held her at arm's length. "I don't ask you to snuff the fire. By all means let it burn, only I can't step into the fire with you. Not until—"

"I'll help you," she pleaded, putting her hands to her breasts, pinching one hard nipple. "Let me use my mouth on you, and we'll make you hard. Or we—"

"No, my goddess, my dearest," he whispered. "It is not that, believe me. Only ... you know how hard it is for me to do what you want. There is no one else I'd rather do this with than you. But I fear if I give in to my lust before I'm fully ready, you will feel it. It will hinder what we do, and we'll both be sorry for having rushed what should have been put off until it could be the shining wonder we both want it to be. I owe that to you." He'd come up with the words the night before, had said them over and again to himself to get them just right, and he was rather happy with how they sounded; he almost believed them himself. *To put my hands on you, to put myself inside you, will sully you, even as my mother let herself be sullied.* The time would come when such a thing would have to happen, when Thomas took the last steps toward bringing about the rebirth of his goddess, when the wooden carving he'd made would unleash its pent wonders ... but that time had to be their first. Anything else would water down the strength of their bond on that worthy day. "One day, soon, I give you my troth, I'll be ready. Only not yet. Please."

Godgyfu gave him a rueful look, her breathing still hard and ragged. "Then you'll understand if I don't wait." It was what she always said now.

"Yes, please. I'm glad to keep doing this for you until I can do more. And this does make you happy, yes?"

"It ... helps. For now." Her high cheeks flushed as she said it, both ashamed and fired by her own words. She lay back in her wonted spot on the bed, her hands already gliding over her breasts and belly, one finger dipping into her navel. All it had taken was that first time last November, after which she'd taken to nakedness like a nine-eyed eel to the mud. Now when she showed herself to him it was with an almost angry steadfastness. Making him look at her—all of her—had become nearly a weapon, one she wielded with a Northman's viking glee. *How far she's come. How far I've brought her. Everything is coming along so well.*

The Worcester pennies were what he was most proud of. There was a tale about Rhiannon—one he'd heard long ago in Wales—in which the great lady was nearly stopped from wedding her beloved Pwyll when the liar Gwawl tricked his way into a betrothal with her. On the very day of what would have been her unwanted wedding to Gwawl, Rhiannon set things right by having Pwyll come to the feast in the cast of a beggar and bearing a bewitched sack that could not be filled unless a highborn lord stomped down upon what it held and bid it be full. When the "beggar" asked Gwawl to let him fill his sack with food from the feast, Gwawl readily let him, wanting to seem openhanded. Bothered by how much food began to melt into the bag, Gwawl asked if the sack would ever be filled, and he was told it would not be until a mighty lord stepped with both feet on the food and bid it be full. Gwawl did this, they drew the sack up over his head, and he could not get free.

Leofric is like Gwawl, and I have him knotted up in a most worthy bag of my own making!

The pennies from Leofric's hoard had been more than enough to get the copper and gold for Godgyfu's likeness. That she had not yet seen the crowned Marie crafted had begun to bother Godgyfu, but he soothed her by letting her know Mannig and his goldworkers were backed up with work the king had already bidden them do for Canterbury. There was even some truth in what he told her: the craftsmen in Evesham *were* working for Christ Church. Not that this had anything to do with the delay, but he let her draw her own answers from what he said ....

Thomas let his gaze slide along Godgyfu's writhing body. She moaned a little, and again Thomas could not help but burn for her. His flesh was as weak as any man's, and he had come to feel it always now when they did this. But he never let himself give in to that darkness within; he was strong where most were weak. He did only what he needed to keep Godgyfu's own fire burning, to keep her sated until the stars were right for her to be born again. Right for him to meld bodily with her so as to give her new life, the life of the goddess dwelling within her. He would shape her into something better, greater. It would be a sundry gift. When the time came, when the gateway between the worlds opened wide enough, he would find the will to do what he must.

He leaned forward, his shadow falling over his goddess. "Your shifting is almost done," he whispered. "Soon you will be shaped anew into a wonder." By then she no longer truly heard him, heeding only her own body's hungry call. It was a hunger she ever sought to fill but which, as with all beings of flesh, never went away.

In truth it might be a few more years before the gateway opened, but he couldn't let her know that. *Keep her thinking I'm on the brink of giving in ....* "Yes, Godgyfu, yes. You look a goddess in truth. A glowing, wondrous goddess."

Her breath came harder, and a part of him was glad he still had some years left with her. Afterward, he knew they would be together forever, but he had grown fond of her smell, of her laugh, of her skin's paleness. Of the closeness they shared when she knowingly let him look upon her in this way. *Damn me, but I've even come to cherish speaking with her, sharing rather than only looking.* It was something he would never have thought could come to pass. For the barest twinkling, he wondered if there might not be some better way—if he should forestall doing what he had planned ....

What foolishness! Such things are of the body, and the body means nothing where we are heading.

LEOFRIC SWEATED AS HE FARED through the woods in the summer heat, cursing beneath his breath at the ache in his head. It felt as though the hunting house was much farther now than the last time he had come this way. *Years ago! I was younger then!* Riding, he'd have been there already, but Thomas had made him swear to come on foot.

He bided his time with another prayer of thanks to Saint Paul for the birth of his son's third child. Alditha was a strong, healthy girl with thick, dark hair and bright blue eyes. A month old, and already she had lungs as loud as her brothers. With the swelling of Ælfgar's brood, it was good their new house was nearly done. If he weren't out here in the heath on Thomas's fool errand, Leofric would have been back in Coventry overseeing the last of the building. But Thomas said Leofric would thank him afterward. *I'd better be thankful, or else I'll wring his scrawny neck.*

Not taking care where he stepped, his foot came down hard in a hollow. A sharp pain shot through his hip, and Leofric had to laugh. Little Eadwin had whacked him there earlier that morning with a wooden play sword, and Leofric's overblown howls had sent Eadwin and Morcere both into peals of laughter. *Ah, they're such good boys.*

The house came into sight at last between the trees ahead. There were two horses tied up outside, one from his own stalls. *That's Godgyfu's saddle.*

Crouching low, Leofric crept up to the house and went around back as Thomas had bidden him. He found the knothole in the wood even as the monk had said there'd be. Scarcely daring to breath, he knelt before the hole and pressed his eye up to it.

At first he saw nothing, but a heartbeat later his eyes settled themselves to the dimmer candlelight within, and his every muscle went stiff. Godgyfu lay sprawled on a bed, naked as a shorn sheep, and she writhed as if in the grip of some fit. But this was no fit. One of her hands worked back and forth between her legs, a wild rubbing. Her moans drifted to Leofric's ears, and beneath it was the wet, slippery sounds of what she did to herself.

So taken was he by the sight, he saw nothing else within the room. Then another stirring drew his gaze—Thomas sitting on a low stool alongside the bed.

Leofric shook—first his arms, then his chin, then his whole body. *It can't be! How? Christ in Heaven, how?* That first time down by the water, Thomas had told him he'd get her to do something like this. Leofric had paid it little mind, never daring to think it could truly come to pass. *Yet here she is, knowingly showing herself to the monk, doing … doing that to herself before him. What must he have said to sway her?* Or could it have been she didn't need much swaying. Had she always wanted to do this? Did she care so little for her own husband that she would show herself a wanton to any man who asked?

An ache crept into his heart. A sadness so deep, so raw, he pushed it away, couldn't bear to feel it.

He thought about rushing in, if only to see the look in Godgyfu's eyes when she saw herself caught. But he didn't rise from the ground. He didn't stop looking. If he went in now, he knew it would all be over—watching Thomas watch her, taking her in bed with Thomas in the roof, all of it. *Without it, I'd go mad. What else could ever come close to what I feel here now, seeing her like this? Nothing!*

And at least, as yet, it seemed Thomas was true to his word. He laid no hand upon her. He was fully clothed himself, hovering over her almost as though warding her, keeping her safe. There was a warmth there, a tenderness. But she merely showed herself to him, and all the devil's monk did was sit and stare, sometimes leaning closer to get a better look. *If ever ... if ever he puts even a finger on her—or she on him—I will end this. I'll kill the monk and ... and ....* What would he do to Godgyfu? Drag her home through the streets naked? Beat her? He didn't know the answer. *She is my wife. My beloved Godgyfu.*

Inside the house, Thomas leaned closer again, and it seemed to drive her into greater throes.

The two never touched, and yet what Leofric saw bespoke a closeness greater than any he himself had ever shared with his wife.

My wife is a dirty wanton! A filthy, dirty—

All at once Godgyfu cried out, her knees drew up toward her belly, and she bucked on the bed like an unbroken stallion.

Whore! Leofric did his best not to cry out along with her. His fist had been pumping fast around his own flesh, freed from his breeches, and now he drew back, away from the wall and spilt his seed onto the turf. The pain in his head took on an unbearable sharpness, then went away altogether, and he sighed. He sat back on his heels, waiting until his breath slowed, until he grew calm again. Then Leofric leaned forward once more against the wood and peered within.

Godgyfu still lay on the bed, but she looked to be sleeping, naked under a sweaty sheen. Thomas sat on the stool, his back against the far wall now, seemingly having lost any interest in the sight before him. Indeed, the man was reading to himself from a book. All was still, restful after the earlier wildness.

Thomas looked up, straight at the knothole, and gave a crooked smile.

Leofric leapt back and scrambled to his feet.

He kept still, staring at the wall, and he frowned. *Is she my wife or Thomas's? I should not be watching them if this is not my wife.* He needed to remember, but for the space of several long, ragged breaths he truly did not know.

Then he laughed at himself. *What ever am I thinking? God's truth it's my wife. This has all been worked out with the monk—I watch him, and he watches her.* The heat had merely been getting to him.

Leofric slunk away, wandering westward into the woods. The setting sun's ruddy light seeped around the boles of the trees like blood; it was getting late, and he needed to get home. He hummed to himself as he walked, a song he'd learned in Canterbury. Then he stopped.

Fear swam snakelike in his belly.

All the trees looked the same across the rolling heathland. For the life of him, he couldn't call to mind which way he had to go, which way led home ....

EIGHTEEN

GLOUCESTER
9 SEPTEMBER 1051

KINGSHOLM WAS A WIDE GATHERING of linked timber and stone buildings near a bend of the Old Severn's western bank within sight of Gloucester town to the south. The spot had once been a Roman graveyard, which Leofric thought made it an odd spot upon which to build a king's hall, but it had become one of Eadward's most oft-chosen spots for meeting with his high-men. They stood now outside the front door—Leofric with his son Ælfgar at his side, Earl Siward, and a grim King Eadward. The Frankish *conte,* Eustace of Bolougne, who had been in England as Eadward's guest since earlier that summer, also stood with them. As the king seethed, none of them spoke. Leofric busied himself peering at the furrowed, stone columns flanking the door; they were old Roman ones carted over from one of the tumbled-down shells in town that ever reminded one of the men who'd lived here before. Even in tatters, the columns did give the spot a look of worthy greatness.

"Earl Ralf comes," Siward said, and Leofric turned back toward the town.

My sword! he thought, all at once knowing he had forgotten to strap it on. But when he put his hand to his hip, he found Bloodwreak's hilt-stone, and he breathed easy.

Leofric and Siward had come the morning before, on the feast day of the Blessed Maiden's birth as Eadward had bidden them. Their hastily gathered housecarls and the sworn fighting-men of their earldoms were settled now in and around Gloucester, mostly on the near bank of the trickling Tweyver that fed the Severn, but some overflowing to fill the fields and farmsteads up against the stone walls that had once been the old Roman fastness's north, east, and south sides. When they'd learned the full breadth of the king's plight, they'd called up even more men, and those newly come had filled the banks beyond Saint Oswald's minster, outside the stone chapman's haven wall near the bridge over the Severn. Newer earthen burh walls linked that westernmost Roman wall to the fastness, and Leofric was glad for it.

Gloucester itself had little to offer—a good ironworks and even better crock kilns that churned out worthy wares to be found throughout the kingdom. It even had a mint to cast the king's new pennies. Mostly, though, it was a farming stead, little bigger than Coventry, but unlike Coventry the strong walls gave this spot a hard shell. It was a good burh, easily warded, and Leofric was happy the king held it now rather than Godwine.

Earl Ralf was at last in sight, riding from the east at the head of some two hundred weaponed men who tread along the Lower Northgate Street toward town. They were men from the southeast Midlands, Ralf's earldom now that Beorn had been killed.

"My stepson has brought enough men, *da ouy?*" Eustace asked. "We can squash this Godwine now?"

Leofric gave the Frankisman a sidelong look. Ralf was the king's sister's son by her first husband, and Eustace had taken that sister to wife in her widowhood. The sister herself, Ralf's mother, had died nearly ten years ago, but the king clearly still thought of Eustace as a wedded kinsman. He wondered how much of the mess they were now in came from that kinship with the king.

"He's right, Highness," Siward said. "We have enough spears to meet Godwine in the field."

When the newcomers reached the other fyrdmen, Ralf sent them south to settle in around the burh's far side. He then spurred his horse up the lane to Kingsholm and soon alit before them. A man rushed out from the doorway to take the earl's horse in hand.

"What the devil is going on?" Ralf asked, dropping to a knee before the king. "I got your word to come with men, and I've been hearing some wild words along the way, but no two tales are the same!"

The king spat. "Godwine has gathered a great host against me."

Ralf spread his hands, opening his mouth but finding no words.

Eustace sighed. "I fear it started with me."

"The blame is not yours, Eustace," Eadward said, his words flat, then he looked back to Ralf. "Your stepfather was on his way home to Boulogne with his men. Before taking ship they bid the men of Dover give them somewhere to stay and rest—put them up before their wayfaring."

"As was our right as the king's guests!" Eustace added, stroking the long whiskers he wore, two bushy tails stretching from nose to ears, though his chin was shaved bare. Leofric thought it made him look like a mad old fox.

"The Dover men forbore giving them rooms," Earl Siward said, "and fighting broke out. Twenty men were killed and many wounded … on both sides. Eustace came to the king with the tale of what had happened, and the king sent word to Earl Godwine that he was to go to Dover and harry the town. Godwine said no."

Ralf sucked a breath between his teeth.

"Worse!" Eadward barked. "A week ago, Godwine, Swegn and Harold gathered a host of men from their earldoms down near Tetbury, right on my doorstep, for they well knew I was sitting here in Gloucester. It is nothing short of an uprising!"

Leofric shook his head. He still could not work out why the king had allowed Godwine's son Swegn back into the kingdom after all the wretch had done. He'd warned the king no good would come of it, but Eadward took no heed. He put his hand to Bloodwreak's hilt, glad to feel it there, knowing he had already done so but fearing he might have been mistaken, that he'd left it in his bedcove when he dressed that morning.

"But what do they want?" Ralf asked.

"They say they're ready to fight the king," Leofric answered, "unless he gives over Eustace and his men to be dealt with for what happened in Dover, and on top of that they ask that Osbern Pentecost and his men be put out of the new *castel* in Ewias."

Ralf turned bright red. "Osbern is my own man! By what right do they bring him into this?"

Leofric sighed. If the young earl had not yet worked out how much Eadward's Norman hangers-on had come to be hated by many Englishmen, he wasn't going to be the one to tell him. He couldn't think how Ralf had seen fit to let one of his own sworn men build a great, Norman kind of fastness right in the middle of Herefordshire near Wales, as though Osbern were some raiding warlord in a land of foes. Godwine and his sons weren't the only ones to have balked at such a misdeed. *I wonder if the fastness is anywhere near those lands Thomas used my loan to reave? I must ask him. Christ, I'd forgotten all about those lands and the pennies both!*

"They've no right to do anything they've done," Eadward answered.

"So we go kick their teeth in!" Ralf said, putting a hand to his sword hilt, and looking every bit as young as he was.

"You'd like that, wouldn't you?" Ælfgar asked, and Leofric turned toward his son in wonder. "Englishmen fighting Englishmen? A good laugh for you Normans."

"Right!" Leofric yelled, raising a hand in warning toward Ælfgar. There was likely truth in what he said, but it would never do for them to squabble among themselves. "Enough of that!" He turned to Ralf, who stood with mouth agape. "Forgive my son, he is somewhat hotheaded and often speaks before he thinks. But I do wonder if it is wise to begin kicking in teeth, as you say."

"Wise?" Siward said, giving a bitter laugh. "That's not the word I'd use. Eadward, you know I'm not one to shrink from a fight, but is this truly for the best?"

"What in Christ's name are you two saying?" Eustace asked, looking at Siward and Leofric as though they'd each grown another head.

Leofric looked to Eadward. "Highness, I can't believe the men under Godwine will fight against you—men who swore oaths before the kingseat. Godwine must know it too. It's only words, to see if he can goad you."

"All the better," Ralf said. "We give him what he asks for and make his men break troth with him! He and his sons will be made to look like the fools we know they are!"

Siward hummed low in his throat. "We *think* they'll break troth. What if we're wrong, and they do fight for him? All the kingdom's best are gathered here in Gloucestershire. Do we truly want to tear ourselves up from within? How long before the wolves form a ring around us from without? The Northmen? The Irish? Osgod Clapa's followers? Each of them nipped at us a year ago, and that was when we were strong. If we let—"

Eadward threw up his hands and cut Siward off by blowing out a loud breath. "I can't worry about wolves in the woods when we've already one in the fold. All of you draw your men up into harrying lines to the south and meet me back here again in one hour! I'm going to my chapel to pray."

They turned to go, Ralf and Eustace with smug grins, Siward more glumly. Eadward spun back toward Kingholm, but Leofric stopped him even as he reached the two stone columns. "King Eadward, a word if you will."

The king turned back with a sigh, but he came. Ælfgar looked to Leofric, and Leofric nodded that it was all right for him to stay too. The others wended their way south over the Twyver.

"Did I not make my wishes bare, Leofric?" Eadward asked. "Why must we speak alone. I called you all here to crush Earl Godwine and his sons. So crush them!"

"Highness, gladly will I do this if it is your bidding, but I need to understand something." Leofric drew a deep breath; this was something he'd long wanted to ask the king but never dared. *The king needs me now, more than he ever has. The kingship itself teeters on a narrow edge, and Eadward knows it. There will be no better time to ask, only ....* He looked up at the sun, and it was not yet noon. Later in the day he knew he would feel tired, his thoughts clouded, and he would not trust himself to craft words the king would understand. *It's still early, though. Saint Paul is with me, and I can do this.* "All my life, even after the Danes left and you came back, I have seen good things going to Godwine and his kin over my own. Earldoms. Kindnesses big and small. You've even wedded his daughter. Now you call me to crush him."

Eadward wrapped the long fingers of both hands around his pale-yellow beard and twisted it before his gut. "The man and his sons took up swords against me when I bid him go to Dover. The Dover folk shamed the kingdom with their misdeeds, and he is their earl. When Harthacnut bid you go to Worcester, you went and did what you had to do. And before our time, my forebear Eadred slaughtered the men of Thetford when an abbot was murdered there. My own grandfather King Edgar bid Thanet be harried over a chapman's slaying. It is the way such misdeeds are dealt with, and you earls are the one's to set things right! All I did was ask the same of Godwine, but because the misdeeds happened in his own earldom, he forsook me. His lord and king!"

"Yes, he was wrong to do so," Leofric said. "But if I may say so, in the past you have always seemed most ... forgiving of Godwine and his kin. Take ... Godwine's eldest ... ahh ...." Leofric snapped his fingers, casting about for the name.

"Swegn," Ælfgar gave it to him.

"Take Swegn," Leofric went on. *How could I forget that wretched oaf!* "You rightly threw him out after what he did with the abbess. He tried to sneak back in the next year and ended up murdering his own kinsman Beorn for not going to you on his behalf. The whole of your fyrd gathered to name him *nithing*—a doom that should have stripped him wholly of his worth, making him unwelcome in any kingdom in the north. But somehow, after less than a year cowering among your foes in Flanders, Swegn was home again, even given back his earldom in some understanding you came to with Godwine." In truth, the more Leofric thought of it, the more he wondered it the king was too forgiving of all his foes, too soft. Emma had gotten back her lands and good stead; even her priest Stigand had found himself the new bishop of Winchester! *Is no one ever truly made to pay for their misdeeds?*

"But now," he said, hoping he did not overstep his bounds, "over this one thing—over Godwine's balking at harrying his own sworn men in Dover—you would go to war against him and his sons? Why the sudden shift?"

Eadward had stood still listening to all Leofric said, his cast giving away nothing of his thoughts. But when Leofric stopped, the king blew a laugh through his nose and shook his head. "All this time, and still you can't see it! Nothing has shifted, leastwise not in my heart. I well know the bitterness you bear toward Godwine, but know that it is nothing next to the hatred I have borne for him from the day I first set foot back on English soil! Do you think I've somehow forgotten his helping to murder my brother Alfred! Worse than murder! They took his eyes out like two apples from a tree so that he died in darkness! Darkness and *agonie*!" Tears welled in the king's eyes. He stopped to take a deep breath and wipe them away with his fingertips.

"Highness, I—" Leofric began, but the king cut him off.

"I'm not done. I'd have put him out of my kingdom the day I stepped ashore, but he was too strong then and only seemed to grow stronger with the passing years. I needed him, needed his backing to bring the Wessex thegns behind me—me, little better than some outlander then, living in Normandy since a time most of those thegns were still in swaddling clothes. Did I want to give Swegn an earldom? Harold? There was nothing I wanted less, but what else could I do? Until I'd strengthened my own stead, I had to keep him happy, lull him into thinking he was a friend. The only good thing to come of it all was my wedding to Eadgyth, for she is a good woman, though I did my best not to see it for a long while. And truth be told, until this mess in Dover, Harold at least has shown himself a worthy earl."

Leofric did not know what to say. It all seemed so bare now; he knew the king was right. *I should have seen it.*

"As for you," the king went on, "yes, I have wronged you greatly. Would that I could have given you and yours much more than I did. I needed you and Siward both to stand against Godwine when I couldn't, and I needed Godwine always to see me as his *complice*—his friend—against you. But no more. You have always been my most trusted earl, whose wisdom I give greater worth even than that of any of my Norman friends. I am strong enough now to slip free from under Godwine's thumb—that is what's shifted. And he's at last stretched his proud neck out too far. I mean to bring the axe down on it, and you and Siward will help me wield it."

God in heaven! Leofric's heart stirred. With the death of Ælfric Puttoc, Archbishop of York, earlier that year, and Bishop Ælfwine of Winchester dead and gone four years now, it had begun to seem Leofric would outlive all his old foes. *Now at last—a way to be rid of Godwine—all I've ever hoped for and more.* He took hold of his sword hilt, heartened when he found it where it should be.

Ælfgar coughed, and Eadward and Leofric both turned to look at him. Leofric had forgotten he was even there.

"Do we know all of what truly happened in Dover? Maybe there should have been some … some nosing about for answers—something to back Eustace's self-serving words before your highness called for a harrying."

Leofric took two swift steps toward his son and rapped him hard across the jaw with the back of his knuckles. "Do you look to outguess your king?"

"Father, I …." Ælfgar bowed his head.

Leofric felt the king's hand on his elbow. "Never mind, Leofric. It's well he speaks as he does. You've never balked at giving me the hard truths, which is one of the things I find most worthy in you. Your son only takes after his father in this." Leofric looked away from Ælfgar, meeting Eadward's eyes again.

"You are most understanding, Highness." He reached up to rub his shoulder where it felt as if he'd pulled a muscle striking his son. *Damn me, but I'm getting old.*

"Understanding?" Eadward laughed. "I'm nothing of the kind. And in hindsight, I may indeed have been hasty, even as Ælfgar says. But we're beyond that now. I bid Godwine do something, and he forbore. Now he's taken up weapons and kindled the south against me. There's no going back from where we find ourselves."

And yet we can't do this, Leofric thought, taking himself aback when he saw that. *Godwine is brought before me like a pig for the spit, and I can't let the king spit him*. “No going back, as you say, Eadward. But I do ask you to think on what war among ourselves will mean. Why let Godwine’s folly weaken the kingdom? Could we not …” He trailed off, thinking. “What about the witan? Gather a witenagemot in London, call Godwine and his sons to stand before it to answer for their misdeeds.” *Now that is something I’d like to see almost as much as Godwine on the spit. The great earl and his sons brought low before all the high-men of the kingdom, likely stripped of his earldom, cast out from England!* He had to hold back a smile.

Eadward sighed. “Very well. I will think on it. Indeed, I will pray on it, and you’ve kept me long enough from my prayers. Tell the other earls to be back here in one hour.” This time Leofric did not stop him.

He looked back at Ælfgar and gave his son a playful swat on the back of the head. “Dolt.”

“Father, the king was of a like mind with me.”

This time Ælfgar did not bow his head, and Leofric was proud of him. All at once it struck him his son had grown taller than him and nigh twice as wide—all hard muscle. *Maybe I shouldn’t hit him lest he think one day to hit me back*. “That’s because you’ve a sharp mind, son. Only you still haven’t learned it’s never wise to tell a king he’s made a mistake. Lead him to it, help him see the mistake for himself, but never come right out and say it, son.” He patted his son on the shoulder and smiled. “I think I see an earldom looming for you.”

Ælfgar’s black beard split in a wide grin of his own, and they headed south to catch up with the others. Hardly had they gone a few steps, however, when Leofric saw Thomas coming toward them, robes hiked up so he could step carefully around muddy patches in the road. “Christ!” Leofric swore. “Go on ahead and let the earls know where things stand. I’ll be along shortly.”

Ælfgar and Thomas nodded and traded a few words as they passed each other by. Leofric stood his ground waiting to hear what the monk had to say. There’d been no choice but to drag Thomas along with him; three years had passed since that day Leofric first peered at them through the wall of the hunting house, but he still didn’t trust Thomas alone in Coventry with Godgyfu no matter that the monk had been true enough to his word and never laid a finger on her in all that time. Nevertheless, thoughts of what Godgyfu did with this man were not what Leofric needed now. It was no time to let his lust draw his mind from the grave business at hand.

“Will there be war?” Thomas asked when he came near.

Leofric snorted. “What do you care? You seem to thrive on mistide and madness like the Northman’s Loki.”

"Oh, I like that," Thomas said, laughing. "But you're wrong. I want things tidy, easily foreseen. It helps me know where to be when there's something I want to see. And as I call to mind, you like watching things too—"

Leofric grabbed the man's robes and tugged him forward, wincing at the ache in his shoulder. "Aye, I like it," he snarled. "You've shown my wife to be a right whore! What man wouldn't like to be made a fool of!" He made a scoffing noise in his throat.

"If you want to stop, then we can."

"No, you little weasel, I don't want to stop." He shoved Thomas away from him so the man fell to his knees. "I want more. Get her to do dirtier things, why don't you? I want to see her on her knees in the mud. Put a Christ-bleeding bridle bit in her mouth!"

Thomas clucked his tongue, but did not stand. "She's a woman—your goddess, Leofric—not some gleeman's animal. Not some dancing bear on a lead. What kind of husband are you?"

Leofric stood there dumbfounded for a stound, pain rushing in to throb behind his right eye. Then he fell atop the man in a red wrath. "You dare ask me that?" His spittle flew as he spoke. He nearly began pounding Thomas's smug face with his fists, then thought better of it at the last; he was within sight of several hundred men and did not want to have to come up with some tale about why he'd seen fit to beat a Benedictine novice to death at the side of the road. Instead he rose, untangled his sword sheath from between his legs, and brushed himself off. "I don't want to see you again until it's time to go back to Coventry. Get out of my sight!"

"As you wish." Thomas rose and turned.

"One more thing," Leofric called after him. "Where are my pennies? You told me I'd see them back twofold once you had the Godwine lands. It's been years now, and I haven't seen one bit of it."

Thomas looked back over a shoulder, then turned and shook his head. "What ever do you mean, Earl? I thought better of the whole thing and made up my mind not to reave those lands we spoke of. I gave the pennies back to your wife years ago."

Leofric stared, trying to find any wit or meaning in the words. "What the devil are you talking about?"

"It was only days after you gave the pennies to me. I was on my way to Evesham for a few weeks and you were away from Coventry, off on your rounds with the hundred moot. I didn't want to leave the bags laying about, so I gave them to Godgyfu and told her to give them back to you, that they were yours."

"Horse shit! She never gave me anything. And that was the Worcester reavings! She'd never have taken it from you!"

Thomas spread his arms wide. "I never told her it was from Worcester. If she didn't give it to you, then the riddle has an easy answer. She must have put it in your hold. She wears the keys to your mint, does she not? Ask her about it. I'm sure she'll tell you it's there."

"Don't you worry, I will!" Leofric shoved past Thomas and strode toward town. He'd wasted enough time with the twisted imp and had worthier things to see to, namely Earl Godwine's downfall.

NINETEEN

COVENTRY
5 OCTOBER 1051

THE DAY WANED, AND GODGYFU was glad they were nearly home. She walked alongside the horsecart driven by one of her housemen. Beornflæd and Abbess Tova sat with their legs dangling over the back, but much as Godgyfu's feet ached, she would not ride. The cart's bouncing only fired her lust, which was an ever-gnawing thing now, mad and hungry. *God help me, if I were alone, I'd throw myself down at the roadside and rub myself raw. Christ, when will Thomas be back?* It was his hands she truly wanted, not her own.

Since sunrise they had wended their way to most of the neighboring steads, bringing alms to those in need, food and clothing for the coming winter. It was what Christ would have wanted, she knew, but more so she did it because of something Thomas had once said. *Rhiannon was known for her open-handed giving, and a queen's greatness is meted by the freedom with which she gives of her wealth.* It was what Rhiannon would have done.

Godgyfu sweated, though it wasn't warm. She wiped her brow with the back of a hand and stuck out her lower lip to blow a stray lock from before her eyes.

"You truly won't ride with us?" Abbess Tova asked. "You look a wreck."

Godgyfu shook her head and made herself smile. *A wreck.* She knew Tova was likely right. She'd lost so much weight over the past year, bones showed sharp in spots that had ever before been softened by fuller flesh. She hardly slept anymore either, so she guessed her eyes were ringed with shadow. "Never mind," she said, and it came out a dry croak. "This day is not about my ease, but about easing the burden of my folk."

Tova snorted. "Grind yourself into dust, and your folk won't have anything left of you."

Beornflæd gave a loud cackle. "I tell her the same, Abbess, but she won't listen."

Godgyfu paid them no heed. She could not, however, hold back a thankful sigh when at last they rounded a bend and Coventry's northernmost houses came into sight beyond the trees. Before long, they neared the market, and Godgyfu bid the driver skirt around it to bring the cart home without them. "We've one more stop to make," she told the women.

The house she led them to was once great, now mostly fallen into tattered shame. It was one of Coventry's few buildings with two floors, spanning nearly half one edge of the market yard straight across from the gateway to the abbey grounds. The market was crowded as ever, and Godgyfu felt dizzy and closed in by all the folk who greeted her and called out blessings. She did her best to nod and smile, but she was glad when they reached the door and she could turn her back on the throng. She knocked, and the door opened straightaway.

Thegn Stenkil was too old and sickly to have gone off with Leofric to Gloucester; he'd paid another to go in his stead. He bowed as low as his twisted back let him, his new young wife Wulfrun and their little lad Oscytel doing the same in the dim room behind him. Oscytel was so thin he looked half a ghost. All Stenkil's older sons and their mother were dead, and he'd no kin left to help him in his need, though he had once come from highborn folk. "Godgyfu," he said, sounding far stronger than he looked. "You gladden us by coming. Wulfrun, get something for the earl's wife! Have you eaten yet? Or maybe—"

Godgyfu raised a hand to stop him. "Thank you, Stenkil, you are kind, but no. I can't stay long. I only wanted to let you know Leofric will take your Oscytel on as a ward if it is your wish to have him raised in our household. The earl is in need of a new cup-bearer, and there are many other things he can find for your lad to do. He'll be taught his letters too and swordcraft and the like alongside Eadwin and Morcere."

The man dropped to his knees. "You give us great worth, and I thank you."

His wife rushed forward to fall at Godgyfu's feet. "Oh, bless you, Godgyfu! Bless you and Earl Leofric both!"

Godgyfu put out a hand and drew Wulfrun back up to her feet. "Leofric always speaks well of your husband's steadfastness over the years, and it is the least he could do." In truth, she hadn't spoken to Leofric of this yet, but she knew if she bid him take the boy, he would. He'd been most eager to please her of late. Leastwise with everything apart from the matter of the heregeld. "Have Oscytel come on the morrow, and we'll settle him in the household."

She turned to go, the man and his wife still calling out their thanks and blessings behind her. Nearby, a little bowl of incense smoldered atop a stall selling outland wares. The smell minded Godgyfu of the leaves Thomas burned whenever they were together, and she felt her breath quicken. The warmth she nearly always had now between her legs grew stronger, began to throb in time to her heart. The swirl of bright hues and loud folk around her made it hard to think.

"This way, dear," Beornflæd said, beckoning.

"Yes," Godgyfu answered. "Coming." Her foot caught on something, and she nearly fell.

Tova caught her, putting one arm about her waist and pressing her shoulder close to Godgyfu's. "You're pushing yourself too much," her friend whispered, her mouth close to Godgyfu's ear. "This has to stop. All of it. What … what you do with Thomas—it is a sin to be with a man other than your wedded husband. It's tearing you asunder. Come to the abbey and pray with me."

Godgyfu drew away from Tova, shoving her aside, ready to scold her for her boldness. Then she saw her friend's stricken cast, the worry in her eyes, and the angry words died on her lips. She took Tova's hands between her own. "I will pray. Later. As for the rest, I … I'm sorry, but there's nothing I can do. I'm weak."

Tova's mouth took on a chiding twist. "You are anything but weak. Though lately one would never know it."

Leaning forward, Godgyfu put her arms about Tova's shoulders and held her as hard as she could, drawing strength from her. *My beloved Tova.* "What would I do without you?" she whispered with lips pressed against her dearest friend's wimple. "But no, I *am* weak. I …." All at once her own words nettled her ears.

What am I saying? I am a godly woman with the strength of Christ in me! With Marie's holy strength! Did Blessed Osburh save me all those years ago for this? To doom myself to hellfire? "Yes, let's go pray in the abbey."

Her friend's cast softened, and she drew Godgyfu toward the abbey gates.

Hardly had they gone two steps when a great upheaval and shouting broke out all about them. The word spread quickly through the crowd: Earl Leofric and his men had come home.

Thomas! All thoughts of prayer rushed from her head, and she drove forward with the rest, making for the high road. She wanted only to taste his mouth, feel his hands on her body. The way his fingertips fluttered between her legs was like nothing she had ever felt. She wanted to put her lips, her tongue, on his skin. On his strong chest and hard stomach. Wanted to grab him and put him inside her.

Godgyfu closed her eyes, and her mind flew back, a month ago, to those last hours she'd whiled with Thomas in Foleshill before he went south with Leofric and the others to Gloucester. She'd had her hands down the front of his breeches under his robes, his flesh swelling beneath her fingers. *My God, he feels like a giant! I need to see it at last—need to feel it inside me, filling me!*

"Come with me to the old Rollandriht stones to the south on the eve of All Saint's," Thomas had whispered, his breath kissed with the smack of the heady brew he'd made for them to share, "and I will give you what you want."

"You said you couldn't yet … you're not ready."

Thomas sighed, nearly a purr, and ground his hips harder against her. "I think I'm ready now. The stars will soon be ready. Together we will touch your godhead."

"Let's do it now! Why wait? Let Leofric and the others go to Gloucester! You needn't go with them! Let my husband find some priest to pray with instead of you!" She made to tug the clothes fully from his body, but he pushed her hands away.

"Not yet. It must be on that day, so the stars themselves will smile on what we do, their light bathing us, making us new." He rose from the bed, tucking his clothes back into place. "And it's best I go away now, lest I'm not strong enough to wait. On the night of the old harvest feast, I give you my troth we will go together to Rollandriht. I'll lay you down on the soft grass among the stones, or maybe even on one of the old stones themselves so we might feel its strength beneath us, lifting us up. On that night, we will be one."

"Yes, my sweet," she said, knowing it was wrong, knowing it was only a way for him to get her to go with him to some pagan stones. *He thinks to have me pray to his old gods on one of their high feast days.* Ever before she'd said no to him when it came to that. But what did it matter anymore? If it meant he would give in and bed her at last, she would go with him to Hell itself. *But God help him if he thinks to forestall me again there!* If he sought to talk his way out of the deed that night, she'd grab him by the ears, knock his head against one of his damned stones, and climb atop him while his thoughts were addled. One way or another she would have him! "Yes, Thomas, that is all I want. To be one with you."

Saint Osburh, save me from myself. It was a small voice, in the back of her head, easily put aside ....

In the market, Godgyfu found herself staring up at a reddening October sky.

"Godgyfu." Tova was calling her name. "Godgyfu!"

She lay on her back in the street. Beornflæd and Tova stood over her, looking down. They seemed so tall, taller than trees, their heads among the clouds.

"What ...?" Godgyfu blinked and sat up.

"You swooned," Tova answered.

Others had gathered, townsfolk making a worried ring about her.

"I'm sorry." She pushed herself to her feet. "Only I was overcome with happiness that my husband's home safe, war staved off." She said it for the other folk. The two woman who helped steady her knew there was no truth in her words. At least Tova knew; with Beornflæd it was hard to say. Her handmaid had never spoken to her of it, but likely she guessed at some of what had been going on between her and Thomas. She put a hand on the old woman's shoulder and squeezed. *Dear, steadfast Beornflæd.*

"Sit a while more, here by the roadside," Tova said, pulling her away from a High Street filling with armed and byrnied housecarls and farmers with leather caps and vests dragging spears behind them or bearing rusty swords or mattocks. It was indeed a blessing from God that there had been no fighting, or many of these men would not have made it home. "Sit until your head's settled."

Godgyfu drew away from her. "No, I must go home to welcome my husband. It's only a little way. Beornflæd will help me. Go back to your sisters."

Tova sighed, but she seemed to know it would do no good bickering over this. "Please take care of yourself!" she called out as Godgyfu left the High Road and wended her way up the tree-lined lane to her homestead.

"Heed what she says," Beornflæd puffed alongside her. "Ye've eaten nothing all day. I'll get ye something from the kitchen."

"Thank you," Godgyfu said, but the last thing she wanted to think about was food.

A small crowd gathered in her house's foreyard, two score folk at least, and it looked a right merry gathering. The first thing she saw was young Eadwin atop her son's shoulders. She made for them, and when the boy saw her, he shouted happily. "Eldermother! Look who's back!"

"I see them," she said. "Welcome home, son."

Ælfgar nodded. "Mother."

She stopped when she found Alditha blocking her way. The girl looked up at her with dark brown eyes wide as plates and a nose as runny as ever. Then she lifted a pudgy hand, held it steady and poked Godgyfu hard in the belly.

"Hello to you too, my little queen," Godgyfu said, laughing.

Across the yard, Leofric chased Morcere in a wide ring, snorting like a moon-mad bull.

Tumbling Eadwine down from his shoulders, Ælfgar handed him off to his wife. Godgyfu stepped closer. "How was he?" she asked, nodding toward Leofric.

Ælfgar sighed. "The same. All was as well as it could be, but there were a few tough times. One night he woke from a dream and didn't know who I was. But mostly he kept himself together. Sharp. I'm more worried about you, Mother. You look awful, like something waiting for the lich-worms."

She batted him in the arm for his bold lip and sought to laugh it away.

"No, truly," he said, "Have you been sick?"

"Don't worry about me. I've been busy, is all." She looked back across the yard. *Thomas.* He stood with Osbern and some other men, talking and laughing. Their eyes met. He winked at her, moistened his lips with the tip of his tongue, and looked away. Her yearning warmth rushed back like a flood. *A few more weeks, and I'll have him!*

Even as her mind whirled with thoughts of Thomas's body atop her, Leofric saw her at last and came bounding forward. His teeth flashed behind his gray whiskers in a wide grin.

"Welcome home, Leofric," she said. "What word?"

"I've one word for you," he answered, and she found herself all at once scooped up in his arms and whirled about. When he set her down, she had to hold onto him lest she fall. "That word is *earl*, which is what you'll have to call your son now!"

She turned back to Ælfgar, raising her eyebrows. He nodded, laughing along with his father. "Harold's earldom," he said. "It's mine now. I leave in the morning to set my new home aright."

Godgyfu looked toward Ælfgar's children, proud of her son but stricken at the thought of losing their fat little faces.

Ælfgar laughed. "Don't worry. For now, I'd have the children stay with you here until things are more settled in Norfolk. Ælfgifu will stay too, and I'll be back and forth throughout the winter."

"Ha," Leofric shouted. "My son, the Earl of East Anglia!" He was beaming, and Godgyfu thought it was the happiest she ever remembered seeing him.

"But tell me!" she shouted back, finding herself drawn into their giddiness. "What happened? I want to know everything!"

"Saint Paul was with us, and the king had a mild heart," Leofric said. "He let the two armies withdraw without fighting, both sides gave over men as troth-wards, and the witan met a fortnight later in London."

"Earl Godwine and his sons were bidden come," Ælfgar took up the tale, "to answer for what they'd done. And the king called up the wider fyrd of all England, so that even the thegns and free folk from Godwine's own earldom were bound to come and stand ready to fight for the king against their own earl!" He stopped to laugh. "Godwine and his sons came to Southwark, and they still had a good lot of fighting folk with them too, but they said they wouldn't come before the king unless he turned over more men to troth their safety. In the end, Eadward wearied of calling for them. He again named Swegn *nithing* and gave Godwine and all his kin five days to leave the kingdom. The last we heard, Godwine and his wife and Swegn, Tostig and Gyrth took ship from Bosham, likely bound for Flanders where Tostig's wife has kin. Harold and his brother Leofwine seem to have sailed from Bristol to go live among the wretches in Ireland."

"Hear that?" Leofric roared, again taking Godgyfu up and spinning her. "We're done with them. All of them gone! Even the Queen! Eadward's sent Eadgyth off to while the rest of her days in Wherwell Abbey!"

Godgyfu shook her head in wonder. Godwine's wife Gytha had always been a bit of an overweening shrew-mouse for whom she would shed no tears, but she could not help but feel a little sorry for young Queen Eadgyth, made to pay for the misdeeds of her father and brothers. "Who is earl in Wessex now? And what of Swegn's earldom?"

"King Eadward's put most of Swegn's earldom under my lordship," Leofric said, "with some few bits given over to Osbern Pentecost. So there's another wrong righted and Mercia nearly whole again!"

"Thegn Odda of Deerhurst has the southwestern half of Wessex," Ælfgar added. "The king's not yet named a man to the rest."

"Mead!" Leofric bellowed. "I want every mead cask tapped! And a feast later this night in the hall!" A great cheer went up, and men ran off every which way to do his bidding.

Godgyfu peered toward the spot she'd last seen Thomas, hoping to glimpse him again, but he was lost in the wild rush. Then she felt Leofric's hands on her, drawing her aside, and she let him lead her until they found a bit of stillness in the herb garden around back. Two chaffinches called to each other somewhere nearby. "I can scarcely believe it's all true. Who ever thought we'd live to see the day!"

Leofric nodded, but he suddenly seemed smaller, less happy. He looked about, squinting against the setting sun's glow, trying to spot the noisy birds.

"What is it?" she asked.

"The monk," he said, and her throat tightened. "Thomas borrowed money from me some years back—from the Worcester hoard—for some fool land he wanted to reave. He says he gave it back to you."

So that's where the money came from! No wonder he hid the truth from me. She had to stop herself from laughing. *The little imp!* She'd been outwitted, but somehow she wasn't angry with Thomas. In the end it was better the Worcester money went to the church anyway—to Marie. *Thomas must have guessed rightly I would feel this way—he knows me so well—and wanted to spare me the guilty tug of knowledge. What does it matter anyway? It let me bare myself to him, got me what I wanted all along.*

"I never knew it was a loan he paid back," she said, keeping her words mild. "And by the Blessed Mother I had no hint it was the Worcester blood-pennies. I reckoned it something Abbot Leofwin owed you from your dealings with him before he became abbot, that Thomas was but his errand-man."

"So you have it?" Leofric asked, his eyebrows climbing his forehead and making the old Worcester scar pucker. "My pennies?"

"I ... I did," she said, thinking fast. "But not any more. It's given over to the Church—to our abbey. We spoke of this at length. Must needs you haven't forgotten the Marie likeness we're having made for the abbey!" She felt guilty, knowing she crafted the flimsiest of tales. Lately Leofric had been so muddled about what had or hadn't truly happened it was easy to wile him in this way.

"I haven't forgotten," he snapped back as she'd known he would. He never wanted to yield that he couldn't remember something, so all she had to do to get him to believe something was hint it might have slipped his mind; then he'd fight like the devil to sway her it hadn't. It worked best later in the day, she'd found, toward evening. "How could I forget something like that! I was speaking to Leofwin about it only the other day, asking if he knew when the likeness would be done. I thought maybe you would know something more of it."

"Yes." This time she needed no wile to make her words ring true, "I've been wondering the same thing." The likeness's crafting had been thwarted by one setback after another, so that she'd given up even asking after it anymore. It would be done when it was done. Or it wouldn't. She didn't care any more.

Thomas is mine, and soon we'll be one.

TWENTY

ROLLANDRIHT
31 OCTOBER 1051

HEATED BY THE NEARBY FIRE, the stone felt almost warm beneath Godgyfu's bare skin. This smaller knot of stones must have once looked like a table, albeit one twice as tall as a man. The four upright stones sill stood, leaning toward each other over Godgyfu's head as though they whispered hidden truths to each other. The fifth stone, the flat board of the table, had toppled down between the others, many hundreds of years ago from the look of it, forming the bed on which Godgyfu now lay. It was a quiet hollow in the wide, rolling green, a spot all their own.

Rollandriht's more worthy sights were a ways east—the ring of rough, shapeless chalkstone slabs called the King's Men and the nearby twisted stone that had once been the King. After the day-long ride from Coventry, Thomas had led Godgyfu among them, telling her tales of how the stones had come there. Years ago, before wedding Leofric, she had gone once to see the great Giant's Ring near Amesbury and had guessed Rollandriht would be something much the same. It was nothing near as awesome, but it had its own sort of loveliness, and strolling among the pitted and cracked stones with Thomas, spotting shapes with him in the stones' yellow and white rag-moss patches, gave them a worthiness in her heart. They'd watched the sunset together from the middle of the ring, and those hours had been as blithe as any Godgyfu had ever spent.

Then the sun dipped fully below the western hills, and Thomas hurried them off to the east. It being the old feast day, the other spots would be filled with the fieldly folk of the hills as midnight drew near. At the fallen table, though, they could be alone. They could do what they had come to do, what Godgyfu had been waiting for. Waiting for years ....

Now it was full night, near midnight maybe, but it was hard to say; Godgyfu's head swam with the thick, sweet draught Thomas had brewed for them. She lay back, letting the night air stroke her skin. A wind sighed through the gaps in the stones above her, the firelight rippling over them so it looked like they danced. Above it all, the stars seemed brighter than was their wont, glowing blossoms which, if only she could stretch her arms a little further, she might pluck from the sky's dark bowl.

"It wasn't truly a table, you know," Thomas said, rising from where he had curled alongside her. "Once this was a doorway, through which the old folk could pass into the faerie world."

Godgyfu smiled. *What tales he tells!*

Thomas stepped away to tend the great bonfire he'd built. It flared up again, brighter and stronger. When he came back to the stone, he had stripped away his robe so he wore only his short, black breeches. The firelight brushed every curve of his muscled chest, the hard ridge of his belly.

She reached out to him. "Come."

For once, without wavering, he did as she bid. Taking one of her feet in his hands, he lifted her leg, pressed the foot to his mouth and put his mouth to her ankle. She shivered as he worked his way upward, brushing his lips along her calf, stopping to lick the soft skin behind her knee, then biting her inner thigh, so that she flinched with the pain of it, quite sure he'd broken her skin. But when he put his mouth between her legs and began to kiss her in earnest, the ache melted away, and she thought she might swoon with the bright, stabbing joy that drove up into her. Soon she was shuddering and let out a mewling sound, the wave of bliss coming nearer—so near she could hardly breathe. All at once, Thomas backed away, rising.

"No," she cried. "Don't stop!"

"We're not done," he said. "But first, it's time for you to see." He reached down among the sacks he'd brought with them and drew something big up and into the light. "Here at long last is what you've been waiting for. Behold! Rhiannon!"

At first she could barely see what it was, so clouded was it by the dancing shadows, by the dizziness brought on from the drink, by her body's own lustful yearnings. Then he turned it so it better caught the fire's glow, and Godgyfu's breath caught. *The pennies! The likeness from Evesham! This is what he did with it?*

Cast all in gold, tall enough to cover Thomas's body from hips to neck, the likeness was of a proud steed with one foreleg out, stepping forward. A naked woman—Godgyfu herself—sat sidesaddle on the horse, looking out with bright blue gemstones for eyes. There was no mistaking the woman for anyone but her, for Thomas had a sundry way of crafting his likenesses so they seemed oddly lifelike. His were not the lovely, weird sorts of wights the great craftsmen throughout the kingdom made with overblown looks and uncanny casts. His works were more like life itself, frozen into stillness, like the Romans used to make. She reckoned it was fair in its own way, but she had often told him how unsettling his wooden carvings were; she always half foresaw them bestirring themselves or speaking. And if this golden likeness were to speak, it would speak with her own voice. She shivered, the fire's warmth rushing out of her.

"You quake," he said. "You feel it calling to you."

"What have you done? This is no work of Mannig and his craftsmen."

He bared his teeth at her, eyes sparkling. "I made it for you. For us. Does it please you?"

"You lied to me. It was to be a likeness of Marie! A holy likeness for the church." This was anything but holy—pagan *idolatria* if ever she'd seen it! He had worked red gemstones into the breasts as nipples and more into a golden helm upon the rider's head. She looked away from it at last, met Thomas's gaze, and the dizziness washed over her so that she fell forward, keeping herself from tumbling off the stone only by grabbing the golden likeness itself.

"I hid this from you, yes," Thomas said. "I know the feelings of seemliness hammered into you by the priests and lords who have hitherto shaped your life; those feelings would have told you not to let me make this thing. For you still don't see you are a goddess worthy of such likenesses! This is my way of worshipping before you. Something that will last even after our flesh is gone from this world."

Everything around her glowed now. She heard his words but they came from the ground, the sky, the wind. His hands were under her then, helping her settle back onto the stone. Lying down, her dizziness lessened. "I … I love you too, Thomas."

He had been wrong to do what he did, but it was love that drove him to it, and the likeness was indeed a wonder. It made her look so fair and lovely, and she wept to see how she looked to him, how godlike she was in his eyes.

He drew close and kissed her, on the forehead then on the mouth, one hand grasping her neck.

She met his tongue with her own, tasting herself on his lips. The yearning came back, strong and hot. *It's happening at last.* She almost couldn't believe it.

"Are you truly ready?" she asked. "I don't want you to rue—"

He shushed her, and he tightened his fingers around her neck so that she could hardly breathe. "Tonight we give ourselves over to everlasting bliss. No more worries or rue."

Then he rose again, and Godgyfu gulped the air. Almost, she had thought she would swoon, and she stared up at the dark heavens, rubbing her sore throat with trembling fingers. "Thomas?" Her voice was small, far away.

"Now we begin," came his answer, and she turned her gaze toward him. Grunting, he lifted the golden statue and put it into the fire. It settled itself on the wooden bale so the horse now seemed to be riding through flames that rose up to lick at the rider.

"What are you doing?" she shrieked. "You'll ruin it!"

He only laughed. "It won't get hot enough to melt the gold. But the flames give the gold life—bring out its earth magic. For burning, we have this." All at once he had the wooden carving in his hands—the one he had begun to make that first day she unclothed herself for him—the naked Marie with her own face, her own body's shape. It had been so long since she'd seen it, she'd almost forgotten he had it.

"I don't understand," she said, pleading with him.

"This one holds you inside it," he answered. "From this one will the fire help set your earthly spirit free." He set the little carving onto a shelf the golden rider's lap made. In a twinkling, it caught, a bright new eye in the flames' wider brightness. Thomas raised his arms and his eyes to the heavens and prayed to the fire, words in the Welsh tongue that meant nothing to Godgyfu. Then he lowered his arms, stuck his fingers into the waist of his breeches, and stepped out of them. His narrow, white buttocks clenched, and notwithstanding her bewilderment, she yearned to feel that flesh beneath her hands, driving him into her.

When he turned, she gasped. Though she had touched him many timex beneath his breaches, this was the first time she'd seen his manly flesh with her eyes. Her breath came hard and fast, the burning ache in her throat only stoking her hunger. "In me," she begged.

Thunder rolled, low and angry, boding rain. He came to her, climbed onto the stone and crouched, eyes gleaming in the firelight. *Like a young wolf in the wold!* Then Godgyfu felt his weight atop her, and her legs went up and around him, drawing him down. She was so ready he thrust no more than twice before being fully within her, pushing, drawing back, then driving forward again.

Her body wept with a bliss deep enough it must surely break her, tear her asunder and shatter her mind into a thousand bits. "My love. My love."

Breathing heavily above her, he began to shudder, and she knew he was soon to release. When she felt his spasms within her, it was too much, sending her over the edge to be with him in a mindless, linked frenzy.

For a long while afterward he lay unmoving, his heart thudding so she could feel it against her breasts. Her own body still hummed, and she sighed almost woefully when he drew himself out of her. It had all happened so quickly in the end, for both of them, she only wished it could have lasted longer. *Maybe we'll do it again.*

Thomas settled down alongside her, thrust one strong arm across her hips and yanked her close. She twisted onto her side to settle against him, feel his warmth against her back. His seed leaked out from between her legs, a warm wetness, and she smiled, staring into the fire through a haze of happy tears.

But the longer she stared, the more her weeping came from something else altogether. Her gaze was fixed on the golden likeness, and she wanted to feel as lovely and sparkling as it looked, wanted this to be the wonderful thing she had dreamed of for so long. Instead, as the breathless madness of their coming together faded, she felt merely hollow inside, as tough she had sold something of herself. She blinked, and through her tears no longer saw Rhiannon on a horse but a golden calf such as the one the folk of Moses turned to when he left them to go up the mountain. *I've given up all I once held dear. Turned my back on Christ and Marie. On Coventry. The Worcester blood money bought this thing ....* The bonfire's flames became the red fires of hell, and a bottomless dread crept into her.

Thunder growled again in the dark heavens. The sound at last drew her gaze away from the fire, and she blinked away her tears, rolling over to look at Thomas. His gaze met hers, eyes wide but not with tenderness. There was a kind of wild, frenzy in his look. Maybe even fear over what they had done. "Oh, I can only—" But she did not finish her thought. Some stirring in the darkness nearby made her sit up … too quickly so that her head swam with the lingering haze of the draught they'd shared.

"Lady," Thomas whispered, "be easy." And his arm around her tightened, drawing her back down.

Shadows moved just outside the circle of firelight. *What?* The shadows drew closer, into the brightness, and she thought at first she dreamt. That she must have fallen asleep alongside Thomas and what she saw was not truly there. Ghostly casts with wide eyes and open mouths stared at her.

No—they were there in truth! Folk stood watching her, masked or hued to look like beasts, but folk nonetheless. Five, maybe six of them. Maybe more. All praying aloud now together, in words she couldn't understand. All watching her as she sprawled naked on the stone. Watching as she and Thomas had been ….

"What is this?" she whispered. "Who are they?"

"Folk from the nearby hills. They're here at my bidding. To watch our faring from this world of flesh into a better world of our making."

This is some pagan rite! Some mass for Rhiannon! And I'm its high priestess! I am damned before God. A sinner! Have I lost my mind? What am I doing?

She made to scramble away from Thomas, off the stone. He grabbed her left wrist, reached for her other arm, and before she even knew what he was doing, he'd slipped the looped end of a a rope around her hands and pulled it tight like a noose.

"What are you doing?"

He sighed. "I had hoped I would not need to do this, but I see now your thoughts are still clouded by the priests' lies. Be not afraid."

She tugged at the rope, but it seemed fastened to something just behind the stone, a wooden stake. Then Thomas grabbed the other end of the rope, tugged on it, and she found herself yanked onto her back, arms raised above her head. She wriggled and twisted, but the rope only dug harder into her skin. She tried kicking at Thomas, but he leapt from the stone and out of reach.

"I beg you be at ease," he said. "These folk love you. You are their goddess, Rhiannon! We are all your loving thralls!"

Fear slithered down her throat and coiled about her heart. "What's happening? Free my hands. Please!"

He came around to the side, stood over her, and stroked her chin with a finger.

No—not a finger. The tip of a knife, cold as ice. "You will not need your hands," he said. "I'll tend to all your body's needs, and soon such needs will melt away. It will all be over soon."

Godgyfu squeezed her eyes shut. *Blessed Osburh, save me.*

She waited for him to say something more. When she heard nothing, she opened her eyes. *Where is he?* He'd slipped away. She could no longer see any of the other folk either, but she still heard their sing-song prayers nearby. Godgyfu craned her neck, looking out into the darkness that ringed her, but the bindings kept her from moving freely. "Thomas!"

Instead of his answering, another sound came—a canny sort of whuffing. A horse's whicker.

A heartbeat later, Thomas stepped back into the light, one hand stroking the beast's neck. At first she took it as one of their own horses, but then she saw this one was younger, a colt still, though almost fully grown. Its coat was a creamy yellow-white, not unlike the hue of King Eadward's beard, and it wore no bridle or saddle.

Thomas walked the horse to the table-stone and wove his fingers through its long mane. He lifted his other hand, there was a flash of steel, and before Godgyfu could cry out, he'd drawn the long knife across the horse's throat. It reared back once, a spray of hot blood washing over Godgyfu's legs and feet, then she no longer knew what it did, for she closed her eyes and screamed. Darkness. Eilífr's seed spraying over her shins. *Mother, no!* A great stream flowed down, all the blood emptying itself from her mother's hanging body in one black flood.

"No!" She lurched up, straining against the rope, but could not get free. She scrabbled with her feet on the rock, kicking her heels, bruising herself against it. When she opened her eyes, the horse had fallen to the ground. Thomas was climbing up onto the rock, crouching over her. She looked toward the fire and the likenesses. The wooden one was gone, burned to cinders. The golden Rhiannon stared out at her as she felt Thomas's weight settle upon her again.

There was a flash, and the thunder rolled again, louder, closer. The first, fat raindrops spattered on the rock. Thomas stroked her face with the flat of the blade, smearing the horse's blood, still warm, over her cheek. "Soon you will understand. With this knife, I'll set you free. Free us both from the wretchedness of this world. The fire will burn away what binds us here, and we shall rise as smoke into our new home."

She wept then, overcome. *My God! Tova was right all along.*

Thomas was still speaking, in her ear now, but she no longer heard. In her mind, she spoke only with the Blessed Maiden. *Pray for us sinful, now and at the time of our death, Amen.*

"Nooo!" Another voice split the night—a great roar as though one of the giants who'd built the broken table were back to set it aright. "Nooo!"

Thomas stopped his whispers, looked back over his shoulder.

Leofric loomed over them.

He pulled Thomas away from her. "I told you not to touch her!" He threw Thomas to the ground.

The other folk came forward then, reaching for Leofric, and he went mad. His sword came out, whistling through the darkness. Godgyfu heard the wet thunk of it biting into flesh, and woeful cries arose all around her. Her husband fell onto the table. He rolled over her, toppling off the other side. There were more shouts, sounds of fighting behind her. One of Leofric's sword blows must have struck the wooden stake, for all at once the rope went slack, and Godgyfu was free.

She leapt from the table, nearly stumbling into the fire, but righted herself. Turning, she saw Leofric locked in a struggle with one of the watchers. Thomas stalked toward Leofric's back, knife raised. Heedless of the fire's heat, Godgyfu snatched up the unburnt end of a flaming branch and, hands still bound, ran screaming toward Thomas. He turned but not fast enough to stop her before she swung. The wood met the side of Thomas's head with a loud crack, and he dropped in a shower of smoldering embers. She let go of the branch. A heartbeat later, Leofric lurched back from the man he fought, brought up his blade, and the man's head flew from his shoulders. Dark blood sprayed as the body fell.

Godgyfu spun away from the grisly sight and ran. But the draught she'd drunk still made her dizzy, and after no more than a few steps, she fell to her knees. With her forehead pressed to the ground, she worked to unwind the frayed rope from her wrists.

Saint Osburh, save me! she thought, over and again. When the rope came fully loose, she looked up.

The night had grown still but for the patter of rain on the stones and grass.

Dead men lay around her, the pagan folk who'd been watching her. The horse's body was nearly within arm's reach.

Thomas slumped against the stone table, no longer holding his knife and one ear ragged and dark where Godgyfu had hit him. Leofric loomed over him, shoving him down every time he scrabbled in the mud to rise. Then Leofric's bloody sword rose—

"Leofric, no!" she screamed.

He turned to look at her, and it was a cast of deepest woe. One of the slain men must have struck him a blow, for his brow was swollen on one side, the skin split.

"It's done," she pleaded. "No more killing."

"This man is a devil!" he yelled, taking another step toward Thomas.

"Please, Leofric," she said. "If you still love me at all, do not do this."

Leofric's eyes closed, and he cried out as if his heart were breaking. Then he cast his sword aside.

"Godgyfu, why?"

She rose, decided she would not fall, and stepped closer to him. His cheeks were spattered with blood, some his own, streaking now as the rain came harder. "How did you find us?"

"What?" He looked bewildered. "Ælfgar. When I saw you and Thomas were gone, I went to our son, and he said the monk once brought him here, that this was where he'd be on this godless, pagan night. But ... why?"

"What ... what ever can I say?" she asked, turning to look at Thomas. His eyes betrayed nothing, no fear, no lust, no anger. *He is a godless man, and I am damned.* And yet she still felt something stir inside her when he met her gaze; it was shrouded in sadness now, an ache that came from his betrayal, his pagan madness, but it was there. "I am as much to blame as ...." She trailed off. As though she heard them for the first time, Leofric's earlier words worked their way into her awareness. "Leofric, what did you mean when you said you told him not to touch me? When did you tell him that?"

Thomas laughed, a chilling sound. "Go on, tell her, Earl."

"He was..." Leofric stopped, and sighed. "Godgyfu, I'm sorry, but you must know the truth now. This man before you is no man, he is indeed a devil. For years now, he has watched your every move. He peers at you when you bathe, follows you to the shit-house. He's hidden himself in our roof like some overgrown woodlouse and watched our bedgames more times than I can say."

"What?" Godgyfu's felt the world breaking up around her. "Wait. What do you say? Watched me?"

"For years. From the day he came to Coventry."

The rain became a cold, heavy downpour. Water dripped into her eyes, and she blinked it away. She opened and closed her mouth, letting the water run inside, swallowing it.

"Is it ... is this true?" she asked Thomas.

"It's true," Leofric answered for him. "Go look! He's got a burrow dug in the thatch above our bed."

Thomas rose from the stone. The flesh hung limp now between his legs, though it was still thick and long. Rain ran down his body and fell from its tip in a narrow line so it looked as though he made water. "Rhiannon, I—"

"My name is Godgyfu!" she snapped. "You've been watching me? When I didn't know you were there? Even after I showed myself to you willingly, still you did this?"

"Must I answer?" he asked, and in the light from the dying fire, for the first time in all the years she'd known him, she saw anger in his eyes—a wild, hopeless anger. "You must know it's true! You knew what we were doing, and now you've betrayed me! Betrayed yourself and all your kind even as my mother did!" He stopped and laughed again, almost a maiden's giggle. "All my work! For nothing! But if we're speaking truth, then tell her everything, Leofric. Tell her how you found me out years ago. But did you go to your wife and warn her? Did you bid me stop?"

"I—" Leofric started, then he dropped his head, and Godgyfu's stomach churned.

"No, Lady," Thomas went on. "All he did was ask that I let him watch me when I was watching you. It got him hard. Harder than ever you can get him with your hand in the dark of your bedroom. What truly fired his lust was seeing you shown in the brightness of day like wares on a stall in the market!"

All at once she was on her knees, folded over forward, retching into the wet grass. The bile stung her throat, sharp from whatever Thomas had put in the draught.

Thomas still spoke, shouting now to be heard over the driving rain. "And not just you, Lady! Tell her, Leofric, about what you make the thralls and handmaids do. About your faring to Blodeuwedd's. About flinging mud at her while she writhes naked. About flogging her with a whip while you flog that shriveled gray lamprey between your legs. About—"

She screamed then, loud and long, a scream to break her throat. Leofric and Thomas looked at her, but she could not bear to look back at either man. Either devil! "Enough!" she yelled, a hoarse rasp.

Leofric and Thomas both tried to speak, one over the other, but she screamed again and leapt to her feet. "No! Both of you get away from me! Get away!"

She ran off into the night. The rain was so heavy now, the night so dark, she couldn't see more than a few steps ahead. Somehow she ran straight into one of the horses she and Thomas had ridden south only that morning—her own mare. She couldn't say where her clothes had gone, but she couldn't bring herself to go back and look for them. Pulling herself into the saddle, she kicked her bare heels into the horse's flanks and rode blindly into the darkness, hoping the horse itself would somehow know which way to go, would get her back to Coventry.

And she was not alone. In the intermittent flashes of lightning, others flew alongside her. Saint Osburh, an edifying glow that kept her mind from breaking. Old Sister Eanfled, who she could not see but who whispered in her thoughts .... *Just a little farther, dearie ....*

Mother. A dark, red shadow.

"I can't go on, Mother." How easy it would be just to lie down and die.

A bright flash! *You can.*

"No. I understand it now—why you did what you did. Sometimes it's all too much." She could let herself sink into the rain-soaked soil. So easy.

I was weak, Godgyfu. Thunder roared and cracked over the inky landscape. *I gave up. But you can't, and you won't.*

"Why? What is left for me?"

The same things that were left for me. I still had you, Godgyfu. I loved you, and that should have been enough.

"Mother ..." she sobbed, clinging to the horse's wet mane, and letting her tears soak into it.

I know it now that it is too late. But it is not too late for you. There are those who love you. Your son and his children. Your friends. Coventry.

"Coventry."

A spear of light thrust into the earth not a hundred feet away, its thunderous boom shaking her bones. *Fight, Godgyfu. Fight ....*

Wailing raggedly into the black night—a wild, ululating sound to mingle with the storm's own din—she kicked her bare heels against the horse's heaving flanks.

Coventry.

THOMAS LEFT LEOFRIC ON HIS knees weeping near the stones. The wretch had dropped like a stone himself as soon as Godgyfu ran from them. *I hope he drowns in his own tears.*

In the guttering fire's last light, Thomas found his robe and his knife. As he leapt into his saddle, he thought about going back and slitting Leofric's throat, ending his woeful life, but to what end? The man was broken. And if instead he could catch up with Rhiannon, there was still time to finish what they'd started. He would use the knife to send them both to Annwn—to the Otherworld, the world of the gods. After that, nothing else would matter, least of all Leofric.

Three times he got close enough to Godgyfu that he heard the thud of her horse's hooves on the wold. Once he thought he heard her screaming. Each time, as he kicked his steed to run faster, the farther away she seemed. It was as though some spell had been cast upon him, keeping him from reaching her. Maybe he only dreamed he heard the sounds—some trick of the rain or of the night or of the blossoms he'd drunk. In the end he gave up, knowing there could be only one spot she'd make for. Home. Her church. Coventry.

He heeled the horse again, riding north. *All my years of work in tattered ruins.* He threw back his head and laughed. *We were supposed to die together. Die and be reborn!*

In time the rain stopped.

He came to the church at dawn on All Saint's Day. All the folk of Coventry were gathering, like sheep, waiting for the abbey doors to open for the feast-day mass.

No one saw him creep into the church porch, where he took up a spot in the shadows behind a stone column. The knife was up his sleeve, though now there was no longer any hope of awakening his goddess. That doorway had closed with the sun's rising. Still, there were other uses for a sharp blade.

He knew this was where she would come, so he was in no way taken aback when he began to hear murmuring in the churchyard. He looked out from his hiding spot and there she was—a golden vision on her white mare. She must have overshot the town in the dark, for she came from the west, through the market, and now rode through the abbey gates in the brightness of the morning sun. She was bedraggled, still naked. Her unbound hair was matted to her skin, wrapped all around her so that it covered most of her flesh, but for her long, white legs, hanging down on either side of the horse, feet dangling free from the stirrups. She was shivering; he could see that even from across the yard. A mist rose off her body, which was blotchy and red from the cold.

Throughout the yard, the townsfolk's murmuring became a hushed stillness, and as one they all dropped their eyes to the ground so as to spare her the shame of being seen as she was.

Not Thomas. He looked at her, and even after all he had seen over all the years he had known her, it was as though he saw her in truth for the first time. She had been brought low, as low as any man or woman could be brought—betrayed by her husband, shamed before the townsfolk—and yet her chin was high, her cast turned up toward the church with pride. He fingered the knife once; would it even pierce her flesh any more? She was already a goddess; it was something she'd had in her all along. A goddess of skin and sweat and blood, a goddess of the world—of the unclean world filled with lust and weakness.

Rhiannon has betrayed me. Betrayed my love. Somehow, the goddess had made herself flesh rather than the other way around. Rather than letting Thomas render the unclean flesh into the purity of a goddess. *Unfaithful whore! All the years—a lifetime of steadfast work—and you break troth with me!*

When her horse neared the church, Rhiannon slipped down into the mud. She stumbled two steps, but righted herself before falling. A townswoman ran to her and handed her a cloak to throw over her shoulders, then dropped her eyes and slipped back among the gathered bystanders.

The goddess flung the cloak over her back and came into the porch.

Thomas stepped out. "Rhiannon."

She looked, but she seemed neither frightened nor glad to see him. Her eyes were dead, like those of a fish caught on a line and thrown onto the bank. "Get away from me," she whispered.

She made for the church doors, but Thomas stepped into her path.

"Why do you turn from me? From my steadfast devotion?"

"There was no devotion, no love," she answered, her dry throat making it sound like a croak. "It was lust. You did what you did to feed your own twisted lust, and I was dimwitted enough to be drawn into your befouled world."

"Lady, no." He reached out toward her, but she stiffened, and he dropped his hand. "It was never about lust. My watching you was because I was so awed by you. When you are with menfolk—even with me—you're not yourself. The men make you smaller. Only when I saw you alone, unseen by you, did I see the hint of your true strength, your inner godhood that has now—"

"Drivel! You watched me in bed with my husband. Even your own lies no longer hold up."

"Listen to me. The flesh was meant to go away. This is not how you should be, Rhiannon. I could have made you better. All that I did for you! But now you—"

She made a scoffing noise. "Enough! It's over, don't you understand. Get out of Coventry. I don't ever want to see you again."

She made to move past him into the church, but he knew she couldn't mean it. Even if she had broken troth with him, she must still see what he had sought to do for her. He grabbed her, tried holding her back, but only made the cloak fall from her shoulders to the ground.

Rhiannon turned toward him, naked and awful in her godly wrath.

She drew breath and screamed.

LEOFRIC RODE INTO THE ABBEY yard on the kalends of November, thinking he would go into the church and confess his sins before the priest. *I've killed men, but they were pagans. I have failed to give worth to my own wife. I am a godless wretch.*

Surely if he made shrift, Saint Paul would go before Christ to beg forgiveness for him.

Paul loves me. The graybeards welcomed me among them as Paul spoke the word of God and told me I may be with them. That I could be newly christened through shrift and be born again with them into Paradise.

His head ached from the blow one of the heathens had dealt him; it still felt swollen between his right ear and eyebrow, but his split skin had stopped bleeding. Leofric alit from his horse and shuffled toward the church. All around him, men and women stood oddly still, staring at the ground or casting sidelong glances at him. *What happens here?*

A scream shattered the morning.

He looked toward the abbey and saw Gogyfu naked on the church porch, Thomas standing beside her.

Naked before Thomas. Before all of Coventry. Before God!

This was the fullness of all his hidden lust brought to its greatest height. A week ago, to have seen her standing naked in the abbey yard would have driven him wild. Now, all he felt was cold and empty. He thought he might be sick. He felt a sadness so deep it left him as one dead. The madness had fled. Too late to matter, too late to help Godgyfu, but it was gone. Blessedly gone.

Slowly, he cast his eye all about the yard and saw that none of these folk even looked at his wife. *All turn away from her shame, giving her more worth than ever I did as her own husband.*

All except Thomas.

Sadness became anger.

Leofric stumbled forward, taking off his cloak. When he came up onto the porch, he wrapped it around Godgyfu.

She looked at him, then looked away, saying nothing.

"What has happened?" It was Abbess Tova. The church doors opened, and she stepped out, Abbot Leofwin and several brothers of Benedict crowding in behind her.

He waited a heartbeat, then another, thinking now Godgyfu would tell all his folk what he had done, what a fiend he was. Instead she looked back at him and raised an eyebrow.

Thank you, he thought.

He turned to the abbess. "I …. My wife and I were set upon by highwaymen. They thought to rob us, and they stripped my wife bare. Godgyfu fled as I fought them off." He fingered the blood-crusted wound on his forehead. Gasps passed among the monks, and Tova, and her sisters drew Godgyfu among them, whispering soothing words.

"Now I come here and find this wretched man looking to shame her further!" He drew Bloodwreak and pointed its tip at Thomas. "He would keep her from coming into her own church! Dare to lay hands upon her! Look boldly upon her naked flesh!"

Thomas gave him a smug half-smile, and Leofric felt his blood boil. *It would be so easy to drive this blade through your heart.* But he could not. Not here on Christ's own doorstep. He had sinned enough for one lifetime and would not let this devil make him sin still more.

Abbot Leofwin nodded. "I saw him peeping at your good wife even as she rode bare into town. That one ever seems to be lurking about where he shouldn't be."

Indeed. Leofric gritted his teeth. "You've had the very devil in your midst, Leofwin. Make no mistake, I will deal with him later." He turned back over his shoulder. "Take him away!"

Osbern and two of his men ran forward and took hold of Thomas, who said not a word as he was drawn off.

Abbess Tova brought Godgyfu within Saint Marie's walls, and when she had melted fully into the darkness within, Leofric dropped to his knees.

He wept, there at the church door. Before all of Coventry, he tore at his hair and his beard. Through his tears, he began to pray.

TWENTY-ONE

SANDWICH
24 JUNE 1052

GODGYFU SAT WITH BEORNFLÆD, BREAKING her fast on the sandy shore. Nearby, a long, wooden wharf jutted out into the Wantsum, the wind whipping a mist up from around its pilings where the water broke against them. She stared out over the shallow, silt-choked harbor teeming with light chapman ships of every length and shape, bringing goods from over the South Sea and loading herring and wool from last month's shearing. The sun rose blood red in the east, the ships' masts and the sloping island of Tenet casting long shadows over the water toward her. Farther out, Eadward's small fleet of longships prowled, awaiting the king's word to sail.

She had been here twice before over the years, but the water no longer looked the same to her. *Nothing is the same.*

Beornflæd smacked her lips alongside her, then let out a loud belch. Godgyfu turned and smiled; her old handmaid at least looked much the same as ever, and it was good to see her again after so long.

St. Osburh, give me a strength like to hers, she prayed and looked back out over the water.

In her mind, she heard again the words she'd had with Leofric the day before. It had been nearly eight months since she'd seen her husband. Eight months since that awful night and the morning she'd come naked back to Coventry. Since then, she'd shut herself up in the Benedictine nunnery at Wenlock—another house that, much like Saint Osburh's, had been burned some hundred or more years ago by viking Danishmen. She and Leofric had paid to build the nunnery anew some years back, and it was as good a stead as any for her to get herself hale, settle her head after what had happened. Abbess Tova had been her only link with her old life; her friend had come often to see her and tell her of Ælfgar and her grandchildren. Indeed, Godgyfu would not have made it through the past months without Tova's help and abiding love. *Bless her.*

After a time she found a sort of happy stillness in Wenlock, and had things been elsewise, Godgyfu might well have stayed there for the rest of her life. Then had come Ælfgar's pistle—his plea for her to come home. Leofric, it seemed, grew more dimwitted and weak by the day, and Ælfgar was in no stead to help him; with his new burdens as earl in East Anglia, he was kept away from Coventry for ever longer stretches. Leofric's brother, the Mouse, had come to stay with him, but the Mouse was a dolt and little enough help to anyone. Leofric needed someone at his side who understood an earldom's lordship, the workings of the kingdom. Her son begged her to come home again, not knowing what it was he truly asked.

Ælfgar, along with the rest of the folk in Coventry, never knew what had happened that stormy night. They all believed Leofric's tale of highwaymen; they thought Godgyfu had gone to Wenlock to make herself well after the fright the robbers put in her. Only Tova knew the whole truth, and they both knew Godgyfu could not keep herself hidden away forever. She agreed to come meet with Leofric here in Sandwich, where the king had called him and where he had been with Ælfgar and Osmund for most of the past month.

A brimfowl screeched as it wheeled overhead, and Godgyfu closed her eyes, seeing Leofric again in her mind's eye as he'd appeared to her yesterday in the bright noonday sun. The sight had shaken her. He looked to have lost nearly half his weight so his skin now sagged and his eyelids drooped. When he smiled his cast looked as if it were all teeth, flashing out from the gray nest of his beard.

"Godgyfu," he had said, and she'd gave him back an uneasy smile. "You are looking well."

At first there had been no talk of what had happened, as though neither of them was yet ready to acknowledge it. Instead their talk wandered to the goings on in the kingdom, to why Eadward needed Leofric there with the gathering fleet. "Godwine seeks to come back," he said. "He's a few ships that have so far kept clear of the boatcarls, and the king now has word he's landed at … where was it? Dungeness, I think."

"He was well loved there," Godgyfu said. "Likely he already gathers men to back him."

Leofric nodded. "Eadward's all but yielded he'll have to let Godwine come home, give him back his earldom. The king fears all Wessex could rise up if he doesn't welcome Godwine back."

"Rodbert of Jumièges must be beside himself," Godgyfu said, sighing. "But then, when has that man not been beside himself over something or another ever since Eadward made him Archbishop of Canterbury?"

Leofric laughed through a wet cough. "If Godwine and his kin are brought home under threat of uprising, they'll be stronger than the king in all but name, and Godwine's hatred for the Frankishmen is well known. Most of Eadward's friends will likely be sent back over the sea, and the king won't be having the Norman duke in his hall again any time soon."

Godgyfu scowled. She'd heard from Tova that none other than young William the Bastard himself, the Duke of Normandy, had come over with many of his men as the king's guest throughout the winter. Some thought the childless king now looked to his old friend as a would-be heir, but it seemed unlikely. *Who among the English would go for that?* "All the more why Queen Eadgyth, at least, should be taken back by Eadward. She sits in a nunnery while Eadward still needs to father a child!"

"At least we won't have Swegn back for a good while," Leofric said. "Word is the big turd's off to Jerusalem on a holy wayfaring of forgiveness, though I dare say even praying before the True Cross won't give him shrift for the evil he's done."

"And Harold?" she asked.

Leofric's brow furrowed. "Who?"

"Godwine's son Harold. Still in Ireland? Or will he get his earldom back from our Ælfgar too?"

He looked at her foggily, and she saw he did not know who she spoke of. *Oh, Leofric.*

But he nodded anyway. "Yes, still in Ireland." He reached up and rubbed at the scar over his brow with his knuckles.

"Your head again? The soreness still comes to you?"

His cast brightened. "No, no. For a blessing, that's gone. The old ache no longer comes."

She nodded, and they sat unspeaking then for a time, Godgyfu thinking of all the things men do to punish those who hurt them. *How often do we end up hurting ourselves even more along the way?*

"I heard what you did to Thomas," she said at last, little more than a whisper. "Was that not ... overdone?"

Leofric's mouth twisted. "I will not say his name. I think of him now as Elymas, the warlock whom God wrapped in a dark cloud when Blessed Paul first went among the folk to spread Christ's word."

Godgyfu gritted her teeth. *Still he babbles of Paul.* "Yes, I reckon he got no more than he'd earned."

"What we all earned, in truth," Leofric said. "We wandered from Christ's path into an empty wilderness."

To that she said nothing. She tried to stoke the anger she felt toward her husband, but it was half smothered by her own feelings of guilt. *Had I not been mad with lust, chasing after Thomas, maybe things would have gone another way. I broke troth with Leofric in thought, if not in deed, long before he ever did with me. Could my aloofness have helped drive him to such depths?*

"Godgyfu, about what happened between us—"

She sought to cut him off, but he raised a hand beseechingly.

"Please, wife, let me say this. I am sorry. Since that dark night, I'm wholly another man. It is as though, like Paul, a blindness was suddenly lifted from me. Before, I was eaten by my own nightmares and lusts. I walked in a fog of sorts ever since ... well, ever since Worcester. Everything from the raid until the night at the stones now seems like something barely called to mind. An awful dream from which I've at last awoken. I was not myself. Now I've given myself wholly over to Christ and his Saints. I ask your forgiveness."

She stared at him for a long while, calling to mind how she herself had thought what a new man he was in those first weeks after he came back from Worcester. *Fetches and faerie changelings are but tales to frighten children, and my childhood is far behind me.* "I'm glad for you, Leofric, truly, if what you say is true. I am also another woman, I think. I rode into Coventry that cold morning, naked as a newborn babe, and in a way I *have* been born anew. I thank Blessed Marie and Saint

Osburh every day for saving me from what might have been a much worse doom. But forgiveness is not something I can give you."

He bowed his head, and she was glad he did not look to push her any farther on it. *I am not without blame.*

"So, then … where do things now stand?" he asked at last, his voice small.

"I have thought long on it. I could leave you for well and good. If I let it be known what you and Thomas had worked out between you, all your dirty games, none would say a word against me were I to live out my days in a nunnery, and your name would be blackened." She felt a bit untruthful in saying this, as she had given herself bodily to a man other than her husband. *Under the laws of Cnut, my flesh could be riven for that!* But Tova had helped her see the greater wrong was not her own; given what she now knew had been Thomas's mark all along, his bedgames with her were nothing short of … well, a kind of rape.

"But I won't do any of that," she went on, meeting Leofric's teary-eyed gaze. "For our son's sake and his children's, and for the good of Coventry, I will not shame you."

"Thank you, Godgyfu," he said, falling to his knees. "Thank you."

"I'm not done." She looked at him cowering before her and nearly felt sorry for him. It was bare as day his mind was slipping from him. *He is old—befuddled and frightened and old.* "I won't shame you, but this is what you must do. As you said earlier, you and I have both sinned greatly. We turned our backs on Christ, but no more! I want the nunnery at Wenlock to get lands and more from us, every year for so long as we both shall live. Also the abbey and church in Worcester to make up for what you did there under Harthacnut. And I have been giving much thought to other worthy steads. We should help the bishop of Dorchester with a gift of land to Saint Marie's Stow. Then there's Leominster, still hurting from what Swegn Godwineson did to their abbess. There are needy churches in Chester, the abbey in Burton-upon-Trent, the—"

Leofric raised both hands to her as if in prayer. "Whatever you wish, it shall be done. I leave it all in your hands."

She nodded. "And lastly, as for us … When outward seemliness bids us be seen together, I will stand alongside you, play the glad wife and let you hold my arm. Other than that, you are never to touch me again, nor am I to learn you've in any way mishandled the thralls or housegirls. Indeed, I want you out of my house altogether, out of Coventry. From this day forward, you will be away at the king's hall or on the king's business as often as may be worked out. Should your burdens as earl bring you back to Coventry, I will stay with Abbess Tova in the nunnery when you are there. She alone knows the truth, and she will tell no one. You'll have Ælfgar to lean on, should you need it, and you have Osmund and the Mouse. It will have to be enough."

He had agreed to it all, wan of cast and eyes filled with shame. Then he'd shuffled away from her, unsteadily, to go pray.

Nearly a day later, the ache of what she'd said to Leofric was all but gone, and she was eager to get home and see Tova. Beornflæd handed her another bit of hornfish on brown bread, and she took it, chewing woodenly. *And if the time comes that it is not enough? Should Leofric need more from me as his wits grow dimmer?* She truly did not know the answer. *I will cross that bridge when my faring takes me there.*

All at once Beornflæd cleared her throat and nodded toward the town. "Here comes the earl with his lad."

Godgyfu looked over her shoulder and saw her husband skipping and leaping down the beach as though his breeches were on fire, young Oswig doing his best to keep up with him. *Dear God, what is it now?* As she watched her husband, she could not help but wonder why, even when he had been sounder of mind and body, she had ever felt she'd needed him—or Eilífr before and Thomas after—to make herself whole. She was stronger than any one of them and now thought of them all as sorry, almost laughable oafs.

Once, years ago, standing in the mud outside the mean cot by the Sherbourne, young Blodeuwedd had said folk could not change, could never be more than they were. Godgyfu had worried whether that were true, but even Blodeuwedd had made herself anew. It had been the happiest news Tova brought to her during her time at Wenlock. As Godgyfu bid her, Tova had gone south to Rollandriht and fetched the golden Rhiannon likeness from beneath the bonfire's ashes. It was given over to Blodeuwedd's keeping, along with one last plea that she consider living with the nuns and give the gold to the Church. But such a life was not for Blodeuwedd; she'd left Coventry within a week, bound first for Bristol where it seemed she had a brother taken as a thrall during a Welsh raid into England some years back. It was her thought to buy his freedom, then go home with him to Wales to start a new life. She'd said something to Tova about having always wanted to take up beekeeping, of all things, and would put a bit of the gold toward setting herself up. It gladdened Godgyfu's heart to think of the girl walking among her hives …

"Come!" Leofric yelled when he drew near. "Another wonder has been sent to me! Last night, after we spoke! Come quickly, so I may tell you and the king both!" Then he turned and ran back toward the town without waiting for her answer.

"We'd better go and see what this is about," she said, rising and brushing the crumbs from her skirts. Beornflæd gathered their things, and together they followed in Leofric footsteps. Before long the sand gave way to packed dirt, and beyond the warehouses lining the chapman's shore, paths crossed each other among Sandwich's houses. The wheezing of a smith's bellows drifted on the wind, but above that sound she still heard Leofric whooping and hollering. Before long they had made their way through the wide middle yard to the town hall, the seat of the Sandwich hundred moot, which had been given over to Eadward and his household while he was in town.

Godgyfu came into the great hall, where Leofric stood before Eadward's kingseat.

"Highness, a wonder has happened!" Her husband shook so, he seemed barely able to stand, and indeed he fell to his knees as Godgyfu stepped up behind him. He saw her and crawled over the floor to lay flat as a worm at her feet. "Godgyfu, it was a truly wondrous thing. Both you and Eadward must come with me to Saint Clement's Church. Pray there with me, I beg you!"

Godgyfu looked awkwardly from Leofric to the king. "Husband, it is not seemly that you tell the king what he must or mustn't do."

Leofric's head came up, rushes from the floor stuck to his beard. He seemed abashed, and he rose, bowing toward the kingseat. "Highness, I know you have much to do. I did not mean—"

Eadward was already waving a hand to brush aside the earlier words. "I will never look amiss on any whose aim is to have me go to church and pray. I was nearly going to hear mass anyway. Now stand up, man, and first tell me of this wonder."

Leofric straightened and beckoned his sworn man forward. Oswig looked frightened half out of his wits to be called before the king, but he did as he was bid and knelt alongside Leofric. "Last night I went to the church as is my wont," Leofric said, "with my man Oswig and two others of my housemen. I made my way as near as I could to the reliquary so my words might be sped faster to Christ's ears."

Eadward nodded, brushing one hand down through his long beard. "I often do the same."

"It was late," Leofric went on, "and two of my men fell straightaway into a deep sleep as I began my prayers. Oswig kept himself awake, though, in fear I think if truth be told, for he was with me once before to witness a wonderwork in this blessed stead."

Eadward coughed. "That other time was in Canterbury, I thought you said."

Leofric was taken aback. He stopped to look about him, seeing his whereabouts anew. "Yes, God's truth it was."

Oh Christ help us, Godgyfu thought. *He scarcely knows what he's saying.* She weighed the likelihood of getting Leofric to come away with her before he made an utter fool of himself, but he was already talking again, even louder than before.

"I had been kneeling only for a short while, when a harsh din all at once filled the church. I thought at first the monk's seats must have crumbled and fallen in one upon the other. But the din abided, growing greater the longer it lasted and shifting in its song so I could hardly think what it might be. Was it not a great roar, Oswig?"

The man nodded weakly, his eyes wide. "Twas mickle loud, lord."

"And then," Leofric said, raising his hands above his shoulders, "in a blink, the din stopped. Before that there was but a lone lamp burning in the church, but now a light shone from the east end—bright white as though the moon itself had newly risen. The light fell upon a spot under the right limb of the cross which stood over the altar, and it grew brighter still as we watched. Soon it shone so bright it filled the wideness of the whole church so the lamp's own light could no longer be seen. The brightness kept up for so long I dared not stare upon it any more, and it was with my eyes fastened upon the floor that the light began to wane at last, and I could see the lamplight once again. By the time the heavenly glow was altogether gone, dawn was nearly upon us. We said our prayers together, Oswig and I, woke the other two men who had slept through the whole thing, and sped ourselves here to share what we saw!"

"A wonder indeed," Eadward said when Leofric fell still.

"Come, then, Highness. While some bit of the holiness may still dwell therein. Let us go pray."

So Godgyfu found herself walking with her husband and the king through the streets of Sandwich, bound for Saint Clement's. Before long, she and Eadward lagged behind as Leofric threw himself more quickly ahead in his keenness.

"I was very sorry to hear of Lady Emma's death," Godgyfu said. "I bid the nun's pray for her in Wenlock."

Eadward nodded. "My lady mother lived a life full enough that it could have been three lifetimes. No need for sorrow. I was, however, most sorry to hear of your own hardships in Coventry. It is shameful such highwaymen are still so bold as to lurk our streets. Once this mess with Godwine is behind us, I will do what I may to further ward wayfarers."

Godgyfu said nothing.

"Though I dare say," Eadward went on after a time, "your husband was right about the heregeld."

She looked at him, eyebrows raised. "Highness?"

"Leofric came to me last year after what happened to you, and he bid me strike down the heregeld, as men with more pennies in their sacks are less likely to turn to thieving. With the Danes no longer a threat, I saw nothing to stop me from doing so, and the way things are going of late it's good men have something to cheer me for. Though since I broke up the standing fleet two years ago, I must find some other way to pay for these ships I now call up against Godwine." He laughed bitterly. "It's always something, isn't it?"

Godgyfu stared, dumbfounded, at the back of Leofric's head where he nearly ran now ahead of them in his eagerness to get to the church. *So he went to the king about it at last. I never thought he'd find the backbone … Coventry will be well.* She had done all she'd hoped to do and more, so that her beloved home was on its way in truth to becoming one of the great towns of England. *Thanks be to God.*

When Godgyfu didn't answer him, Eadward turned and saw where she set her gaze. "He's getting old now—and such men are sometimes wont to bouts of …. Well, we had another word for it in Normandy. Dimness, I think we would say here. But your husband is still one of the shrewdest men in England. You should know—and I hope he knows too—how much worth I still give his wisdom. He is my truest earl. And don't think I can't see how much of his worth flows from your own sway."

Godgyfu nodded, acknowledging the king's words. Again, she found nothing to say.

When they came at last to the church, Leofric waited for them in the doorway. He beckoned them to come with him to the chapel on the church's north side, near to where a priest was saying mass. A gold and green wallcloth, thickly woven, hung behind the chapel's altar. A small cross stood on the floor in the northeast corner, but only a hand's width of the cross could be seen beneath the hanging; the rest lay behind it, up against the wall.

Following Leofric forward, Eadward and Godgyfu were about to kneel, when Leofric spun back toward them. "Christ in heaven, do you see it?" he hissed.

Godgyfu looked about, seeking whatever it was her husband spoke of.

"There," he whispered. "A hand over the cross. I thought at first some churchman stood there blessing us, but the hand passes through the wallcloth itself. And I can see the cross behind it, for the cloth grows ghostly."

Godgyfu looked again but saw nothing, least of all some ghostly hand. She met Leofric's gaze and saw the holy awe shining in its depths. Her heart broke in her chest. "Yes, Leofric, I see it now," she lied. "That is no earthly man."

Leofric shook, a rough quaking, then he fell to his knees, weeping openly.

"Fear not, Earl Leofric," Eadward said, putting a strong hand upon his friend's shoulder. "It is a wonder we now witness. Christ himself come to give his blessing and to heal our bodies and souls."

The king's words drove away Leofric's shivers. Tears spilled into Leofric's beard, but there was no fear in him. Godgyfu sought to hide the tears in her own eyes, but she felt them on her cheeks. She looked at Eadward, and the king too wept.

Leofric crossed himself and turned back toward the altar. "See the fair fingers, long and thin, each nail cast from pearl. What a lithe wrist and strong forearm beneath that sleeve. Oh, Blessed Paul, ward me! A man comes from the shadows behind the hand! It is the Healer! Lord, I cannot look upon you!" He threw himself forward, hanging his head down, lower, until his forehead touched the cold stone floor. He shook, but the sobs Godgyfu heard were not ones of woe but of deepest bliss. A gladness borne of heaven.

The king knelt alongside his earl. "Keep this to ourselves," the king whispered. "For the nonce, bring up what has happened here to no one."

Godgyfu knew the king said it because he wished no one else to learn his earl was half mad. Eadward needed a strong friend in Mercia with his hold on the Godwine lands and indeed all the rest of his kingdom so unsteady.

Eadward was ever a holy man. Maybe some bit of him wants to believe the wonders Leofric beholds are true.

Godgyfu stared at her husband, at his quaking shoulders.

Maybe they are true. Maybe he is touched by God. Maybe God has touched us all.

Godgyfu crossed herself, knelt on the stone floor, and whispered a prayer.

EPILOGUE

WESTMINSTER, LONDON
CHRISTMAS DAY 1067

WITH THE MASSES DONE, THE Christmas feast was now well and truly underway. The mead flowed, songs were sung, and an army of servants brought great mounds of food out to the long tables. Overseeing it all, King William sat laughing loudly with his closest advisors and highborn nobles.

Far from the place of the king, at the hall's opposite end, the benches of one table groaned under a dozen English thegns and one lowly Norman chevalier named Roger who'd been unfortunate enough to miss the Norman invasion fleet's departure the year before and so had squandered the opportunity to distinguish himself at Senlac near Hastings when William's armies overran King Harold and the English defenses. But Roger had finally come over during the first week of December with William himself when the king returned to his new throne after some months setting things in order in his dukedom across the English Mere's narrow sleeve. There were rumors of impending revolt throughout the conquered realm and even noise from King Sveinn that sounded very like the prelude to a Danish invasion. Roger hoped one of those two possibilities would give him a chance to make a name for himself and impress the king. In the meanwhile, he bided his time among the brutish thegns, drowning his embarrassment in wine and mead, listening for any hints of rebellion in their incessant prattle as the king had ordered him to do, for Roger was among the few Normans to speak the English tongue.

He grabbed another cup from a passing servant and poured the mead down his throat as he stared across the wide space. Suspended from the second-floor gallery at the front of the hall, Harold Godwineson's fighting-man banner was on display, muddy and bloody from the field at Hastings. It very succinctly showed the fate of an upstart earl who thought to sit a dead king's throne in place of that king's rightful heir. Not far from the banner, King Eadward's widow Eadgyth sat, smiling gracefully at whatever William's half-brother Odo whispered in her ear. That Eadgyth was Harold's sister was not a mark in her favor, but Roger thought her a pretty enough wench, if a bit old for his tastes. And as the widow of the last *true* king before William, William liked having her about to add a sense of legitimacy and continuity to his infant reign; Roger prided himself on the shrewdness of this insight even as it came to him.

"Did you hear the great lady Godgyfu has died?" one of the thegns seated across from Roger asked.

Roger turned and looked at the man, a corpulent boor with a bright red beet for a nose. "Who's she, some English cunt?"

After a moment's silence, the thegns all began to stumble over each other to answer him.

"A great and godly woman, she was," answered one man with a wicked scar—probably a gift from Senlac. "Gave much and more to churches and abbeys throughout the kingdom. Her and her husband Leofric both. They were the eldermother and elderfather of Harold's queen Alditha."

Roger spat on the floor. "That Alditha was no queen, but the wife of the oath-breaking usurper. And used goods to boot. Wasn't she first married to some hairy Welsh mud-king?"

The scar-faced man blushed, his wound all but glowing. "The Earls Eadwine and Morcere are also the sons of Godgyfu's dead son."

Roger nodded his head with slightly more grudging respect. "English earls. We'll see how long they hold onto their earldoms now that England's but a part of Normandy. Perchance King William would like to reward one of his great chevaliers with a juicy plum, nevermind your dead English cunt of a countess and her brood of shits." He smiled broadly, reveling in the wounded looks he engendered.

"I'll thank you not to speak so coarsely of her," a rich thegn from Saint Albans said, emboldened by drink. He was better groomed than the others and wore a fine ermine-lined cloak about his shoulders. "Twas Coventry Godgyfu loved best, you know. That's why she rode naked that time. They laid her to rest in her own abbey there alongside her dead husband."

"Naked?" All at once, Roger's interest was piqued. "What do you mean naked?"

The thegns nodded knowingly at each other

"It was some penance she did," the beet-nosed one said, "and she weren't naked nohow. She walked barefoot in her shift, as did her husband, to humble themselves before God and beg forgiveness for reaving church lands in Evesham and Worcester."

"You're daft," another man said. "She wore no shift. She was naked as the day she was born, and it was some highwayman that dragged her by her hair before the church, a hostage, so none would grab him before he could reach the church door and claim the right of *sanctuarium*."

"I heard she wore a fisherman's net around her," muttered a young thegn, scarcely old enough to grow a beard, "but you could see *everything* through the holes!" He tittered, his eyes bright with desire.

The Saint Albans man gave an exaggerated sigh and raised his hand. "If you're all done with your witless rot, I'll tell you what *truly* happened. It was back years ago, when the Coventry folk were starving, not rich like they are now. Earl Leofric still lived then—though I think he died five or six years later, a few years after Earl Godwine died. Anyway, Godgyfu went to her husband the earl and begged him to take away the geld that was doing them in."

"What was it, the horse geld?" someone asked.

"No," the well-dressed man answered, cocking his head to consider. "It must've been the heregeld, because King Eadward put an end to that right after her ride."

"Bugger the gelds!" Roger barked. "Get to the ride. I thought you said she rode naked on horseback?"

"Aye, her husband told her he'd ask Eadward to strike down the heregeld on the day she took off all her clothes and rode naked through the middle of town—meaning he'd never ask, as no godly woman would ever do such a thing. But Godgyfu called the earl's bluff and got on her horse without a stitch of clothing.

King Eadward was there to see it, and her bold ride so stirred him he went straightaway to his geld men and told them the geld would be no more."

Roger snorted. "Ballocks! What was the king doing in some backwater privy-hole like Coventry?"

"He must've been there to visit Saint Osburh's shrine," Beet-nose suggested.

"Wait!" Roger said. "You expect me to believe an earl's wife rode naked through the town for every common villain to see? And saintly old Eadward to see as well? What was she, some bawdy strumpet?"

The Saint Albans man suddenly rose and lunged toward Roger, gripping him by his cloak. "I warned you, Norman!"

Roger mashed a fist into the man's gut and laughed as he doubled over and sat back on the bench. "Easy, before you hurt yourself, man. Your story's nonsense."

"Do you call me a liar?" the thegn demanded, knocking over his mead cup and rising again.

"I call you an idiot! Were you there to see it?"

"*I* was." Everyone turned to regard the shriveled old man in monk's robes who'd been sitting quietly in the corner and who now spoke up for the first time.

"Oh, that's rich!" Roger laughed. "And what did you see, blind man?" For plainly enough, the man was blind. Not just blind; his eyes were two scabbed-over, red holes where someone had done him the favor of removing his apples from their sockets.

"I still had my eyes back then. Lady Godgyfu was divine—her skin so pale it was like the first snow of winter, her body wrapped round about by the falling locks of her ruddy hair. So proud she looked upon her white mare. That is how I will ever remember her, a goddess whose body glowed with heaven's light."

"Me too," Roger said. "I'll remember her that way the next time I've no maid to mount!" He made a pumping gesture with his hand, and everyone laughed awkwardly, even the Saint Albans fellow. "What do you make of *that*, monk?"

The old man smiled sadly and turned his head away. "I'm no monk, only a novice."

But no one was listening.

HISTORICAL NOTE

Lady Godiva (Godgyfu in Old English, a name meaning "God's gift") and her husband Earl Leofric did indeed dwell in Mercia during the mid-11th century. Nowadays, along with her image being featured on the chocolates that bear her name, Godiva is mostly remembered for a tale in which she rides naked on the back of a horse. What are we to make of this tale as it relates to everything else history tells us about the Anglo-Saxon noblewoman?

In truth, little is verifiably known about Godiva. She was a wealthy, landowning woman of the period, married to Leofric, the Earl of Mercia. Leofric effectively controlled most of central England in the name of the king and was one of the three major earls in power when Edward the Confessor's ascension to the throne in 1042 ended nearly three decades of rule by conquering Danish kings (the other two earls were Godwine of Wessex and Siward of Northumbria, who also play a role in this book). By all accounts, Godiva was highly respected, and she generously endowed the Church with her land and wealth. In particular she and Leofric are remembered for having founded a great abbey in the town of Coventry, which seems to have been their primary place of residence. Godiva's grandsons, Edwin and Morcar, were earls at the time of the Norman Conquest

(October 1066 onward), and her granddaughter Ealdgyth (Aldith) was King Harold Godwineson's queen when Harold fell at Hastings. Godiva outlived her husband by at least a decade, seemingly alive to witness the arrival of the Normans, but she had died by the time of the Domesday land survey in 1086. Her death might have taken place any time during this twenty-year span (1066–1086), and I have chosen to place it near the earlier end of that range.

Had this been the sum total of Godiva's legacy, impressive though it is, it seems unlikely chocolates would be named after her today. But a little more than 150 years after her death, the earliest surviving account of her legendary naked ride appeared in *Flores Historiarum (Flowers of History)*, by chronicler and monk of St. Albans Abbey, Roger of Wendover. In this account, we are told:

> The countess Godiva, who was a great lover of God's mother, longing to free the town of Coventry from the oppression of a heavy toll, often with urgent prayers besought her husband, that from regard to Jesus Christ and his mother, he would free the town from that service, and from all other heavy burdens; and when the earl sharply rebuked her for foolishly asking what was so much to his damage, and always forbade her ever more to speak to him on the subject; and while she, on the other hand, with a woman's pertinacity, never ceased to exasperate her husband on that matter, he at last made her this answer, "Mount your horse, and ride naked, before all the people, through the market of the town, from one end to the other, and on your return you shall have your request." On which Godiva replied, "But will you give me permission, if I am willing to do it?" "I will," said he. Whereupon the countess, beloved of God, loosed her hair and let down her tresses, which covered the whole of her body like a veil, and then mounting her horse and attended by two knights, she rode through the market-place, without being seen, except her fair legs; and having completed the journey, she returned with gladness to her astonished husband, and obtained of him what she had asked; for earl Leofric freed the town of Coventry and its inhabitants from the aforesaid service, and confirmed what he had done by a charter.

The tale received further embellishments over the centuries, but it was not until 1678 that another equally famous figure was added to the mix. In this version, the people of Coventry, wishing to spare their noble and beloved Godiva any shame, hid themselves away indoors during her naked ride, shutters closed so that none would see her nakedness. Only one man, a tailor name Thomas, peeked out at her, and he was immediately struck blind (or in some versions dead) for his voyeuristic transgression. Thus did the concept of a Peeping Tom have its origins. And while Thomas was likely only added for reasons of storytelling or as a buffer and scapegoat to insulate the reader from the prurience of vicariously seeing Godiva's nakedness, I could not resist including him in my book despite there being very little historical basis to suppose he ever existed. Nearly all of Thomas's own deeds and actions, then, are likewise the products of my imagination, although fans of Chaucer's *Canterbury Tales* might have noticed the inspiration I derived from "The Shipman's Tale" when weaving Thomas's financial grift against Leofric and Godiva ....

While it is possible Roger of Wendover had access to a now-lost antecedent text recounting some or all of the details of the naked ride, any such text, even if it existed, is likely to have been apocryphal. The ride is very unlikely to have ever happened. First, it seems highly improbable a powerful and pious noblewoman of the time would have willingly engaged in such a scandalous act. Also, while there was indeed a rather contentious tax during Godiva's lifetime, this was the national "heregeld" collected by the king to finance the military, so it was not a tax an earl could have unilaterally struck down. Even had the tax in question been some local tax, Lady Godiva owned the lands of Coventry in her own right, so it would arguably have been up to her and not her husband to relieve Coventry's people of the financial burden.

One goal in writing this book, however, was to start with the assumption that the ride did indeed happen but to return the improbably anachronistic episode to a more historically grounded context. My hope was to reexamine the woman behind the legend and the passions that drove her, bringing her own story and motivations to the fore.

Turning then to the history within this work of historical fiction, Godiva's parentage, birth, and early life are shrouded in mystery and largely unknown. The biographical details of Godiva's parents in *Beheld* are thus entirely of my own invention. Historian Joan C. Lancaster suggests several possible theories regarding

Godiva's early life, and I have preferred a theory that our Lady Godiva was the same person as a Godiva who, during the reign of King Cnut, was the widow of an unnamed earl whose lands she bestowed upon the church when the earl died; this Godiva later gave additional lands at Barking (her own lands or inherited from her parents) to the church when she was apparently near to death. From among the likeliest of Cnut's earls to have been this Godiva's first husband, I have chosen Earl Eilífr, who did indeed spend some time in Constantinople as a Varangian Guard and may even have died there. If this Godiva was the same person as the famed Lady Godiva, then she would likely have been a mere girl at the time of this first marriage (not at all uncommon at the time), and it is not beyond the realm of possibility that she survived what she might have believed to be a terminal illness so that she was Eilífr's widow when she later married Earl Leofric.

We know nothing whatsoever of what this Godiva's illness might have been, but for those interested in the medical basis of her illness as portrayed in my prologue, I chose to afflict her with kidney stones that had grown to a sufficient size to cause ureter obstruction and the excruciating pain known as renal colic. She might well have believed herself dying under such circumstances, but her subsequent recovery would have been quite possible ... with or without a saint's intervention.

Speaking of Saint Osburh, historian Stephen Bassett makes a well-reasoned argument that Osburh more likely belonged to the 7th rather than the late 10th and early 11th centuries. But as this theory is something of an outlier, I decided that it made for a more dramatic scenario to keep to the prevailing thought that Osburh was martyred in 1016 at the nunnery she founded, while fleeing Danish raiders so as to save the holy items of her church.

As for Earl Leofric, much more is known of his life and deeds from the historical record, and all of the various military and political machinations in which he is involved in my book are firmly established. Oddly enough, one particular aspect of Leofric's personal journey that might seem fanciful or woven from whole cloth is in fact derived from one of the few sources contemporary to Leofric's own time. Specifically I refer to the episodic mystic visions he has throughout *Beheld.* An astounding Old English manuscript known as *Visio Leofrici* ("The Vision of Leofric") dates from the 11th century and recounts in detail each of the holy visions that appear herein, including the locations where these visions supposedly took place. As a novelist, having such a document at my disposal was like manna from heaven, and I knew straightaway these visions would have to feature prominently in my story. Fortunately they dovetailed perfectly with my decision to depict Leofric as struggling with wider mental, emotional, and perhaps even mystical issues. I am greatly indebted to historian Peter A. Stokes for his recent retranslation and analysis of the "Vision" in *The Review of English Studies* (Oxford University Press 2011).

I must confess, however, to taking authorial liberties with Leofric's personality and offer my apologies to the earl's legacy for having suggested he suffered from voyeuristic and candaulistic obsessions. These are entirely of my own invention, inspired by the fact that the (likely apocryphal) tale of Godiva's naked ride casts him as the one who suggested she ride naked through town. There is nothing in the historical record to suggest Leofric suffered from a broken mind, although it is likely he might have felt some amount of guilt for having had to attack the town of Worcester, within his own earldom, when King Harthacnut ordered that the town be punished for the murder of the king's tax collectors (an event that does indeed derive from the historical record). It is for this reason that I chose to have Leofric's mental decline begin in Worcester. Further inspired by the Welsh myths and legends of the *Mabinogion* (which would likely have amused Thomas, I suppose), I even have Leofric wander into the mists when he becomes separated from his men after the fighting in Worcester, much as happens to Pwyll in the Welsh legend, emerging a changed man albeit not having been replaced by the king of the otherworldly realm of Annwn ....

Most of the other primary and secondary characters in *Beheld* likewise derive from the historical record, with the notable exceptions of Abbess Tova, Sister Eanfled, and the various other nuns and lesser priests of Coventry (who are fictitious, although men and women like them would indeed have been present in the town), Leofric's housecarl Osmund, Osmund's son Oswig, and the various ceorls and lesser thegns of Coventry and the surrounding villages (who are merely composites of the sorts of people who would have filled these roles), and Godiva's steadfast handmaid Beornflæd and the Welsh prostitute Blodeuwedd (who are both entirely of my own invention).

Finally, I'm afraid Emma, mother of King Eadward, emerges from my story in a distinctly unflattering light; to serve the story, I chose to credit some of the less flattering of the conflicting historical accounts of her deeds, motivations, and reputation. But it must be stated that Emma was an absolutely astonishing figure, Queen of England, Denmark, and Norway through her marriages to Kings Æthelred and later King Cnut, and at the center of the events that shaped England during the first half of the 11th century. As a panacea to her depiction herein, might I suggest the Emma of Normandy Trilogy by novelist Patricia Bracewell.

If you'd like to delve even deeper into some of the research and history behind Beheld, *consider subscribing to my author newsletter at* **CHRISTOPHERMCEVASCO.COM.** *As a subscriber, you'll gain access to exclusive bonus material like genealogies, historical maps, essays, suggestions for further reading, and more!*

DRAMATIS PERSONAE

KINGS OF ENGLAND *(DANISH INVADER KINGS IN GRAY)*

Æthelred II, "Unraed", reigned 978-1013, reclaimed throne 1014-16

Sveinn Forkbeard, King of Denmark 986-1014, England 1013-14

Edmund, "Ironside," Æthelred's son by Ælfgifu of York; reigned 1016

Cnut, Sveinn's son; King of England 1016-35, Denmark 1018-35, Norway 1030-35

Harold, "Harefoot," Cnut's son by Ælfgifu of Northampton; reigned 1037-40

Harthacnut, Cnut's son by Emma, King of Denmark 1035-42, Wessex 1036-37, England 1040-42

Eadward, "Confessor," Æthelred's son by Emma; reigned 1042-66

QUEENS

Ælfgifu of York, first wife of King Æthelred II

Ælfgifu of Northampton, first wife of King Cnut

Emma of Normandy, second wife of Æthelred II; subsequently second wife of King Cnut

Eadgyth, wife of King Eadward; daughter of Earl Godwine
(see House of Godwine below)

FOREIGN ROYALTY

Gruffydd ap Llywelyn, Welsh king of Gwynedd and Powys from 1039

Haraldr Sigurdsson, succeeds his nephew Magnus as King of Norway in 1047

Magnus, King of Norway from 1035 to 1047; claimant to Denmark's throne on Harthacnut's death

Sveinn, nephew to Cnut and to Gytha Thorkelsdottir; claimant to Denmark's throne on Harthacnut's death

William the Bastard, Duke of Normandy from 1035

HOUSE OF LEOFWINE

Leofric, Earl of Mercia from 1028; son of the eponymous Ealdorman Leofwine

Godgyfu, widow of Earl Eilífr; weds Earl Leofric early 1029

Ælfgar, son of Earl Leofric and Godgyfu, born late 1029

Ælfgifu, weds Ælfgar in 1045; cousin of Ælfgifu of Northampton

Eadwine (b.1046), **Morcere** (b.1047), **Alditha** (b.1048), **Burgheard** (b.1049) (Ælfgar's children)

Godwine the Mouse, Earl Leofric's eldest brother

Æthelwine, son of Godwine the Mouse; mutilated as a hostage at age seven by Cnut in 1014

Northman, Earl Leofric's deceased older brother, executed by Cnut in 1017

Leofric, Northman's son; a monk in Peterborough

Eadwine, Earl Leofric's deceased younger brother; killed in battle by Gruffydd ap Llywelyn in 1039

HOUSE OF GODWINE

Godwine, Earl of Wessex from 1018

Gytha Thorkelsdottir, Earl Godwine's wife; Sveinn Forkbeard's great-niece; Earl Eilífr's sister

Swegn (b.1019), **Eadgyth** (b. late 1019), **Harold** (b.1020), **Tostig** (b.1026), **Gyrth** (b.1029), **Leofwine** (b.1030), **Gunnhild** (b.1035), **Aelfgifu** (b.1039), **Wulfnoth** (b.1041) (Godwine's children)

OTHER EARLS AND NOBLEMEN

Beorn, nephew of Gytha Thorkelsdottir; brother to Sveinn of Denmark; succeeds Thuri as earl in southeast Midlands in 1045

Eadric Streona, ealdorman in Mercia from 1007; betrayed the English when Cnut invaded; slain under Cnut in 1017

Eadwulf of Bebbanburh, ealdorman of Bernicia from 1038, murdered by Harthacnut in 1041

Eustace II, Count of Bolougne from 1049, a Frenchman, married King Eadward's widowed sister Goda in 1035 (making him stepfather to Ralf of Mantes); came to England as Eadward's guest in 1051

Eilífr Thorkelsson, a Dane; earl in Gloucestershire under King Cnut; wed Godgyfu in 1023; died in 1027

Harold, son of Earl Godwine *(see House of Godwine above)*; named earl in East Anglia in 1045

Hrani, a Dane; earl in Herefordshire under King Cnut; earl in Magonsæte under King Harthacnut

Odda of Deerhurst, a major English thegn, made earl over the southwestern half of Wessex in 1051

Osbern Pentecost, a Norman knight, follows King Eadward to England; sworn to serve Ralf of Mantes

Osgod Clapa, a powerful thegn and major landowner in East Anglia, outlawed in 1046

Ralf of Mantes, a Frenchman, son of King Eadward's sister Goda, comes to England with Eadward; succeeds Beorn as earl in southeast Midlands in late 1049

Rodbert fitzWymarc, came to England with King Eadward; made Eadward's staller (constable)

Siward, Scandinavian-born, earl in Yorkshire from 1033 and of all Northumbria from 1041

Swegn, son of Earl Godwine *(see House of Godwine above)*, made earl in southwest Midlands in 1043

Thuri, a Dane; earl in southeast Midlands, appointed by King Harold Harefoot in 1037

CLERGY

Æfic, Prior of Evesham Abbey; friend and spiritual advisor to Godgyfu until his death in 1038

Ælfric Puttoc, Archbishop of York 1023 to 1041 and again from 1042; Bishop of Worcester 1040 to 1041

Ælfsige, Abbot of Peterborough and an ally of Emma of Normandy; dies in the summer of 1042

Ælfwine, Bishop of Winchester from 1032

Æthelnoth, Archbishop of Canterbury from 1020 until his death in 1038

Bergulf, priest of Saint Michael's church in Coventry

Cynric, priest of Holy Trinity/Saint Marie's church in Coventry

Eadsige, Archbishop of Canterbury from 1038 to 1051

Eanfled, a nun at Coventry's minster church in the 1020s

Eawynn, a young nun of Coventry

Leofwin, Abbot at Coventry from 1043

    Ringwaru, Abbot Leofwin's wife

Mannig, a monk of Evesham; Abbot of Evesham from 1044; one of the kingdom's most renowned artists

Offa, a priest in Coventry in the 1020s

Osburh, founded a nunnery in Coventry; slain by Cnut's Danes in 1016; later venerated as a local saint

Rodbert of Jumièges, Abbot of Jumièges, Normandy; came to England with King Eadward

Sigrida, an elderly nun of Coventry

Stigand, former priest of Queen Emma; bishop of Elmham stripped of see by Eadward in 1043; later bishop of Winchester

Tova, "abbess" in Coventry from 1035

OTHER

Acca, a poor man of Coventry, newly raised from ceorl to thegn

Sigrida, Acca's wife

Alfkil, an elderly ceorl of Foleshill, a village neighboring Coventry

Alric, miller in Coventry, dies in 1044

Gytha, Alric's widow

Beornflæd, Godgyfu's handmaid

Blodeuwedd, a Welsh prostitute living in Coventry

Coenwulf, a ceorl of Allesley, a village neighboring Coventry

Culfre, Coenwulf's sister

Feader, one of Harthacnut's geld-collectors, murdered by a Worcester mob in May 1041

Hrolf, a ceorl of Coventry in the service of Earl Leofric

Osmund, an Englishman; Earl Leofric's chief housecarl

Oswig, Osmund's young son, taken on as a houseman by Earl Leofric

Stenkil, an elderly thegn of Coventry

Wulfrun, Stenkil's second wife on the death of his first

Oscytel, their young son

Thomas, of Norman/Welsh descent; a newcomer to Coventry in 1041

Thurstan, one of Harthacnut's geld-collectors, murdered by a Worcester mob in May 1041

ACKNOWLEDGMENTS

A SINCERE THANK YOU TO Steve Berman, who offered Godgyfu a place among the many other memorable characters who appear between the covers of Lethe Press books.

I also extend immense gratitude to the beta readers who each read one of my early drafts of *Beheld* and offered perceptive and inspiring critiques: Alan Smale, Genevieve Valentine (who also helped me find my title), Kameron Hurley, Livia Llewellyn, Tracy Berg, and Vincent Jorgensen.

For feedback on the opening chapters, I'd like to thank the members of Wellspring 2012 not already named above: Bradley P. Beaulieu, Brenda Cooper, Debbie Smith Daughetee, Eugene Myers, Grá Linnaea, Gregory A. Wilson, Holly McDowell, Kelly Swails, and Stephen Gaskell.

Finally, my wife Megan has been an indispensable first (and second, and third, etc.) reader, my staunchest champion, and my toughest critic. It is impossible to thank her enough.

CPSIA information can be obtained
at www.ICGtesting.com
Printed in the USA
BVHW030434010422
632949BV00002B/127

9 781590 217146